STARSTRUCK

STARSTRUCK

MCKENZIE BURNS

Cover design copyright © Nicole Luisi and McKenzie Burns

Edited by: Emily B. Rose
Proofread by: Emily B. Rose, McKenzie Burns

Internal formatting design © McKenzie Burns

ISBN: 9798990265806

To my fellow fangirls.
Keep dreaming of your own happily ever afters.

OTHER WORKS BY MCKENZIE BURNS

From the Shadows

Through the Flames

Legacy of the Night

WORKS WITH APPEARANCES BY MCKENZIE BURNS

Magic & Moons: A Fantasy Anthology

Chaos & Curses: A Collection of Unfortunate Tales

AUTHOR NOTE

I am a firm believer that love stories come in all shapes and sizes. While many books showcase that happily ever afters are easy to find, that is often not the reality for most people.

That being said, this love story involves mentions of past sexual assault and the trauma that follows. No assault is depicted on page, but readers are advised to proceed with caution.

STARSTRUCK

NINE YEARS EARLIER

PEOPLE ALWAYS TOLD me life could change in the blink of an eye, but I never really understood what that meant. I figured that if life were to change so drastically, it'd be impossible not to see it coming. I was no philosopher, but I never thought the perfect state of life I'd found myself in for the last four months could be impacted so quickly.

I was wrong. So very wrong.

I got voicemail again, and after the two half-started messages that ended in cowardice and three that started with good intentions, but ended with five seconds of a silence, I hit the end-call button before the robot lady could even finish her instructions.

The blaring sound of the intercom startled me back into the

bustling Heathrow Airport terminal, and I realized how desperately I needed to get my shit together. I didn't have much time before we boarded, though the London weather had given me more time than I would've otherwise had. While many would've considered a three-hour flight delay a continuation of my curse streak, I didn't. Somewhere out there, a higher being was looking over me, giving me a second chance—or twelve— to do this. Yet I'd done nothing but chicken out each time I got even remotely close to what I needed to do.

What I needed to say.

I stared at my phone, hoping it would light up and save me the further embarrassment. I didn't even know how to put into words what I'd been thinking about for the last two weeks, what I'd been feeling. Words were supposed to be my thing. I'd crafted hundreds of fictional conversations, yet nothing came to me when I actually needed it. As much as I loved the English language, there was no way I could articulate it all.

I barely registered the intercom calling my boarding group, and I felt myself going through the motions of boarding in a haze.

He knew I was leaving. We'd been counting down the days, dreading the moment I would head back to America at the end of my study abroad term.

Part of me wished I had fallen into a movie, and despite all the security protocols, he would come bounding through the terminal, scoop me into his arms and kiss me before I could step on the jetway.

But this wasn't a movie. My incredible reality had turned into one I wanted to escape forever—and I was, in the form of an eight-hour plane ride across an entire ocean. By the time my group was called and I held my boarding pass out to be scanned, my phone still hadn't lit up.

I sighed as I sat in my seat, my legs twitching in a way that probably made the man beside me just as nervous as I felt.

I swallowed.

As the turbines grew louder and we made our way across the taxiways, I ignored the request to put my phone on airplane mode and did what I knew I had to do.

I opened my messages and typed one last text.

I'm sorry. I love you.

CHAPTER ONE

HUNDREDS—SOMETIMES THOUSANDS—of people passed through an event or comic-con on any given day, so the probability of running into someone I knew shouldn't have shocked me. So far, it had only happened a couple times. Once when I saw the manager of the bar and grill I used to work at, and once when my third grade English teacher stopped by to check out our merchandise. The shock factor was much greater with my old manager, given the fact that he was in full cosplay of some character from an anime. Mrs. Harris probably wasn't as surprised to find one of the biggest nerds she'd ever had the pleasure of teaching working at a publishing company booth, surrounded by books.

But still, everyone is surprised when they see someone in

public that they weren't planning on running into—regardless of that person's significance.

I work for Starr Publishing and Media. It used to just be Starr Publishing, way back in the day before I graduated college with enough qualifications to apply to my dream company. The media came later, when electronics started taking over, even in the world of books. It didn't matter to me. I'd fantasized of working for Starr ever since I'd been a little girl and went to my first book signing. I'd stood in that line in awe, not only because I was going to meet one of my favorite childhood authors, but because the company was kind enough to put on an event that let me do so.

Obviously, Starr wasn't the only publisher in the world to have organized a signing that I attended, but they were the first. Therefore, that made them the best.

Now, I was on the other side of the table, watching over our attending author as he chatted with con-goers about the latest fantasy thriller adventure for sale that day. All day I'd been restocking piles of a book I'd yet to read by an author I didn't particularly like touring with.

Jackson S. Albrecht.

He was just as pretentious as his name made him seem, often mansplaining plots as though I hadn't been engulfed in the fantasy book scene since pre-Mrs. Harris. But Mom had always taught me to pick my battles, so instead of outwitting him with my knowledge of more fantasy lore than a twenty-eight-year-old should probably know, I sat back and nodded. Smiled politely. Reminded myself that I'd wanted this job—had *dreamed* of this job my whole life—and had gone into thousands of dollars in student loan debt to obtain it.

Besides, Jackson wasn't *awful* to be around when he wasn't working. I definitely wouldn't consider us friends, but I could deal with him in more casual settings.

When the fans were around, that's when the inner diva came out.

"Jordi, we're running low," Jackson announced, gesturing with his eyes to the books in front of him in a way that communicated his silent, less customer-friendly message: "Why the hell haven't you noticed this problem yet?"

It was begrudgingly received, and I sighed before I moved to the back of the booth to where we kept our stock.

"The con floor shuts down in thirty minutes," my colleague, Tori, muttered to me while I crouched down to retrieve a new stack of books from one of the many boxes under the table. A scantily clad warrior woman with devil horns stared back at me from one of the glossy covers.

Funny, since Jackson's main argument against my taste in books was the amount of smut within them. I wasn't getting any action in real life, so I needed to fill the void somehow. I'd never stoop as low as to see what he'd come up with, though. Or why the woman on his cover was dressed the way she was.

"Is this supposed to make me feel hopeful or depressed?" I

asked.

Tori's eyes lifted from her inventory clipboard. "Thirty more minutes with the monster, then we're free to drink obscene amounts of margaritas, courtesy of Starr." She set the clipboard on the nearest table before placing her hands on my shoulders. Her curly, shoulder-length blonde hair bounced with the movement, and her blue eyes locked with my brown ones. "You've got this, girl."

I chuckled and shook my head before I left her to go appease Jackson, a stack of books in hand.

"Thank you," he said, cheerily. The politeness meant there must be a customer approaching. I tried to ignore them as I went about setting up the books in a way that met Jackson's absurd standards. "Hello, sir, are you here to check out the newest book in my series?"

"Oh, no, I just wanted to see if—Christ. Jordi."

Holy shit.

My eyes slowly lifted from the woman on Jackson's cover to the voice that had just addressed me—even though I already knew the answer.

Under different circumstances, I might have prolonged the moment, relishing in the awe written on Jackson's face as he tried to comprehend how this beautiful black-haired, tan-skinned, monochrome-clothed man knew me, not him. Or maybe it was awe of a different sort, since our new booth visitor was kind of a big deal.

That much was apparent from the con-goers gawking as they walked past, whispering to each other as they blatantly stared at the back of his head. Male. Female. It didn't matter. These people were now in close proximity to Alfie Fletcher, and they were taking full advantage of the moment.

Alfie was one of the biggest fantasy TV stars of the twenty-first century: Cain Luther from the ultra-popular show, *Crimson Curse*. When it came to British TV, *Curse* was one of the best shows available. We're talking *Doctor Who* level popularity, but for people who liked sexy vampires and lots of fictional melodrama.

So, naturally, I'd been a fan—along with millions of other teenage girls.

Apparently despite the show having ended years ago, the fans still lingered.

I didn't necessarily consider myself one of them anymore, since I'd stopped watching the show before the final season had aired. But that didn't mean I couldn't go toe to toe with the mega-fans in some themed bar trivia.

I only realized I was lost in a daze when Alfie's brow rose, and damn if it wasn't the sexiest thing I'd seen since…

Wow, I really needed to get out more.

I forced a smile. "Alfie. H—" I wanted to smack Jackson upside the head with his brick of a book for laughing when I knocked the stack I'd just organized over. I scrambled to right it before finishing with, "Hi."

He stared at me, dumbfounded, for a moment more before the smallest of smiles curled into his dark stubble-covered cheeks, his brow still furrowed in confusion. Like he couldn't believe this situation. Honestly, I couldn't say I felt much differently. "Hi," he replied.

I glanced back over my shoulder to see if Tori was witnessing the scene. Ever the gossip enthusiast, whatever task she'd been engrossed in before was now on hold, her eyes wide and focused on Alfie. At least her attention wasn't on me.

"What, uh—what brings you to Tulsa?" he asked when the silence stretched a little too long.

"Oh, um, this book, I guess." I picked up the novel at the top of the stack. "I hear it's really good."

"The whole series is amazing," Jackson interjected. "There's five more before this one if you're interested."

Alfie, ever the gentleman, gave Jackson a polite nod before returning his attention to me. I noted the three security guards standing a little ways off from the Starr booth.

"I feel like I should be the one asking you why you're here," I continued as I replaced the book.

"We're coming up on the fifteen-year anniversary of *Curse*," he explained, then gestured to the space around us with a few casual flicks of his wrist. "The network is planning all sorts of celebratory rubbish, so we're doing some promo tours."

"We?"

"Well, just me for now," he explained. "The rest of the cast will join at some of the later stops."

"Starting off strong," came a seductive drawl from over my left shoulder. Seconds later, Tori's manicured hand reached out past me, and Alfie reluctantly took it. "Victoria Wilson. It's a pleasure to make your acquaintance."

Oh, for the love of—

"Do you want a book or not?" Jackson seethed through a well-fought smile. I had to give him credit. He'd allowed someone else to take the spotlight for much longer than I'd anticipated.

"Um, I'm sorry," Alfie said, even though he definitely didn't need to. "I don't think I'll be getting a copy today, but, uh…" His eyes drifted past our mangy crew to the banner behind us. "But maybe I'll see Starr Publishing at another event sometime."

"And media," I corrected, and immediately hated myself for it. "Starr Publishing and Media."

He nodded once before amending, "And media."

"You'll most definitely be seeing us again," Tori butted in. I fought the urge to elbow her in the side.

"Brilliant." Alfie turned to me. "Stay in touch?"

Trying to act nonchalant amongst the stampede happening inside me, I nodded and managed to squeak out, "I'll try."

Why he wanted to see me again was more confusing than him calling out to me in the first place. Given the last time we'd seen each other…

Alfie accepted my answer, though, and with one more nod to Tori, a wave and smile to me, and complete ignorance of Jackson, he walked away with his bodyguards trailing behind, swallowed by the sea of nerds that had heard the news of his appearance in our aisle.

I watched him until he was too far gone in the crowd. He looked like a model out of some grunge magazine shoot or on the album cover for a punk rock band. Unfortunately, his manners didn't match his persona. Maybe if they did, it would have been easier to calm my heart down.

"Excuse me?"

I turned to see Tori, her hands on her ample hips.

"Sorry, is that half hour up? We can head out for—"

"No, no, no." She waggled her index finger at the spot Alfie had just vacated. "You aren't going to explain why Alfie Fletcher talked to you like you're best buddies?"

"Alfie Fletcher…" Jackson mused. "Wait. Is that the guy from that show? The ridiculous one with the vampires." Despite the disdain in his voice, I could see from his sidelong glance that he was almost as curious as Tori was, now.

"Ridiculous to some classless viewers, but a work of art to those of us with taste," Tori fired back. She turned to me again. "Well?"

I sighed before I pulled my phone out of my back pocket. Ten minutes were left before our slotted time was up and we could finally go home.

11

My eyes slid to Jackson. "Either you can pack up on your own or we all agree to leave now, because I'm not doing any explaining without alcohol in my system."

Jackson picked up on the invitation, knowing it was rare. I would have felt bad leaving him behind, especially after seeing his intrigue over what had just happened.

Besides, blatantly making plans in front of someone involved in the conversation then not inviting them was a level of rude I didn't want to hit.

He was out of his seat in seconds. "I'll come, but I can't be hungover tomorrow. It'll make my signature sloppy."

"SO TELL US more about how you and that piece of British man-candy are connected."

I loved Tori. I really did. And even though we were co-workers, I considered her one of my friends. However, I'd never considered her my most *subtle* friend.

Jackson leaned forward on the table, his lips around the straw of his margarita and eyes wide with intrigue. If I thought *I* needed to get out more, he *definitely* did.

I followed his lead, however, and took a big sip of the strawberry and tequila goodness that had been given to me. I needed the liquid courage to get through this. Plus, it gave me time to figure out just how I wanted to craft my story. Tori's bluntness came packaged with an inability to keep secrets. I knew she never meant any harm—I'd heard enough office secrets passed along in innocent conversation—but this was one secret I couldn't risk getting out. Not even for my sake, but for Alfie's. Despite the years that had passed, I still cared about his image.

Besides, it was a secret that I'd been keeping for nearly a decade. And having Alfie himself be the one to remind me of it all again…

I couldn't confess it. Not yet. Not before I had time to process everything myself.

It was time to keep my ten-year lie going.

I lifted my head and focused my attention on my two impatient yet eager companions. "I was a pretty crazy fan. He might remember me from the fan forums."

"I was on those forums too," Tori admitted, surprising me. She'd never struck me as the obvious fangirl type. She seemed like more of the hidden-guilty-pleasures kind of girl. "If you used your real name and not some embarrassing username, you're braver than Bloodsucking Biyotch over here," she said, gesturing to herself.

Appalled, Jackson turned on her, but I saved that argument from ever starting by asking, "How many of those o's were zeroes?"

"Every single one of them." My smile widened at Tori's pride. "But you can't change the subject. If Alfie fucking

Fletcher was on those forums…well, I just hope he never finds out that I'm Bloodsucking Biyotch because he could definitely sue me for one reason or another."

Not wanting to ask further details about that—for personal and HR reasons—I decided to divert. "Then maybe it was the fan letters. I'm pretty sure I sent a school picture or two."

"Did you write a romantic haiku on the back?" Jackson asked.

"Have you done this before or something?" Tori retorted.

"You don't reach my level of literary fame without dabbling in the other artforms."

Tori rolled her eyes before she asked me, "Were you hoping to show him what he was missing out on?"

"Something like that, I guess."

"You're cute, Jords." Tori leaned down to take a sip of her drink.

"Apparently whatever you did worked because he sure seemed happy to see you." I didn't miss the bitterness in Jackson's voice.

With a one-shoulder shrug, I replied, "Sometimes celebrities take a liking to the superfans, you know? It's probably out of pity, but still."

I'd said it as an excuse, but in reality, I didn't doubt that Alfie had, in fact, spoken to me out of pity. Why else would he have bothered? I didn't deserve any sort of compassion from him.

Also, those stories weren't *completely* false. I'd been on the forums, and I'd unfortunately sent some embarrassing letters and pictures to Alfie's fan club address while I'd been in high school, complete with braces and side bangs. As far as I knew, though, he'd never seen any of them, and I'd gotten close enough to Alfie that he would've told me. I could picture exactly how it would've played out: the two of us sitting in whatever flat he found himself in at the time, the sounds of London surrounding us. We'd be talking casually, but he would find some smooth way to make a comment about my high school photo. I would've gotten defensive out of embarrassment, but he would've loved it, hugging me closer as we laughed and—

I sucked a deep breath in through my nose, trying to bring myself back to reality. To Tulsa. To Tori and Jackson. To the giant margarita I intended to drown my problems with.

Tori hummed to herself then shrugged while Jackson continued to eye me suspiciously.

"I don't know," he said. "Romance isn't my forte—"

"Shocking," Tori snuck in.

"—but he seemed pretty interested in talking to you."

"Who said anything about romance?" I asked.

Jackson pointed to his eyes then mine. "It's all in the look. That's why I pick my cover models, you know. Eyes sometimes say more than we can convey with words."

Wow, I hated to admit it, but Jackson S. Albrecht might've had a point with that. An oddly poetic point.

Tori slapped her palms down on the table. "Who are you to talk? Your *cover models* are there for one reason, and one reason only." She grabbed her bountiful chest through her blouse to indicate what she meant.

Jackson shrugged. "Sex sells. I might not write romance, but I'm also not an idiot."

"Yeah, unlike Jordi who totally brushed off Cain fucking Luther." She dramatically gestured to the drinks, chips and salsa in front of us. "We could've been sharing these with him!"

I tried to remain casual, shaking my head as I did with all of Tori's eccentric comments. "Next time I earn the attention of a celebrity, I'll be sure to extend an invite."

Unless, of course, that celebrity was named Alfie Fletcher.

CHAPTER TWO

WHEN MONDAY ROLLED around, I realized how little sleep I'd gotten the remainder of the convention. I'd been kept awake each night by my thoughts, the memories I'd tried so hard to suppress rising to the surface to taunt me. Now, they weren't only trying to break free while my eyes were shut, but while I very much needed to keep my eyes open at work.

I attempted to blink myself awake as I stared at the spreadsheet on my too-bright screen. No use. Then my attention drifted to the *Crimson Curse* coffee mug that sat on my desk. Mom had gotten it for me before I'd left for my study abroad trip in college, and I hadn't had the heart to get rid of it, even when I moved to Chicago. So, despite the uneasy feeling I got every time I caught sight of the show's title scrawled in a font that looked like dripping blood, I'd made it my work mug. My job provided enough distractions that I didn't usually pay it too much attention, and if I turned it a certain way, I was met with blank white ceramic.

This was not one of those times, and each time I took a desperate, much-needed sip of my liquid lifeline, the script taunted me. After so many years, I'd thought I'd gotten used to ignoring it. Apparently, all it took was one run-in with Alfie to erase any prior progress.

The stalkerish Google searches probably didn't help either. I'd already spent the better half of my morning researching what Alfie had been up to in the years since I'd last seen him. With *Crimson Curse* no longer on the air, the paparazzi gave him less attention, but not so little that I couldn't find anything. Given Alfie's nature, though, what I'd managed to find wasn't anything shocking. No drunken scandals. No leaked nudes. Only some articles about charity work and potential girlfriends that ended up being figments of media imagination. I would know. I'd read those articles with uninterrupted interest. I could've written a full report on them if I'd been asked to.

Unfortunately, I had to write my sales summary instead.

"Did you break out the reruns of *Crimson Curse* when you got home?" Tori asked as she waltzed into my cubicle, creating one more distraction. "I know I did."

I clicked over to my calendar before checking the time. I needed to be at the event follow-up meeting in twenty minutes. Nothing like procrastinating.

"No, I'm pretty sure those are hiding in my storage unit," I replied. I was also pretty sure they'd remain there for all of eternity. Never mind that I could probably also find them on no less than three streaming platforms.

"Fair enough. You can just use the real-life Cain Luther to get off, unlike the rest of us."

I choked on the latest sip of my coffee and broke into a coughing fit before finally managing to shriek, "Tori!"

Outside of work, my mind rarely left the gutter, but I liked to think of myself as a professional at the office. And that meant no sexual comments about sexy vampires from TV. Especially not ones named Cain Luther.

Tori only shrugged. "I'm just saying. You won't catch me saying this often, but Jackson was right. He couldn't take his eyes off you."

I rolled mine in response. "He definitely could. We hardly talked for five minutes, and I'm sure he was just being polite. Did you happen to notice all the phones pointed at him?"

"I did, but I'm pretty sure *he* didn't. Actually, I'm pretty sure he would've stayed there all day talking to you if he could have, cameras and all."

I gave her a pointed look for the use of her *dreamy* voice. She was mocking me, and I didn't have time for it.

I turned back to my computer, aware that my most recent Alfie search was open in one of my browser tabs. I scrolled through my email aimlessly, hoping Tori would lose interest and I could go back to half-preparing my report and half-researching Alfie's latest charity work. I was noticing a trend that he liked working with children. As if I couldn't already name a million perfect qualities he possessed…. Guess that one was added to the list.

"So, when are you guys meeting up next?"

Tori hopped up onto my desk, making it her new seat. She sipped the froofy specialty coffee she'd brought with her, waiting for the response I didn't want to or know how to give.

"Tor, I have to finish this report."

"I see no spreadsheet," she retorted. "We've worked here for how long together now? You know Lynn won't care if you turn it in tomorrow instead of today."

"Easy for you to say. You're already headed for a promotion at the end of the year."

"And when I get more power, I'll bring you right up with me. Now, answer my question."

"Sorry to disappoint, but there won't be a next time with Alfie."

"Why not?"

I'd found, through my research, that Alfie still resided in London, but I couldn't tell Tori that. It would be too obvious that I'd spent my day cyberstalking him. So instead, I said, "He said he was on tour, remember? We probably won't be in the same city…ever. Tulsa was a coincidence."

"Well, then when are you getting in contact with him?"

"I can't."

"Why not?"

"Do you know how much it costs to send international texts?" And since I hadn't expected to ever need to do that, I hadn't purchased a phone plan that allowed it.

Tori's brow rose. "Texts? Girl, I was talking social media."

Shit. I probably should have realized that. Texts would have been the preferred option of communication, though. His was the one number, despite everything that had happened and the many phone upgrades since, that I couldn't bring myself to delete. I liked to go through purges now and then—clear out the names I knew I would never reach out to again. Alfie's never made the cut.

The idea of sliding into Alfie's DMs, however, made me feel like the boys that I hadn't talked to since college. The ones who only communicated with me when I posted pictures in bathing suits or low-cut shirts.

Sleazy.

Of course, that wasn't my intention at all. Far from it. If I *did* communicate with Alfie, I hoped he wouldn't see it that way, either. But who could be sure in the modern era of messaging?

"Does he even have any accounts?" I asked, because I truly didn't know.

Tori set down her coffee and pulled out her phone. "He most likely has an Instagram."

It took all of two seconds for Tori to start engaging in

research of her own. I tried to ignore her, continuing to pretend like I had any intention of starting my sales summary.

"Ha!" she finally shouted triumphantly, then turned her phone screen towards me. "Here he is. A little over a million followers too. Not too shabby. Not that I can really say anything with my four hundred something."

I couldn't help stealing a glance at Tori's phone. Sure enough, there was Alfie's face staring back at me from a six-picture grid and his profile photo. Looked like he was a big fan of the black and white filter. I couldn't say it surprised me.

I watched from the corner of my eye as her finger found the follow button. As it went from blue to grey, a smile lit Tori's face.

"Do you think he'll recognize my name?"

"You introduced yourself as Victoria, remember?"

"That's right…well, that just means I'll have to slide into his messages too."

"I never said I was doing that, Tor. *You* just assumed I was going to."

My beloved colleague rolled her eyes in the most dramatic way possible. I turned away, not wanting to hear what was to follow, then found myself with no choice as she grabbed the back of my spinning office chair and swiveled me in her direction again.

"At least give him a follow," Tori said. "That puts the ball in his court, you know?"

"How?"

"If he gets notifications or checks his followers, he might not know *my* name, but he sure as shit would recognize yours."

"I highly doubt he's paying that close of attention to that." Of course, I could only speak to the version of Alfie that I'd known before, but he didn't strike me as a man who worried about frivolous things like follower counts and likes on a post.

Tori shrugged, completely unfazed by my logic check. "At the very least, it will keep you connected if you *do* decide you ever want to reach out on your own."

She wasn't wrong. Not to mention I could play the "I keep forgetting" card for all of eternity with Tori when she undoubtedly decided to follow up on the progress I never intended to make.

However, I *did* need to make progress on my report by the time my boss expected it. The only way that would be accomplished was if Tori left me alone. And the only way Tori would leave me alone was if I satisfied her.

I sighed and reached for my phone. I went into my app and followed the same steps she had, aiming my screen at her once Alfie's profile also read "following" for me.

"Happy?"

Tori smirked. "Very."

"Good. Now will you please let me work on this report? I have ten minutes to make it look like I at least attempted to get it done on time."

"You would've had more time if you hadn't argued so much." Tori hopped off my desk. "You'll see, Jords. I know what I'm talking about."

"Yeah, okay…"

Anyone else might have been offended by my standoffish tone, but Tori only laughed.

"Good luck at your meeting," she said. "Can't wait to hear an update."

With that, she walked away, and just by the sing-song nature of her good-bye, I knew the meeting results weren't the update she wanted.

I'D THANKFULLY MANAGED to crank out enough of the report that Lynn didn't fire me on the spot. I promised to have it completed by the end of the day before she let me go on my way.

I was halfway down the hall, on the way back to my cubicle, when someone called out, "There she is! The woman of the hour!"

After nearly jumping out of my skin at the sudden booming voice in the otherwise quiet hallway, I turned around to find Jackson coming my way with his team in tow. I looked behind me again. I was pretty sure no one else was around, and I was correct. But there was no chance Jackson would sound so excited to see me.

"Don't look so surprised." Jackson grinned as he led his team right up to me. I smiled politely at them while I continued to wonder what alternative universe I'd stumbled into. I hoped Jackson didn't think this was normal now. Two rounds of margaritas did not a friendship make.

"What can I do for you Jackson?" I asked, then it dawned on me. "If you're all looking for the numbers from the weekend, I just spoke with Lynn. I have to finish some stuff, then I'll send it around to—"

"It's not the numbers from the weekend that we want to talk about," one of Jackson's team members said. I believed she was his publicist. "It's the numbers from after."

My brow furrowed. "After?"

Jackson beamed. "Your little friend is a miracle worker."

"My…? What are you talking about?"

Another member of Jackson's team handed me his phone. I hadn't intended to grab it so violently, but after one glance how could I not have?

On the screen was a picture of the Starr booth from the Tulsa convention. It looked like a screen shot from an Instagram story, complete with the on-screen caption, "Can't wait to dive into this great new series!"

The name in the top corner? Alfie fucking Fletcher.

"My… friend…" I repeated slowly.

"How did you get him to do this?" the publicist asked.

My head popped up in a panic. "I swear, I can have him take it down." At least I thought I might be able to. The last thing I wanted was an angry PR team blaming me for some unwarranted post. They were probably freaking out over the potential invoice that would come. Influencer marketing was *not* cheap.

"Take it down?" Jackson asked. I swear he looked like he wanted to faint from the idea. "Why would we want him to take it down?"

My eyes nervously scanned the group in front of me as I said, "I just… I thought… You like that he posted this?"

"We just had a celebrity that we didn't have to pay post about one of my books." Jackson let out a singular, incredulous laugh. "Sales have been through the roof! We've had people buying the whole series in one go."

I had a difficult time hiding my shock at the news. I knew celebrity influence was a real thing, but seeing so much success for one of Starr's authors after just one post…

Out of all the incredible talent signed by the house, why did it have to be *Jackson* that got the free publicity?

Pushing my personal vendetta aside, I forced a small smile. "That's amazing."

"How do you get him to do it again?"

"Again? Jackson, I wish I could take credit for this, but I didn't get him to post anything to begin with. I just help run the signings. I don't do any of the other marketing for—"

My phone buzzed, and worried it was an upcoming meeting notification—I'd completely forgotten to check my schedule for the day amidst everything else—I somewhat rudely checked it.

It wasn't a meeting. It was an Instagram notification.

ALFIE FLECTER has requested to follow you.

I hadn't quite processed the first notification when another one popped up. *ALFIE FLETCHER would like to send you a message.*

It took until Jackson cleared his throat for me to realize I was staring at my phone while still surrounded by him and his team.

"I, um…" I started then held up my phone. "Sorry. Emergency. We can set up a meeting time, maybe, and talk about this?"

"I'll get something set up," Jackson's agent, Marcus, said. I'd gotten to know him a bit from the first few events he'd attended. After that, he'd left Jackson to Tori and I. "We have some planning meetings for the next few novels this afternoon. Maybe we can loop this into the discussion."

"Perfect." Lies. It was not perfect. My heart was beating rapidly for many reasons I needed to handle, and another meeting wasn't helping any of them. But neither was this drawn-out conversation.

I excused myself again, and made my way past the group. Once I was sure they weren't going to turn around, I took off toward the bathroom.

CHAPTER THREE

THE STALL DOOR echoed in the vacant bathroom when I slammed it shut behind me, promptly locking it. I sat down on the toilet, pants up. Privacy was necessary if I was going to handle the mental rollercoaster currently running inside my head. A place where no one could see the frantic facial expressions I knew I was making as I went through every possible scenario for Alfie's still-unknown message.

First, I needed to be the bigger person and accept the follow request. Well, Alfie had already become that person. Twice, actually. Once when he'd held a civil conversation with me, and again when he lifted the twenty-first-century version of a white truce flag with a follow on social media.

On the other hand, I'd been standoffish in Tulsa, and I knew it. I couldn't blow my chances at reconciliation by ignoring him here too. Even if the only thing to come from said reconciliation was some mental stability and the chance to wash away some of my guilt.

I sucked in a deep breath as I unlocked my phone and didn't let it out until I quickly made my way to Instagram and hit the blue ACCEPT button for Alfie's request.

Next, I moved to my messages where, in the requests, I found the reason for my nervous heart palpitations: *Hey what's up?*

That was it. The simplest message I'd ever received from anyone, let alone Alfie. Maybe he was just as nervous as I was. Treading lightly. Not getting his hopes up that I would respond.

I intended to, but had absolutely no idea how.

It took me three attempts at crafting the perfect message before I finally hit send: *Oh you know. Working.*

My lips trilled as I let out a frustrated breath, my phone grasped screen-down on my lap. I stared at the inside of the stall door, distracting myself with the fine print on the manufacturing sticker. If I'd thought Alfie's message had been lame, what did that say about mine?

My phone dinged a moment later, announcing a new notification.

alfiefletcher: *Starr Publishing's STAR employee? ;)*

The old-school winking emoticon almost had me melting.

j_wright22: *haha I'm trying my best!*

Play it cool, Jords. Play. It. Cool.

alfiefletcher: *Have you been keeping busy since you got back from Tulsa?*

Not wanting to divulge that he was the reason for my most recent praise at work, I said, *Yeah, we never seem to have a break in publishing,* before sending a follow-up message.

j_wright22: *How about you? Is your hand alright after signing all those autographs?*

alfieflectcher: *Lol it's still there but barely*

j_wright22: *And the jet lag?*

alfieflectcher: *You're currently speaking to post-nap Alfie which is the best kind of Alfie there is*

I couldn't help the giggle that escaped while I read his message. He'd always been such a dork, and it seemed that hadn't changed.

I was halfway through typing my response when a notification banner dropped down, announcing a text from Tori.

Where'd you go? I thought your meeting with Lynn ended a half hour ago? Can't find you anywhere!

Shit. I hadn't realized how much time had passed between the end of my meeting. The conversation with Jackson and Co. hadn't felt very long. And I couldn't have been chatting with Alfie for more than a few minutes. Then again... my first message alone had taken a few minutes to craft. I might have accidentally utilized my lunch hour without realizing it.

I texted Tori back: *Yeah, ran out to get a real coffee. Couldn't stand the water in the break room anymore.*

Her reply of three laughing emojis satisfied me enough. I left Alfie on read while I made my way back to my desk, only realizing once I sat down that I hadn't actually gotten a fancy coffee.

Double shit.

Oh well, with my level of caffeine addiction, Tori would likely believe I'd chugged it with the same enthusiasm as a frat boy shot-gunning a beer.

After figuring that excuse out and clicking around on a few things to continue my farce of working that day, I pulled my phone back out. I knew it wasn't the most appropriate office etiquette, but if I was caught, I figured Tori would back me up. Or Jackson, now that Alfie had singlehandedly doubled his book sales overnight.

But as I stared at the messages, thinking about how to respond once again now that I'd been thrown off my rhythm, new worries started to form.

It felt too normal. All of it. Alfie following me and messaging me and… was it just my imagination making it seem like he was flirting with me a little bit? His last few messages were filled with the same dorkiness that I'd known almost a decade ago, and it was that dorkiness that had attracted me to Alfie even more than I'd already been. He was *real*. What I'd known of him before that was the same superficial infatuation as any other fangirl. Yet, I'd been lucky enough to get a new glimpse into the world of Alfie Fletcher—a taste of who he was when the cameras weren't rolling.

Even after everything that had happened, he was still allowing me into that private part of his world.

I didn't deserve it. But dammit, I wanted it more than anything else.

I stared at my *Crimson Curse* mug while I thought of how to proceed. If I kept messaging Alfie, there was no doubt whatever feelings I'd managed to suppress would come bubbling up like volcanic lava after years of dormancy. With even just these few messages, I could feel the butterflies taking flight each time my phone lit up.

There was no way in hell that I could go without seeing Alfie if we kept talking. It was just like when I was in London: one taste wasn't enough. Once you got involved with Alfie Fletcher, it was impossible to not get caught hook, line, and sinker.

I unlocked my phone and went to Instagram again, but instead of going to Alfie's messages I went to his profile… followers… perfect. There were plenty of fan accounts, just as I'd hoped.

Lucky for me, I knew how fans worked. I'd been one of them, after all. I just needed to find the right account to tell me the information I wanted.

When I found it, I got to work.

I KNOCKED SOFTLY on the office door, just in case the person who resided behind it was on a call. When I was met with a muffled, "Come in," however, I pushed it open and put on my best I'm-happy-to-be-here smile.

"Jordi," Lynn said, clearly surprised to see me back so soon after our meeting. Well, two hours after, but that was fast for me. "Finished with that report already?"

"I am," I announced, proud of the work I'd accomplished when I finally closed out of my many Google searches and put my phone away. "I also wanted to propose a new plan based on a conversation I had a little bit ago with Jackson and his team."

"Oh?" Lynn's brows came together as she pushed her laptop to the side, her full attention on me. "I didn't know you were meeting with them today. Was Victoria involved?"

"It just kind of happened," I said. "We ran into each other in the hallway, and I haven't had time to sit with Tori yet. She's been in meetings all day, and I was going to talk to her after I met with you."

Lynn grinned. "Skip the middle man and go straight to the decision-maker?"

I chuckled as I shrugged. Something like that. I knew Tori would approve of my half-selfish plans disguised as work the second I proposed them to her. It was Lynn that would take a little more effort. She was *way* less in-the-know of my personal life.

"I like the initiative." Lynn sat back in her chair and crossed her arms over her chest. "What do you have for me?"

Like the professional I was, I opened the laptop I'd brought with me and pulled up the quick presentation deck I'd created. It hadn't been hard to get a response from Jackson's team when I'd reached out to them, asking for the updated sales numbers. It was clear Lynn was impressed with what she saw the second I flipped to them. I'd decided it was best to start with a bang, putting them on slide two.

"This isn't what we discussed earlier today," she said.

"No, it's not," I agreed. "There was an instance where a celebrity posted about Jackson's book. I didn't learn about it until after we met."

"And this is the result?" Lynn asked, pointing to my laptop screen. I nodded. "Jesus, Mary, and Joseph…"

"I was impressed as well, and after running a few additional numbers from the report that we *did* discuss earlier…" I clicked to the next slide and Lynn's eyes widened further. "These are the total impressions and sales I projected given convention attendance, celebrity influence, and combined totals should we go through with my proposed plan."

That's when Lynn's attention finally strayed from the screen, back to me, looking a little more worried. "What're you thinking, Jordi?"

"Budget permitting," I started, already knowing her top concern from years of working with her, "I'm suggesting a book tour."

"You know those are reserved for new releases for the larger ticket authors."

Oh, how I would have loved to see the look on Jackson's face if he'd heard Lynn say that.

But she was right. Jackson was big, especially now with the Alfie Effect in place, but he wasn't the most prominent author Starr had signed in recent years. Social media made it easy for certain authors to go viral, and even though we were a small publisher, we'd been lucky to have been hit with some of that success. Those authors were the ones we pushed most often, knowing there was a higher return on investment.

But...

"Each of those authors started at a level equal or lesser to Jackson," I reminded her, and was happy with the face she made in return. "To his credit, Jackson's been doing pretty well on his own without the virality. But now that this has happened, I think it would work in our favor to start a tour for him. His book *did* just come out a few months ago. It's still fresh enough, and with his series so far along, it opens more opportunity for sales. Readers won't just buy one or two books. There's greater potential for them to buy up to six books just because of the recent influence. In fact"—I pulled up the next slide with more numbers from Jackson's team—"it looks like most people already are."

Lynn examined the bar chart that depicted the average

number of books per order as she chewed the inside of her cheek. Marketing and events always got the short end of the stick when it came to budgets, and I knew she was looking for some sort of excuse not to say yes. Thankfully, every single number so far had played in my favor.

"Do you have dates planned?" she asked. "You know it's hard to get booth space so close to when conventions take place. And the cost is likely higher because we've waited so long."

"I thought of that, too, and looked at a few dates for domestic conventions coming up that Starr has gone to in the past." I flipped a few slides, so I could get to the appropriate information to back-up my answer. "It's unrealistic to plan for anything within the next two to three weeks since we'd likely need to order more stock anyway. But once we get out a little further, there's plenty of conventions with perfectly reasonable booth rental prices."

They also conveniently aligned with Alfie's tour schedule for the *Crimson Curse* reunion, but Lynn didn't need to know that.

Lynn waggled her fingers, letting me know she wanted control of the slide deck. I happily slid my laptop her way and waited patiently while she flipped through, likely searching for something that would work in her favor. The only thing I added in was potential conflicts with already-scheduled events, but the members of the Starr team were professionals at stepping up to help if needed.

Finally, Lynn sighed. "You make a convincing argument, Jordi. Have you gotten confirmation from Mr. Albrecht that he's available?"

"Not yet. I wanted your approval first before I got his hopes up."

Lynn chuckled. "Good point. Well, I don't see any reason not to approve, honestly. I'll need to bring it to the rest of upper management, though, since I'm sure we'll need a few thousand extra if we're going to make all these dates work. If not, we'll see what we can manage on our own. Sound good?"

It sounded more than good.

After agreeing to a time when Lynn would try to have a definite answer by, I collected my laptop and prepared to leave. I stopped myself at the door, though.

"Um, Lynn?" She looked back up at me. "I forgot to ask earlier, but, um, did you happen to have time to look at that thing I sent you?"

Her head tilted to the side. "The thing?"

"Uh, yeah. The, um, thing that I wanted you to look over and maybe pass to Mr. Singh?"

"Oh, right." My stomach dropped the moment Lynn smiled in that apologetic way of hers. "I haven't had a chance yet, but I will soon, okay? You know how crazy things have been lately. And it sounds like they're only going to get busier," she finished with a warmer smile and nod at my laptop.

"Yeah," I said with a nod of my own. "Yeah, of course. I

appreciate you even taking the time to look."

The apologetic smile returned. "Of course."

With that, I left to get back to work. Hopefully my proposed tour would have a more positive outcome.

CHAPTER FOUR

ATTENDEES OF THE Albuquerque Fantasy Expo buzzed with excitement as they walked around the show floor, dressed to the nines in their intricate cosplays inspired by their favorite fantasy movies, shows, and books. I recognized probably too many, but none as well as the fans lined up in front of the Starr Publishing and Media booth, waiting for their chance to have Jackson S. Albrecht sign their book. Or in many cases *books*—with an s.

My excitement was just as high, but for a different reason. Or maybe it was anxiety. Or maybe I'd finally consumed enough coffee on an empty stomach to give myself a heart attack. Could twenty-eight-year-olds even have heart attacks? Probably, but it seemed like an anomaly.

Great. I was about to be an anomaly.

"Would you stop fidgeting so much?" Tori asked. "The customers are staring."

"Sorry," I said as I tried to distract myself from my thoughts by peering over at the dwindling stack of books beside Jackson and deciding it was time for a refresh. "I just really need this to work."

"I'm honestly surprised accounting was able to reallocate the funds for this little tour of yours." Tori held up the table cloth at our back table—the one where we had books for sale by non-present authors—so I could remove a new box of Jackson's titles. "I never did see the presentation you showed Lynn, you know. Must have been impressive."

"The numbers don't lie, I guess."

"Yeah, apparently. Hey." Tori got my attention then nodded off in Jackson's direction. In a hushed tone, she asked, "You *really* didn't have anything to do with that *coincidental* post a few weeks ago?"

Word had gotten around the office pretty quickly about Alfie's non-sponsored sharing—no thanks to Jackson and his ego. Tori was the only one who'd questioned me about it. The rest of our colleagues were too much in la-la land to assume there was any sort of connection between one of the top actors of the previous decade and anyone they knew.

He was Alfie Fletcher, after all, and we were a publishing house staffed primarily by millennials who had either watched the show or held enough pop culture knowledge to know it was a big deal. Fantasy was our top-selling genre. And even Starr—before my time, of course—had fallen into the trap of all things vampire when *Crimson Curse* had been at its prime.

I heaved a box of hardcover books into my arms. Thankfully, I'd spent most of my life carrying around large stacks of books, so it was surprisingly easy at this point.

"I swear, I did nothing."

"You're still talking to him, though?"

I gave a one-shoulder shrug—the only movement the box in my arms would really allow. "Here and there. But nothing too intense."

Tori smirked. "Remember when you didn't even want to follow him?"

"Shut up," I muttered with a small smile so she didn't think I was actually mad at her. Then I went to restock the books.

In reality, we really weren't talking too often. We'd chat for a few days, then it would die, then all of a sudden, my phone would light up again with a new message. It was never me. When Alfie didn't reply, I let the conversation end, regardless of my disappointment. It wasn't my place to force him to keep talking to me. It was miraculous that he'd humored me as much as he already had.

Still, each time I didn't hear from him for a few days, I got nervous my phone wouldn't get that beautiful notification banner alerting me to a new message from Alfie Fletcher ever again.

Now, was one of those times. Hence why I was shaking in my boots. Or rather, gym shoes. I'd learned my lesson early on to dress for comfort over fashion at conventions.

I'd concocted a brilliant plan for work, yes, but I'd only done it in hopes of having a not-so-coincidental run in with one of the top guests at the convention. So far, I'd seen nothing of the real Alfie, only Cain Luther cosplayers that had shown up for Jackson's signature.

"This was your best idea yet, Wright," the author in question said to me between guests.

"Don't let it get to your head," I replied as I stacked the last of the books on the pile beside him. "We've still got a lot of tour left."

"I'm gonna need to get a wrist brace in that case."

"I'd recommend you preserve your wrist where you can then," Tori said, jumping right into the conversation. She always had perfect timing.

"What does that mean?"

"You mean to tell me you have scantily clad women on your book covers and you can't even catch a sexual innuendo when it slaps you in the face?" Tori fired back.

"Not all of us read erotica in our spare time."

"No, you just probably fantasize about it while playing with Little Jackson."

I grinned when Jackson's face actually scrunched up in disgust.

"Let's keep it PG, okay?" he said. "In front of customers."

"Then how about you pay attention to those customers instead of giving me too many perfect opportunities to make comments like that?"

I don't think I would have been surprised if Jackson stuck his tongue out at Tori after that, but to his credit he only narrowed warning eyes at her before plastering on a customer service smile and started up a conversation with the next guest.

"Hey, Tor?" I asked when I was sure he was distracted. She turned to me. "Now that you're up here, would you mind watching stock for a second? I have to run to the restroom."

"Yeah, not a problem. Just promise you won't be gone long. I can't stand staring at his smug face."

"His back is to you."

"I know, but I can still feel his little beady, judgmental eyes. It's freaking me out."

I chuckled and patted her shoulder. "Stay strong, soldier. I'll be back soon."

I ducked out from under the square of folding tables we'd set up and into the wilderness of the con. It was approaching early afternoon, so there were plenty of attendees. Probably the most I'd seen so far.

Props from various cosplays blocked my path as I swerved through the crowd. Why, of all days, did it seem like everyone on the convention floor had decided to wear the most grandiose outfit possible? Any other time, I might have lingered to admire them. But today, I was working with a time limit.

I hadn't been lying that I needed to take a bathroom break, but my bladder could still wait a little longer. My impatience, on the other hand, could not.

"Excuse me?" I asked a passing fae warrior. "Do you know where the celebrity autograph booths are set up?"

Once he directed me towards them, I made my way through the bustling aisles of seemingly endless vendor booths. I sometimes forgot how many spaces were rented out, since I was usually trapped at the Starr booth.

It was only when the signing area came into view, that I saw the problem.

Lines. So many lines.

I scanned the row of banners, searching for the one with Alfie's name and headshot. When I finally found it, my brow furrowed. Hm. Shorter line. But also no Alfie.

Upon further inspection, I saw he wasn't scheduled to come back out for another half hour. I counted twelve people already waiting for that moment to come.

Bathroom break. I was on a bathroom break.

Ah, fuck it.

The previously last person in line gave me once over as I siddled up behind them. I probably looked insane, dressed in my business casual attire with my vendor badge. Did I get special access to things like this as a vendor? I'd never tried to test the power of my badge before, but didn't think this was the best time to do so.

The anxious con-goers didn't give me much time to contemplate my options anyway. Within five minutes of me jumping into the line, it had easily doubled. If I left to find out about potential special privileges, I'd only have to wait longer if I ended up needing to come back.

I'd eaten a pretty sketchy burger for lunch. Food poisoning seemed like a reasonable excuse for my extended absence. I'd just have to deal with Tori potentially killing me for leaving her alone with Jackson for so long.

If she did that, though, she'd have to work the rest of the stops on her own. It really wouldn't be in her favor.

The people in the front of the line stood up—they must have been camping out a *long* time—and I looked up from my phone clock, where I'd anxiously watched it tick up, minute-by-minute. My heart skipped instantly.

Alfie had emerged from behind a curtain, joined by a woman with a spiky black-and-blonde pixie cut, and was smiling beautifully at the crowd. If he saw me among the others, he definitely didn't show it. Instead, he dutifully waved at everyone before situating himself in his chair and began getting all his markers in a line. I couldn't help but notice the way his grey long-sleeve shirt hugged his muscles as he moved.

"The things I would let that man do to me," said the teenager in front of me.

And while it was odd to think of someone who was

potentially still in high school say that sort of thing about a thirty-one-year-old man, I couldn't help but agree.

In fact, I had probably already done those very things with the man in question.

It was at that precise moment that I realized where, exactly, I was. These fans were probably prepared to pay hundreds of dollars to get an autograph and picture from Cain Luther. I, on the other hand, just wanted a quick hello and small talk.

I was truly going insane.

The line beside me started to cheer in the same manner my line just had, and I looked to the front to see who was there. Shit—that was April Evans. And on the other side of her was Elliott Smith. And to round out the big four, Louie Foster sat on Alfie's other side. I'd forgotten he said the rest of the cast would eventually catch up with him on the tour.

The butterflies in my stomach turned into a full-on elephant stampede.

Alfie nodded at Pixie Cut, and the line started moving as she motioned the first person forward. I tried to keep my attention on Alfie, rather than the other actors. There was no way they'd remember me. And even if they did, almost a decade had passed. We all looked different than we had in our early twenties. Besides, I was likely the last person they'd expect to see.

Pixie Cut returned a credit card to the teenager in front of me before she allowed the girl to move over to Alfie's side of the table. Like the gentleman he was, Alfie looked up to greet her, but his eyes strayed, checking who would be next in line to meet him. He fumbled with his already uncapped marker when he saw it was me, drawing a thick black line across the Cain Luther headshot he was supposed to sign. I offered a polite wave while he seemed torn between saying something to me and giving his full attention to the girl who'd just paid for it.

"Oh, um, wow." He chuckled, and it sounded nervous even from where I stood a few feet away. An embarrassed blush tinted his cheeks soon after. "Would you mind getting me a new portrait, Lisa?" he asked Pixie Cut. "I'm so sorry. I don't know what got into me just then."

Lisa did as she was asked then waved me forward.

"What would you like to get today?"

"Uh, Lisa?" Alfie interjected before I could say anything. "Hold on for that one."

Once again Lisa followed orders, but it was clear her interest in me had grown. I offered her a shy smile while I picked at my chipping manicure.

"How about a selfie?" I heard Alfie say to the girl in front of me. She beamed as he stepped out from behind the table and grabbed her phone from her.

I watched as they took their extra pictures and she gave him a hug, looking like the happiest person on earth. I'd felt the same way the first time Alfie had hugged me.

Then the girl walked away, giggling with the friend she'd

brought with her, and Alfie turned to me.

"What the hell?" he said with a smile.

"Hi," I replied like an idiot. My brain was overheating, along with the rest of my body.

"Hi," Alfie repeated, then it was my turn for a hug. It lasted much longer than the girl's, keeping me enveloped in a strong embrace that smelled woodsy and sweet all at once.

When we pulled back, I dared a glance at April's booth. Her eyes widened when she registered who I was before they went back to normal and she greeted her next fan with a bright, toothy smile.

"What are you doing here?" Alfie asked as he made his way back behind his booth. His smile still hadn't faded.

"Working," I said. "But also I think I'm supposed to pay for an autograph or something?"

He chuckled. "That *is* what most people do after they wait in this line. Or get a picture. Or both." Apparently startled by something he'd said, his eyes widened and he held up his hands. "Unless, of course, you, uh, you don't want anything. It might be… weird?"

I smiled at his blundering. "I supposed if I've waited then I'll go all-out and get both."

I turned to Lisa, since she seemed to be the one who took the fan orders. She started tapping the screen on her tablet, but Alfie stopped her again.

"This one's free."

"No way, Alfie. Your time isn't free."

He capped his marker and crossed his arms on the table, brows raised and hazel eyes set on me in a challenge. "Then I'm not signing anything," he whispered, probably so the rest of the line didn't hear.

"Half-off," I tried.

"Ninety-nine percent off."

"Alfred Fletcher…"

His smile finally faded at the use of his full name. I hadn't even meant to say it. It was just something that happened naturally. Like before…

"I'm giving you five dollars," I said pulling out the bill I knew I had in my back pocket. "Mostly because it's all I have on me right now, if I'm being honest."

That brought the smile back. "Sold."

I watched as he pulled a random Cain Luther photo and uncapped his marker again.

"To Jordi," he narrated as he wrote. "My favorite fan."

I watched as he scribbled his signature below his sharp handwritten note. I'd been nervous, unsure of what I would get. Thankfully, he'd kept it pretty simple.

"Here you go, Jordi," Alfie said as he passed the photo to me with a smile. "When do I get your autograph in return?"

Blush heated my cheeks. "I'll be sure to let you know."

"How about that picture now? Lisa, would you mind?"

I handed Lisa my phone as Alfie came around the table again.

I couldn't tell if I was imagining every single set of eyes in the line on me, or if they truly were watching me, wondering who I was to Alfie. Why he was spending so much time on me.

My whole body tensed when his arm slipped around my waist, casual as ever, and memories flooded to the forefront of my mind. How this very same hold had gone from comforting to protective. Reminding others what was his, not theirs. They still hadn't listened. And I hadn't done enough to remind them either.

"Relax, Jords," Alfie whispered. "Smile."

We posed for the camera as Lisa took a few pictures then handed my phone back to me.

"You here all weekend?" Alfie asked. I nodded. "I'll have to find your booth again."

"Yeah, that would be great," I said. "We won't have to worry about holding up a line to talk."

It seemed Alfie had all but forgotten about that part of his job because he finally acknowledged the waiting fans. "An old friend," he said, with an apologetic wave.

That seemed to be enough to satisfy their curiosity—or perhaps annoyance—over why I'd hogged so much time. Still, I didn't plan to take any more of it.

"I have to get back to work, but it was great to see you."

"Much better than direct messaging."

I smiled. "Yeah." I agreed for many reasons, a key one being the opportunity to hear his beautiful accent.

"I'll stop by when I can," Alfie said.

He leaned in again and for the briefest of moments, I froze, unsure what was about to happen. But instead of getting what my subconscious wanted, my more sensible self was satisfied with the second hug I was given. Only this time it was accompanied by a kiss on the cheek.

I knew it was a European thing, but still, my American brain read too much into it. I pulled back much quicker than I should have, especially given the audience. With one more wave at Alfie, I hurried away.

I hadn't even remembered to grab my autographed photo.

CHAPTER FIVE

"WHERE WERE YOU?"

Tori managed to scold me before I'd ducked all the way back under the Starr tables. I understood her frustration. I'd all but run back when I realized I'd been gone pretty much a full hour. And despite our friendship, she was still my superior at work.

"I'm so sorry," I said, panting. I wiped at the sweat that was forming on my hairline. I didn't even want to check my pit stains. "There was a line and then I think that burger I ate didn't agree with me."

Tori grimaced. "God that sucks. You could've texted me. Do you need to go back to the hotel or are you fine?"

"I took some meds so I should be okay," I lied.

"Okay, well, in that case—not to put you right back to work, but we're running low on additional stock of the non-Jackson books. I've been manning things for him, so if you wouldn't mind maybe putting some new stuff out in the back and watching that for a while, I'd really—Oh, you've *got* to be kidding me."

My face twisted in confusion before I turned around, following where Tori stared past my shoulder. I'd thought it would be some absurd thing Jackson was doing. Maybe a crazy cosplay. Instead, I saw Alfie Fletcher walking straight up to our booth, toothy smile in place, as he waved a piece of paper around by his head.

I hadn't been to the eye doctor in a while, but even my worsening vision could tell it was the autographed headshot I'd left behind.

"Really, Jordi?" Tori whisper-hissed to me. "Bathroom?"

"I did go to the bathroom," I defended. And there had been a line—some cosplays were *really* difficult to pee in, I imagined. "But there might have been a detour beforehand."

Neither of us had time to say anything more before Alfie was at the booth, standing in front of us. Like the professional she was, Tori put on a smile. A chorus of muffled excitement rose from the line that awaited Jackson, and even the author himself had relinquished being the center of attention to watch what was happening.

I, on the other hand, had a hard time figuring out what to do with my face, caught between wanting to smile at Alfie, but also still fighting off the mortification of being caught in my lie.

Our new celebrity guest slapped the photo down on the table in front of me, still smiling. I noticed the rise and fall of his shoulders from heavy breaths, making me think he'd rushed it over.

"You forgot this," he said, then pointed to where he'd written something extra with an arrow pointing between 'favorite' and 'fan'. It now read, *To Jordi, my favorite and most forgetful fan.*

I tried to ignore the giant lurch from my heart when I read it.

"I wish I could stay to chat with you and Victoria, but I have a panel to go to," he said. "Wanted to deliver this before." He patted the headshot twice. "Talk soon, Jords."

I'd wanted to say goodbye, but I just let out a ragged breath instead as I watched him fast-walk away with security guards in tow. He waved politely at his fans, causing more excited squeals to erupt from Jackson's autograph line.

"Holy shit, he taped a five to the back."

I hadn't even noticed that Tori had grabbed the headshot, but sure enough, when I turned to fully face her, she was removing a five-dollar bill from the back of the picture. The same five dollars I'd used to pay for it in the first place.

Alfie Fletcher, you little shit.

"You know," Tori went on as she stared at the image. "I was kinda pissed that you lied to me. But now I just have *so* many questions."

"Can we save it for when people aren't flocking our booth?"

Because sure enough, the surprise appearance from Alfie had brought about a renewed crowd—both in Jackson's line and in front of the books I was supposed to be monitoring.

"I think I'm suddenly understanding why you were so eager to start this tour."

"Yeah?"

"Yeah, and honestly I'm relieved it wasn't for Jackson's benefit." Tori bent down and removed a box from under the table we were standing behind. When she plopped it in front of me, she added, "But I'm going to be asking those questions I mentioned a little bit ago later tonight. I'll bring wine."

I tried to smile, hoping it hid the true anxiety I was facing internally. I'd already gotten out of the situation once. This time, I'd all but willingly put myself in front of the firing squad.

At least I would get wine before I was impaled with questions I didn't think I'd be able to lie myself out of the second time around.

AS PROMISED, TORI showed up at my hotel room door with a fresh bottle of wine in hand. I'd just gotten out of the shower and was midway through brushing my hair, but she didn't seem to care and burst in like it was her own room.

"Therapy session starts now," she announced as she slammed the bottle down on the desk that came with the room and promptly began searching for glasses. "We might be drinking this stuff out of coffee cups. Or from the bottle if you're into that."

"I'll grab us some glasses," I said, not sure if I was desperate enough for straight-from-the-bottle.

I'd been mentally preparing for this conversation since I got back to my hotel room. I'd known it would eventually have to happen, but I'd hoped that we would've gotten a little bit further in the tour. Beggars couldn't be choosers, I guess. Besides, I'd basically signed myself up for failure the minute I'd decided to visit Alfie's autograph booth without thinking of a good enough excuse beforehand.

After Tori filled each of the glasses I managed to find by the hotel room mini bar, she passed one to me then took a seat on the bed.

"Spill," she said. "Not the wine. Drink the hell out of that. Spill all the tea about you and Cain Luther, though."

"Can you at least call him Alfie? It feels weird hearing the fictional name."

Tori shrugged. "I'll call him whatever you want as long as you tell me what's going on between the two of you because 'super-fan' isn't gonna fly anymore, Jords."

I rolled my eyes. "Where do you want me to start?"

"There's a *start*?" Tori's eyes widened to golf ball size and when she inched forward on the bed, spine erect with excitement, I thought for sure she'd go against her own advice and spill her wine on the pristine white duvet. "How long *is* this history?"

"I don't know, like… six months? Give or take."

"Why were you in London for so long?"

"I was a study abroad kid. British terms are longer than American ones."

"Oh no."

"Oh yeah."

"Was that semester your whole personality for the next… I'm gonna be nice and assume you only talked about it for six months."

"You are kind because it was my personality for a solid year afterwards."

Tori groaned and I laughed as I took my first sip of wine.

"Okay, okay, enough about you being a dork!" she said. "You were with Alfie that *whole* time?"

"Define 'with'."

"Dating."

"Yes."

That time Tori did flail so much that a few drips sloshed over the side of her glass and stained the duvet.

"Okay, no wine if we're going to have to pay for damages or something," I said, reaching for the glass, which she promptly pulled away.

"No, I'm done, I promise." When I tilted my head and gave her a good stare, she added, "I think. I promise to try to refrain from extreme movements while the drink is in my hand."

I still didn't believe it, but I went back to our main purpose for being there by again asking, "So where do you want me to start?"

"Well day one, obviously."

Damn, she really wasn't going to let me get out of this without revealing every little detail.

That didn't mean I couldn't leave out a few things though. Same as I'd always done.

"I don't even know where to begin," I admitted.

"Where did you guys meet?"

"At a club near Piccadilly in London."

"How romantic." Tori smirked over the rim of her glass while she took a sip.

"It was, like, the definition of a meet cute." I blushed, fighting back a smile, before I added, "He spilled his drink on me."

That moment would remain tattooed in my memory forever.

The vision of flashing lights, blaring music, and overcrowded dance floor filled my mind as if I were actually there, not in some random hotel room. I'd spent hours that day debating which of the four dresses I'd brought with me to wear on our first night out. Ironically, those same details came to mind when I thought of when everything had ended, too.

Mortification over what he'd done aside, he'd looked absolutely divine, with his casual suit on, tie loose, jacket open.

I'd decided then and there that America really needed to pick up on the trend of men looking like they wanted to go to a country club instead of a dancing club when they went out. But I quickly realized that most men probably couldn't pull off the look the way Alfie had. Like he still did, if any of the picture's I'd seen on my Instagram deep-dives were any indication.

"Shut up." Oh, *now* Tori was invested. Even more so than she'd already been.

"Yeah, and I mean you heard him talk, right? He's such a softie. I swear you would've thought he'd broken my foot or something."

"I would have definitely pegged him as more of a bad boy," Tori mused, swirling her drink.

"*Everyone* sees him as a bad boy," I agreed. "Until they get to know him."

"And him ruining your clothes was apparently the way to your heart?"

I chuckled. "Well, after he spilled his drink on me, we engaged in some small talk, but it was my first night out in London with the group, so I didn't want to be away too long. I excused myself, and honestly didn't think I would ever see him again, but then lo-and-behold my group had stolen his party's reserved booth."

"Shut *up*."

I continued, "They brought over this bouncer, but then Alfie saw me and I gave this shy little wave because I was half scared that I was going to get kicked out of a club in a foreign country and half afraid of literally just being in his presence—"

"As one would be."

"—but Alfie told the bouncer that we were cool and told his friend that he knew me. And that's how we ended up blending our groups and getting free bottle service."

"You're making it seem like the free alcohol was the best thing to come out of the night."

I rolled my eyes again. "Alfie and I talked the whole night and exchanged numbers and he asked me to hang out the next time I was free."

"What—like your schedule was so packed?"

"I had class, Tori. I wasn't there to drink and meet British men the whole time."

"Sounds like you did study abroad wrong to me."

"No, I did it just right because Alfie *loved* the idea of study dates."

"And how much time was spent actually studying?"

"A lot when we were first getting to know each other."

"And after you knew each other?"

I gave a one shoulder shrug. "About half. Maybe less."

"That's my girl." Tori extended her glass and I clinked my own against it. "I can't believe you didn't tell me you boned Cain Lu—sorry, Alfie Fletcher."

"It's not exactly work appropriate conversation, Tor." I lifted my glass just below my lips, staring at its contents as I added,

"It's also not the most casual conversation piece."

"And what changes things now?"

I gestured to bottle on the nightstand. "We're drinking wine in our pajamas, for starters. Also, I knew this tour was going to be dangerous territory and I'd have to reveal my secrets eventually."

"Then you know I have to ask," she said.

"What?"

"You dated for six months, and from the little you just told me, it sounds like things went well. So, how did it end?"

That was it. The question I dreaded. The one that would bring forth the memories I'd tried to suppress so far inside the recesses of my brain that they would never be able to escape.

It was also the first thing she'd asked that I planned to lie about.

"My schooling ended and I was set to go back to tiny-town USA." I shrugged. "We just figured distance wouldn't work. Especially given his schedule and with me still needing to finish another year of school."

I'd recited the speech about why everything had gone bad in the shower a few times, fearing the worst. I'd gotten rusty over the years, forgetting what excuses I'd spun for the people closest to me as to why my relationship had ended.

My practice seemed to have worked because Tori nodded slowly, letting all the information soak in while she took a long sip of her wine. It was followed by a prolonged hum that completely wiped away any hope that had begun to bubble in me. I'd thought I'd put a solid end to the questioning by spoiling the end of the story. What more was there left to tell? We worked in publishing. Tori should have known as well as anyone when a story had met its conclusion.

"What's that face for?"

She shrugged. "I'm just not convinced."

"Of what? That we dated?"

"No, I'm sure of that." She snorted and shook her head. "I'm *really* sure of that seeing how Alfie has had such a hard time keeping his eyes off you on these... *coincidental run-ins.*" She finished her statement with air quotes.

I knew my cheeks were turning red as a sudden rush of embarrassed heat overcame me. "I'm sorry..."

"As your superior at Starr, I should probably report this to Lynn, you know." Tori watched me under her lashes. "You're using company dollars to continue some decade-old unrequited fling."

"I know..." If that happened, I could kiss my career at Starr goodbye, along with the other request that I'd put in with Lynn.

"But as your friend and general busybody who's now very invested in this, I'm going to say nothing."

My heart leapt so much that I was sure it would come out of my mouth if I so much as breathed a little too heavy. "Seriously?"

I tried not to laugh at Tori's apparent offense to that

comment.

"Maybe we *aren't* friends," she said. I could tell she was teasing. "Maybe as soon as we get back from New Mexico I should go straight to Lynn's office and—"

Tori squealed when I dipped my thumb and index finger in my wine then flicked the liquid in her direction. When she faced me again, I was thankful to see her smiling.

"I think this tour is gonna end up being successful," she finally said when our laughter had subsided.

"Yeah, it seemed like Jackson was getting a lot of attention today. Which we know is only gonna boost his ego, but—"

"No, no, no," Tori interrupted. "I'm not talking about that diva. I don't give two shits if he sells enough books to keep getting series extension contracts."

"How professional."

Tori smirked. "Says you."

"Touché."

"That's what I'm talking about, though," she said. "I'm basing the success of this tour on whether or not you get in Alfie's pants."

"Well, that sounds predatory."

"If he gets in yours?"

"I don't think it's gonna sound great any way you phrase it."

"But you know what I'm trying to say!" She clutched her cup in both hands. "It's clear he's into this flirting thing you've got going. We just need to get *you* more on board."

"I organized this tour, didn't I?" How much more obvious could I have been about the whole situation?

Tori reached for the bottle of wine and refreshed her glass as she said, "That's the easy part. You didn't actually need to talk to him to do it, and if it did go wrong, work would have been your excuse, right?"

"Right."

"See? So now the hard part is actually doing whatever it is you're apparently so afraid of."

"Afraid?" I huffed a laugh. "I'm not afraid of Alfie."

"I never said you were afraid of Alfie. I just said you were afraid."

"Yeah, which means…?"

"Which means I see the way you get all shy and eager to run when he's around," Tori accused. "I've been around the block a few times, Jords. I'm clearly no expert in love, but I can tell there's some sort of unfinished business going on here."

The way she watched me over the lip of her glass, brows raised knowingly, made me equally irritated and embarrassed. I'd been caught red-handed, but there was no way in hell I was going to admit it. Mostly because I hadn't decided for myself what I wanted to do.

Sure, I was on this impulsive tour, but Tori was right. I'd tried to make a move by going to Alfie's signing line at the con, but what good had come of it? Some small talk, awkwardness, and a signed headshot?

I remembered the way it had been when I'd first met Alfie. It hadn't been smooth by any means, but it had immediately been easy. We'd chatted and laughed as he fumbled over his apologies, which continued later when our groups had blended together. That's when the flirting had come into play, and I'd happily obliged. Not because he was a celebrity, but because he was... I didn't think I had a word for it. I suppose because he was Alfie, and while I'd been infatuated with him, yes, I'd also been curious how someone who played someone so menacing on TV could be so sweet in real life.

From the beginning, things had been simple. Then they just weren't. No matter what my original intentions for this tour—this potential second chance at fixing what I'd ruined—had been, I was so afraid I'd never silence my guilty conscience.

"I'll see what I can do," I said.

"If you don't do it for yourself, then do it for your favorite co-worker here." Tori set her glass down after she emptied the rest of its contents. "I'll be the world's best wing-woman if you need me to just so I can live vicariously through you."

The following gestures definitely wouldn't have been approved by HR, but I laughed all the same. I needed to. I'd gotten too in my head and needed it clear if I was going to make any sort of progress the next day at the con.

CHAPTER SIX

"HOW DO YOU think it fell?" Jackson asked as he sipped on his grande extra shot americano with three pumps of cinnamon syrup and a splash of oat milk. I knew because I'd ordered ahead for him, Tori, and I, but Tori and I had yet to have a sip of our own drinks.

That was a problem for many reasons, one of the main ones being Tori would happily bite anyone's head off before the jumpy bean juice kicked in. Especially during a con weekend. Extra especially when things didn't go as planned—as was proving to be the case.

Tori and I stretched onto our tip toes again, trying to get the pop-up banner featuring Jackson's headshot and his latest book cover to stay up. The small hook at the top of the pole kept coming undone just as we tried to secure the bottom into the holder in the base. If I was counting correctly, we were on attempt number seven.

"Maybe someone hijacked it," Jackson answered his own question. "I bet it was that romance author down the way. I saw the way she was eying our set-up."

The banner snapped down, creating the loudest sound known to mankind yet again. The booths around us had stopped giving us concerned looks a while ago. They were busy going about setting up for the day, and offering to help us was the least of their worries. Time was money, after all, and booth space wasn't cheap. Considering many of the people surrounding us were small presses, artists, and small businesses I didn't blame them for leaving the established publishing house to fend for themselves.

When I glanced at Tori to see how she was faring, I was surprised to find no steam blowing out her ears. I couldn't help imagining those old cartoons where the character's face got red and the little imaginary thermometer above their head exploded.

Thankfully, she didn't turn her anger on me.

"Jackson," she said, her voice actually scary enough to send a chill down my spine. Oh, he was in for it. "How about instead of conjuring conspiracy theories, you actually help set up the giant picture of your face."

Jackson curled his lips in and shook his head. "Can't." He held up his hand. "Have to keep this fresh for a long day of signing, and that death trap has snapped one too many times. Safety hazard."

Ever the professional, Tori managed a tight-lipped smile. I figured she wanted to pick up the banner and wallop Jackson across the head with it before our next attempt at setting it up, but she thankfully refrained.

"They just *had* to get the six-foot banners," Tori muttered as she turned back to the challenge at hand. "They know how tall we are. Why pick something that has a foot on the people who'll be setting it up?"

"I think we almost got it the last time," I said, trying to defuse the tension. "If we just make sure to keep the pole as straight as possible then we should be able to—"

I'd jinxed us with too much positivity before coffee. This time it was bad.

I should have learned my lesson from the seven prior attempts, but as the banner unhooked yet again, I saw my life flash before my eyes. Or at least the lives of a few of my toes. I should have known better than to use the base as leverage. Now I was going to pay the consequences, and probably have a super fashionable boot for a few months. Not to mention be sent home from the tour.

All the plans—the hopes and dreams of overcoming my insecurities about rekindling with Alfie—were about to crumble to dust. All because of a stupid—

"Whoa, careful there!"

A pair of tanned hands appeared from behind me, grabbing the banner mid-air before it had the chance to crush my toe bones. Tori's gaping mouth told me enough about who my knight in shining armor was before I turned around—as if I hadn't already figured it out for myself.

I half turned and watched as Alfie popped the banner into place, using his height advantage to make sure the hook stayed secure at the top of the pole when he noticed it might come undone.

The hook wasn't the only thing that would come undone. I'd forgotten how nice Alfie looked in long sleeve shirts, especially the dark ones like the one he'd shown up in today. They could try as hard as they liked to hide the muscles underneath, but they never succeeded.

"You showed up just in time," Tori said.

Alfie offered her a small smile. "I wanted to stop by and say hello before I'm trapped at a table all day. Though I suppose I shouldn't complain."

From where he stood behind me, I could feel the heat radiating off his body. We were close. Too close to be casual. I noted the position of his hands, half in his front pockets, and the tension in his wrists. If he wanted to, he could make the smallest move and at least one of them could settle on my hip, and dammit it if I didn't want it to do that.

That hug and Euro-kiss—and lack of caffeine—had messed with my head. I was too accustomed to the way I used to act with Alfie.

"Well, good morning to you too!"

Jackson bounded up, conveniently forgetting the wrist he needed to protect and greeting Alfie with the most enthusiastic handshake I'd ever seen. Alfie returned it with less gusto, but with a smile. What sounded like a surprised laugh escaped him.

"Good to see you again, Jason."

Tori and I shared a glance while we tried to hide our laughter. "Jackson."

"Oh, right, Jackson." Alfie shook his head in an I-should-have-known-that way. "Easy enough to figure out, what with all the books."

I watched as his eyes scanned the booth space and the collection of titles already on display from the day before. We'd have to set out more before the con doors opened for the day.

"You're welcome to grab yourself a copy if you'd like," Jackson offered. "I'll even give it to you half off and sign it for free."

Were it not for our present company, I might have brought my palm to my face.

Tori did instead.

"Uh, thanks, mate, but I'll have to, uh, take a pass this time. Small suitcase. One carry-on. Can't afford to pack too much else."

"Of course. I should've thought about that." He made a *doh* face to likely hide the hurt of celebrity rejection. "You're still welcome to stick around and—"

Alfie turned away from Jackson and back to me. The politeness could only last so long. "I'm pretty packed this morning with signings and photo-ops, but I saw some pretzels and cheese sauce yesterday that looked delicious. Maybe we can enjoy them for lunch?"

I tried to hold back my chuckle as Tori asked, "Don't they feed you celebrities better than that?"

Before Alfie could reply, I said, "Alfie has the palette of a kindergartener."

"Ah."

"So… pretzels and cheese sauce?" Alfie asked again, timid. Like he expected me to deny the invitation.

"It's a tough offer to pass up," I teased. "But I, uh, I'll have to check if I can take a break at the same time—"

"I'll make sure she's on her lunch break when you're free," Tori interrupted. With his brows raised, Alfie looked between the two of us. "I'm her boss. What I say goes, and I say she deserves a break. She was proactive enough to get us on this little book tour to begin with."

Oh no.

I watched Alfie curiously, wondering if he'd picked up on what Tori had said, but it didn't seem like he had.

"How convenient," he replied. That time his hand did find my hip and gave it a little pinch. I fought the urge to lean into his warmth. "I'll stop by here beforehand?"

I nodded, but Jackson took the opportunity to reinsert himself. "Yes! Please, come by this booth whenever you'd like. And know the offer still stands for that free signature."

If only he could shut his self-centered mouth. I could tell Alfie didn't like it; he'd never enjoyed the celebrity treatment, but even less so when he knew he was being used—which was exactly what Jackson was doing oh-too-obviously.

"I'll keep that in mind." He pinched my hip again. "I have to go, but I'll see you later."

He gave Tori and Jackson a polite wave before he sauntered off in the direction of the signing tables. There were likely green rooms for the celebrities behind the curtains so they didn't have to mingle with the con-goers—not that Alfie had done a great job of avoiding them thus far.

"He's marketing gold," Jackson commented, and I didn't have to look to know Tori had given him some sort of glare. "How you got him wrapped so tightly around your finger, Jordi, I'll never know, but my books and I thank you for it."

"Go rest your wrist or something," Tori said, physically shooing him away. Then she moved beside me and nudged my arm with her elbow. "What did I tell you?"

"I don't know." It could have been any number of things coming from her.

She pointed her thumb at herself. "World's best wing woman." Then she leaned in closer to whisper, "You're welcome."

I rolled my eyes. I'd only thank her if I managed to make it through this.

JUST AS HE'D promised, Alfie showed up at the Starr booth later that afternoon—with a gaggle of fangirls and a few security guards in tow.

"Ready for that break?"

I turned to Tori, making sure it was still okay given the sudden influx of potential customers. She nodded. "Have fun you crazy kids!"

Alfie was still chuckling after I ducked under the booth and made my way over to him. We fell into step beside one another as we ventured toward his beloved pretzel and cheese sauce.

"I like that one," he said in lieu of a proper greeting. "She's quite the character. Your boss, she said?"

"Not quite," I explained. "She's a step above me in the corporate hierarchy, but my true manager's name is Lynn. Tori and I are partners in crime for these sorts of things more so than manager and managee."

"In regards to these sorts of things…" His tone made me nervous before he even asked the question. "Did I hear the word *tour* thrown around earlier?"

Shit, he *had* picked it up. "Yeah, you did."

"And is that a local tour or…?"

"We're in Albuquerque," I reminded him.

"Touché, Miss Wright. Where are you headed to next?"

I bit my lower lip before I answered, "Phoenix."

For a second, I thought he'd tripped, but it turned out I'd managed to stop Alfie dead in his tracks. I watched as the security guards that tailed us adjusted their distance accordingly. There had once been a time when I'd been used to having some random guy join along with Alfie and I, but not any longer.

"Phoenix, Arizona?" Alfie asked, and I nodded. He hummed to himself.

"What?" I asked, as if I didn't already know he'd started putting some sort of mental puzzle together.

The corners of his lips curled up in a small smile. "Sounds like we'll be seeing a lot of each other."

"It's just one more stop," I lied, trying to play it off instead of succumbing to the embarrassment of getting caught.

"Where are you headed after Phoenix?"

"I'd have to check the schedule."

"Dallas, maybe?"

"Why are you so curious?"

"Why are you avoiding the question?"

"I'm not avoiding it. I just don't remember."

The charming yet devilish grin that split his lips made me swoon, so much so that I almost didn't care about our proximity or his hand on my lower back. His face very, very close to mine. I could smell his cologne. Woodsy yet sweet.

Same as he'd always smelled.

"Are you stalking me, Jordi Wright?" He said it with enough sarcasm that most of my worries about being caught faded.

"That's a serious accusation," I replied.

"What if I told you I didn't mind?"

Heat made its way to my face. I knew my cheeks were as red as a tomato without needing to see them, and that knowing grin he still wore wasn't making it any better.

"My break won't last forever," I said. "Do, um, you still want to get your carbs and cheese?"

I didn't bother looking at him, but his brief pause told me that I'd shaken his rhythm. "Yeah, the more cheese and carbs the better."

We fell into a silence, and I took the opportunity to finally look around the convention we were passing by. Aisles upon aisles of creators were set up, trying to sell their merchandise and artwork to the con-goers. As a self-proclaimed nerd—more so about books than other forms of pop culture, but a nerd all the same—I was already creating a mini shopping list in my head. Thankfully for my bank account, I'd likely never find an opportunity to go purchase it, but I'd always been more of a window shopper than someone who actually followed through anyway.

"Did you see something?"

The question shook me out of my quiet mental-shopping trance. "Huh?"

Alfie nodded backward at an aisle we'd just passed. "It looked like you saw something that interested you."

"Oh." I hadn't realized he'd been paying attention. I figured he'd been just as distracted as me. "I, uh—I thought I saw some earrings that looked like the ones from my favorite movie."

"That animated one with the handsome wizard?"

I turned to him, surprised he remembered. We'd watched it together at one point, but I hadn't thought it had left any sort of impression. I ignored that altogether, though, a smirk curling up the corners of my lips as I said, "Handsome?"

That made Alfie smile again, any awkwardness I'd previously created erased. "I'm not immune to the charm of animated men." He shrugged. "Would you like to stop to look at them?"

"Oh, no, it's okay. We're on a mission for your lunch, remember?"

"I don't mind making a detour. I think I've got the time." He pulled out his phone to check what it said, then glanced back over his shoulder, likely trying to locate our buff companions. "And if I don't, one of them will stop me."

I smiled. "It's okay, Alfie. I'm more interested in food than jewelry at the moment. I haven't gotten a chance to really eat anything today either."

"Do you ever eat at these things?"

"I pack granola bars," I said. "Then Tori and I take turns going to get food. Jackson takes a break at some point too, so we get to relax, but the booth still gets some traffic without him there."

"I can imagine you probably get more without him there."

I couldn't help snickering. "So you've noticed his appeal too?"

"I don't know how you do it, Jords," Alfie said, smiling while he shook his head. "He seems like a nightmare."

"He's definitely a diva, that's for sure."

"And how did he become what he is?"

"What do you mean?"

"I guess out of all the authors signed to your company, why choose Jackson as the one you feature?"

"We host events with other authors too, but those are usually at a smaller scale. Jackson has a pretty big following, believe it or not, so the publisher justifies paying for these more expensive events. Right now, he's practically blowing up."

"Really?" Alfie genuinely seemed surprised.

"Celebrity influence is a very real thing."

It took him a moment, but then his face showed his understanding. "*I* did this?"

I nodded. "In part, yeah. But like I said, Jackson already had a decent following. You just expanded it to millennial fangirls."

As if they'd heard me, some of those very same millennial fangirls chose that moment to make themselves known. A small gaggle of them were standing at the edge of one of the marketplace aisles, phones poised and recording. I tried to keep my face down as Alfie gave a courtesy smile and wave in response to having his name called. The *Crimson Curse* cast was one of the top-billed attractions of the con, so it made sense that plenty of fans would be in attendance.

I was honestly surprised we hadn't been stopped more. I'd learned there was some form of convention etiquette when it came to celebrities, so perhaps that was what had saved Alfie from being bombarded mid-floor. That, and the burly men that seemed to keep growing in number around us the further we went on our search for a soft pretzel.

"What, uh, happened to Harry?" I asked.

I turned my head up to him and noted the quick rise of his eyebrows, as if he was surprised that I'd asked. "He, er, retired a few years ago actually. Lives in the countryside with his wife and dogs now. He'll share pictures with me now and then. I think he's up to his third grandchild too."

"That's so sweet."

"Little girl. Big brown eyes," Alfie said with a hint of a smile. He turned down to me then, meeting my eyes. "He'd be happy to hear that you asked about him." He looked away again. "He'd be happy to hear we're talking again to begin with. He always liked you."

My eyes moved to the ground where I tracked each of my steps. "I liked him too. He was great to have around." I paused, then, "Do you miss having him as your bodyguard?"

"Sometimes," Alfie admitted. "He was with me through the big *Curse* craze, so he became a rather big comfort to me.

Almost like having my dad with me at all times. Telling me what was right and wrong. Helping me out of sticky situations. But he was never too overbearing. He still let me have some freedom."

I chuckled when he stole a backwards glance at the entourage following us. I remembered when Alfie and I went on our first few dates, Harry hanging around wherever we'd decided to go, trying to act as nonchalant as possible from a few tables or barstools over. But eventually he'd left us alone, allowing us our privacy, despite Alfie's fame. I'm sure it bothered him to no end, leaving his ward on his own to face the potentially adoring—or potentially brutal, depending on the crowd—public. But I saw it as a sign of trust. He'd wanted *me* to be the one to protect Alfie.

I wondered how true Alfie's statement of Harry liking me still was, after everything that had happened. If they were as close as father and son, he'd likely been told a good portion of the details.

"Do you remember when he gave you the silent treatment for a week?" I asked when we finally made it to the food stall with the soft pretzels. The line wasn't too long, thankfully.

Alfie actually laughed at that—a joyful sound that came with a suppressed memory being brought back to light. "Christ, I forgot about that. It was because I snuck out to see you, wasn't it?"

"Did it happen more than once?" I asked incredulously, my

own smile appearing.

"Don't worry about that, love," he said, nudging me with his side. "But that was particularly for when I'd snuck out of an event to meet up with you and your friends, I believe."

I nodded. "We were at a dingy little pub and you showed up in a tux."

Alfie laughed to himself again. "By the end of the night I'm pretty sure you were wearing my coat and one of your friends had my bowtie on her head."

"Grace," I said. "It was definitely Grace."

"She was a character. Is she still like that?"

"Somewhat. She's out in Colorado working in sales for some start-up, so I think she's traded the drinking for a more…green recreational activity."

"Ah," Alfie said, understanding my explanation. There were kids around, after all. "And what about the other one? I'm completely drawing a blank on her name."

"Olivia?" I asked, and he nodded. "She's moving around a lot, actually. She ended up marrying a guy in the military right after we graduated. Grace and I were in her wedding, but it's hard to meet up since she's never in one place for long. She just had her second kid not too long ago too."

"Her and Harry's granddaughter could be best friends."

I chuckled, smiling as I began to ask, "How are your friends doing?"

As soon as I finished talking, I realized my mistake. My smile transformed into a horrified frown as Alfie's body visibly tensed. The ease and comradery that had just flowed between us dried up like the Sahara all because of one stupid question. One that I should have known was the number one off-limits topic. I realized I didn't even care about the answer. My social auto-pilot had taken over, and asking about his friends had seemed like the next logical step in the conversation.

I, of all people, should have known better. I *really* should have known better.

"What can I get for you both?" the pimply, greasy-haired teenager at the counter asked in a bored voice. I would have also given up on outstanding customer service if I'd been handing out snacks all day.

"Hi, the lady and I will do two of your pretzels with that cheese sauce."

"We're out of the cheese."

Of course they were.

"Uh, that's fine. Just the pretzels then."

He rang us up and the teenager handed over our food and Alfie and I stepped out of line. He lifted his pretzel to me.

"Cheers to delicious salty carbs, even if they aren't doused in cheese."

I tapped my pretzel against his, forcing a smile. I could tell Alfie was too, and something told me his attitude change wasn't only caused by the missing cheese.

CHAPTER SEVEN

I COULDN'T SLEEP. No matter how hard I tried, that lovely R.E.M. that I needed so desperately wouldn't come. Maybe it was a blessing in disguise, not so much for the next day of the con, but for the regret that had continued to follow me after Alfie and I had parted ways.

There were a million other people I could have asked him about—his parents, his sister, any of his *Curse* castmates. Quite literally *anyone* else. Yet, I'd still managed to screw up and ask about the one group of people with the baggage.

I was sure he would have answered "fine" for most of them, then given updates similar to my own about marriage and kids and jobs. It was hard to imagine that he'd cut them *all* out of his life.

I saw my hotel room light up behind closed lids. When I

opened them, I found my phone brightened with a fresh notification. An Instagram message.

alfiefletcher: *You wouldn't be against sneaking out would you? For old time's sake*

My eyes shifted to the time. Just about midnight. Looked like I wasn't the only one struggling.

IT DOESN'T MATTER what city you find yourself in. There will always be somewhere that's open late and offers greasy fries.

Alfie had already ordered what looked like an extra-large portion of them—maybe even two extra-larges—and had dumped them all on a napkin-covered food tray by the time I'd arrived. I'd Googled the meeting spot before I called a rideshare to drop me off. It hadn't been that long of a drive, but apparently Alfie's hotel had still been closer than mine.

I counted seven little white dipping sauce cups on the table too. Ketchup, mustard, ranch, honey mustard, barbeque, and the ketchup-mayonnaise mixture he loved. Just like ranch was my American thing, that condiment concoction was his British one. I knew that one would need a refill because I secretly loved it too.

Alfie paused with a fry mid-way into his mouth when I pulled back my red chair and sat down. We'd chatted about where to meet up, each doing our own searches, before finally settling on a place that mimicked a 1950s diner. It even came with a jukebox that was currently playing *All Shook Up* by Elvis. The oldies lover in me resisted the urge to mouth along to the lyrics.

"Sorry I didn't wait," Alfie said, lowering his fry. "I haven't eaten much other than that pretzel today."

I huffed a laugh. "Please, Alfie. You can have all of these if you want."

He raised a brow. "You're not hungry?"

I shook my head. No, I hadn't had much other than that pretzel either. I hadn't even had more than a few sips of my coffee. Stress made me anxious and anxiety suppressed my appetite.

Though sitting here with Alfie after he'd been the one to initiate our evening junk food run made it dwindle a little.

He nudged the tray in my direction. "At least have a few. I ordered the supersize option thinking you'd have some."

Not wanting to make him feel bad, I grabbed a few fries and dunked them in the ranch he'd brought back, since I figured that had been done with me in mind too. The man remembered my true midwestern obsession.

Alfie finally popped his fry into his mouth. "I'll tell you what was keeping me up if you tell me what was keeping you up."

"That's not how this works, buddy." I reached for another fry, this time dunking it in the ketchup-mayo. "*You* invited *me* out. That means you go first."

"Pushy," he replied with a smirk. "Fine. I couldn't sleep

because I was thinking about our conversation earlier."

The fry I'd just swallowed threatened to come right back up. "Oh?"

"I was rude and never answered your question."

"Which one?" I asked, even though I already knew.

"The one about my friends."

I nodded slowly, trying to buy my time on how I wanted to handle this conversation. "So, how are they?"

"I still see Louie and Elliott often," he said, referring to two of his *Curse* castmates. "They're a part of this tour, actually. We went out for drinks last night and they asked how you are. I guess April told them you were here." His brows furrowed. "I hadn't realized you two had seen each other."

"I think she saw me when I was in your line yesterday," I explained, remembering the small bit of acknowledgement I'd received from April Evans. "But that's good you all still keep in touch."

"Yeah, and Noah will join sometimes too, especially when there's a big football match on. We'll go out to a pub and watch it together." He paused, probably waiting for the next logical question from me. When I never asked it, he said, "I don't speak to Josh anymore."

I grabbed another fry, despite a fresh wave of nausea bubbling in my stomach. Food sounded repulsive at that moment, but I needed some excuse not to talk. Chewing provided that.

"I figured you should know," Alfie continued, his voice soft. Gentle, like he was testing the waters.

"No, I, um—yeah, that's good to know," I said. And because my skin suddenly felt like it was covered in fire ants, I changed the subject. "How're your parents?"

Apparently, I'd made my stance on talking about the previous topic of conversation clear enough. Alfie cleared his throat, his demeanor shifting from serious to… not quite as bubbly and excited as I knew he could be, but close. There was a reason he'd become such a successful actor.

"Mum and Dad are great. They just moved out of Chelsea, actually. They're over in Surrey now. Englefield Green, if you know where that is. They claim they didn't follow Izzy to school, but I don't think they could handle both their kids being out of the house soon. Her schedule allows for a lot more free time than mine."

"Are you not in Kensington anymore then?" I knew, at one point, his parents had lived relatively close to him in London.

"No, I am. Just returned. I've been over in Mayfair for the last few years."

I aimed a small smile at him. "That's longer than normal." If there was one thing about Alfie that I remembered, it was his terrible habit of not being able to stay put in one place for long. He never left London, but I swore he'd probably lived in nearly every single part of it at this point. "Is the new place just as dark and moody as the apartments I've been to?"

"Darker and moodier," Alfie replied with a wink. He grabbed another fry and swirled it around in the mayo-ketchup. "I thought about moving to America this time, actually. Los Angeles or New York or Chicago. Big cities with lots of production, you know? And I always remembered you saying you loved them."

"Los Angeles would have been nice," I said. "Outside the city, though. Towards the beaches and stuff."

I'd once wanted to move to LA as well, before learning about the astronomical living costs. A job in publishing wouldn't have supported me well enough to survive in So-Cal. A job in publishing wouldn't have necessarily been available there, either. I'd been lucky enough to land with Starr, one of the few houses located in my home state of Illinois.

I'd been drawn to the romanticized side of California, anyway. Waking up in a tiny beach-front property, a freshly brewed cup of coffee beside me, listening to the waves as I worked on my manuscript, some indie pop playing softly in the background...

Those daydreams only made my mind wander to the project currently in Lynn's possession, causing a whole new wave of anxiety to tease me.

"I'm in Chicago now," I said, trying to distract myself again. "Starr has an office located there. It's not in the Loop in a fancy skyscraper or anything, but we have a space in a small office building."

"That's awesome, Jords. I'll have to visit sometime and you can show me around."

The thought of Alfie visiting my tiny, one-bedroom apartment in Chicago made my heart flutter. That meant he wanted our time to be spent outside of my mild-stalking-disguised-as-a-book-tour. He hadn't seemed to care earlier, and he didn't seem to care now, so I supposed I was in the clear.

"Definitely," I agreed, then dove back into the fries to avoid having to expand any further.

The odd thing was Alfie not saying anything either. I peered up at him from under my lashes and noticed he was biting his lower lip while he stared down at the food in front of us. Damn was it sexy. Once upon a time I'd bitten his lower lip too, tasted his tongue, seen his—

Down girl. More thoughts like those and I'd regret not having my battery-operated boyfriend waiting for me back at the hotel. This was a work trip, after all, and I was a professional.

"So," Alfie finally said.

"So," I repeated. Just when I'd thought we'd steered clear of the intense talk, it sounded like my companion wanted to start it up again.

"I wasn't completely honest with you earlier. When you asked what was keeping me awake."

I raised a brow. "How so?"

"I was concerned about that conversation earlier, and…and

I said what I wanted you to know."

The look on his face made me believe he'd actually only said part of what he'd wanted me to know, but I let it slide. An old diner in the middle of Albuquerque was not the place to have that full conversation, nor was that conversation one I was mentally prepared for yet. Besides, Alfie and I would be seeing a lot more of each other at the conventions coming up. Even tomorrow—or later today, I supposed—we'd have the chance to go somewhere and—

"I'll be leaving for the airport in about five hours."

Scratch that last thought. "What?"

"I'm only a Friday and Saturday guest," Alfie explained. "I'll be stopping in New York for a quick photoshoot, then I'm headed back to London for a charity event."

I tried to disguise my disappoint by letting out an admittedly awkward laugh then saying, "I'd think you'd want to sleep with all you have going on."

"Trust me, I was trying. But I couldn't shake the feeling of the way we left things today, and I wanted to make sure I saw you again."

"You'll see me again, Alfie, don't worry. You caught onto my grand plan, remember?"

He tilted his head. "I didn't want to wait weeks before we could clear the air, Jords."

We've already waited nine years, was what I wanted to say. But instead, I stayed quiet, chewing my own lip this time. I fought the urge to look at Alfie, to see if he was watching me the same way I'd watched him. He probably was. And a part of me hoped his thoughts had wandered in the same direction mine had. I'd feel less guilty.

"I'm glad you told me," I admitted because I was. I couldn't have imagined walking into the con the next day and getting no visit from him. Not that he was under any obligation to make visiting me a priority. But it had been a nice surprise, the last few days, seeing him make a point to stop by the booth, no matter how brief.

"We'll see each other in Phoenix, though," he said. I couldn't tell if he was saying it as a fact, or wanting me to reassure him that yes—this wasn't the last time we'd see each other.

"Yeah, we will."

"And once you check the schedule, we'll probably see each other in Dallas too."

I smiled at the way he recalled my bad lie from earlier. "I suddenly remember that we will, in fact, be in Dallas also."

"And after that?"

Under the table, his foot brushed mine. I would have thought it an accident if it hadn't lingered there, creating the smallest bit of contact between the two of us. Yet, it made my heart nearly beat out of my chest.

I moved my other leg, tangling us together. "After that, we'll take it one con at a time."

WE STAYED AT the diner until it closed at two in the morning. By then, it was just us and a few groups of what appeared to be fresh twenty-ones, out for a greasy drunk snack after a night at the bars.

It turned out that Alfie had walked from his hotel to the diner, a fact I learned only after I started to call a car to pick me up. He insisted on waiting the full fifteen minutes with me until my driver showed up, even though I assured him I would be perfectly fine. The only other people around were the sixty-something-year-old man running the counter at the diner and a few people who couldn't even stand without wobbling. The safety odds were in my favor.

It's very hard to argue with a beautiful man with a beautiful accent, though. So, he stayed.

Our light conversation picked back up. We talked about everything from good restaurants we'd eaten at recently to our families. I hadn't realized how much we'd actually learned about each other in the short time we'd spent together all those years ago. I was pretty sure even my best friends had forgotten some of the details he'd asked me about. Hell, even I had.

It was only when the car that had been assigned my ride pulled up along the curb that I realized our time together was over.

"Please let me know when you're back at your hotel," Alfie said. "I'll be packing, so I'll be awake to see it."

I smiled. "I will. I promise. And, uh, thanks for inviting me tonight."

"There's no one else I'd rather devour a tray full of chips with."

We both chuckled as we went in for the goodbye hug. I'd already gotten a snuff of his cologne earlier, but now I was fully emersed in it. I inhaled a big whiff, trying to cement the scent in my memory. It smelled so damn good.

I pulled away, ready to get in the car, but Alfie's arms were still around my waist. I looked up to find him staring down at me.

Butterflies pooled in my stomach at the affection I was met with. His hazel eyes were soft, muscles loose, and when he reached up to brush the backs of his knuckles along my cheek, I thought my legs might stop working.

In a voice as tender as his stare, he asked, "Would it be okay if I kissed you?"

I couldn't imagine ever denying him my consent, but it warmed something in me that he asked.

I nodded, afraid that if I spoke my voice would betray me. I could already feel it tightening with the tease of tears.

That sensation was replaced by another the moment Alfie slowly leaned down and settled his lips on mine. It was at that precise moment I understood why I'd been so nervous to rekindle any sort of anything with Alfie. It was the same exact reason why I could never fully let him go in the past nine years. Even with all the guilt and heartbreak, his kiss still had the same effect on me as it had almost a decade before.

Fireworks. Loads of them. A Fourth of July finale.

Even though the kiss didn't last long, it was enough for me to be left craving more when Alfie pulled back.

"I'll see you when I see you," he said.

I smiled up at him as I repeated, "I'll see you when I see you."

The second the car started to pull away, my fingers went up to my lips, where the ghost of Alfie's kiss still lingered.

Yes. He definitely had all the permission in the world.

CHAPTER EIGHT

IT WAS CRAZY to think that Alfie had left the comic con that weekend to go to a photoshoot and a charity event, whereas I went back to a two-by-two cubicle.

He'd messaged me that he'd landed safely in New York the next day, but since I'd been working the booth, I hadn't seen it until after the con floor closed. He'd posted a behind the scenes, black and white photo of the set on his Instagram story, but I'd still told him to have a great time, as though I hadn't seen it—and as though I didn't know he absolutely *hated* photoshoots. Funny, since I also knew his mom was a retired model from Italy. It explained a lot about his good looks.

Other than that, I'd tried to stay off social media, knowing what I'd end up doing if the doom-scrolling began: another deep-dive into Alfieland.

I'd never been left in such a state of infatuation after kissing someone. In the years since Alfie, there'd been plenty of guys I'd gone on dates with; some shy, some pushy, some that fell somewhere in the middle of that. None of their kisses, no matter how sweet or tender, had left me feeling the way I had on Saturday night. I didn't know if it was because I'd kissed easily the most beautiful man I'd ever laid eyes on or because of our history, but I did know one thing for sure.

It had been a mistake. A huge one. Colossal. Because now I was left in this confused state of smittenness that couldn't be sated in any way until the next convention. And even if I did decide to do something more with Alfie when we saw each other next, I knew that would be a mistake too.

The further we went, the further we'd fall back into our old ways, and I wasn't sure if I was ready for that. No matter how much my body was telling me I wanted it, and no matter how clear Alfie had made it that he was aware of my reservations, I didn't know if I was capable of it. Of being the person that I knew a man like Alfie Fletcher—who was sweet and funny and handsome and beyond considerate—deserved.

I was... damaged.

My phone vibrated on my desk, drawing me from my thoughts.

I made a confused face as soon as I saw whose name showed up. Olivia.

It was a text in the group we shared with Grace. With

everyone's schedules and our locations scattered across the country, my college friends and I didn't text too often. The occasional life updates, and Liv loved to send pictures of her girls. Grace would send pictures, too, mostly of the mountains and tell us we needed to come visit A-S-A-P. Then we would talk about dates that would potentially work, end up with someone having a conflict, never book a plane ticket and go silent yet again. We still loved each other, though. Adulthood had just made it hard to catch up in person instead of virtually.

I opened it, expecting to see some picture of Olivia's toddler in a new princess dress or her infant covered in baby food. Instead, it was a link to a TikTok. That was new.

An accompanying text followed it.

Ummmm care to explain this Jords?!

The fact that I was being asked to explain something about a TikTok concerned me more than anything. I wasted no time opening it, and my stomach dropped as soon as it started to play.

Somehow, Oliva had stumbled across a video taken by someone who'd attended the convention this past weekend. It was a short clip—no more than five seconds, max—in which the girl recording called out Alfie's name and he politely gave her a wave as he walked past.

And there I was, clear as day, walking beside him.

Grace Draper
When did you reconnect with Alfie Fletcher?!?!

First I want to know how this ended up on Liv's feed

Olivia Loughman
I went down a Crimson Curse rabbit hole

Olivia Loughman
BUT NO CHANGING THE SUBJECT!!!

We ran into each other a few months ago

Grace Draper
Where do you just "run into" Alfie Fletcher?!?!

At a convention. Maybe we should video call later?

I needed this conversation to end. First, because I could see it lasting a while, and I knew I shouldn't stay on my phone for extended amounts of time when working. Second, I needed time to figure out how much I wanted to divulge. Grace and Liv were a whole lot different than Tori. They knew Alfie and

I. They'd been there when we'd first met. When we'd first started going on dates. They'd stayed up with me into the wee hours of the night drinking cheap Tesco wine as we talked about the insanity that had become my life. My Lizzie McGuire moment, if you will.

They'd have questions. Lots of them. And unlike Tori, they'd know *exactly* which ones to ask.

Olivia Loughman
YES!! I'll make sure Derek is around for the girls

Grace Draper
I'll be around tonight too!

That temporarily solved that problem, I supposed. Now to return to the other problem at hand.

I opened my app back up to where the video was still on loop, not bothering to watch it. I'd been through this once before and knew the video wasn't the issue. The comment section was.

Who's that girl???

Does Alfie have a girlfriend?!

Nooooo!! Dain forever <3 <3

He can't be with anyone but April! They're meant for each other!

Classic fangirls and their shipping. Honestly, I'd expected worse. I'd run into the same kinds of comments on *Crimson*

Curse online chatrooms and Tumblr pages years before.

I was glad it seemed like the target demographic of those websites was not the same one that I was subjected to now. I didn't want to risk the chance of any of them recognizing me from past photos that had ended up online. I'd grown up for sure, but I hadn't changed all that much, looks-wise. It wouldn't have taken a rocket scientist to do a little sleuthing, put two and two together, and figure out I was the same person. Alfie's ex and now his... something.

I would have labeled us as friends—we'd definitely moved past acquaintances—but friends didn't kiss each other. And if they did, it was an accident. A test to make sure there was definitely nothing more there.

Given the way my body reacted the moment his lips had touched mine...

"Jordi."

My hands turned into jelly and my phone clattered onto my desk, making me appear more guilty than I actually was. Lynn smiled, though, as she stepped into my tiny space, coffee clutched in both her hands, and leaned casually against one of the cubicle walls.

"What're you up to?" I didn't miss the way her eyes slid to my phone, letting me know she wasn't interested in the work I was doing. Which at that moment—and for many moments before—was nothing.

"Sorry, my friend sent me something," I said. Not a lie, but I wasn't about to tell my boss it was a video of me with one of the millennial generation's biggest stars. Especially when she was the one who'd gotten approval for the tour that helped me see said star in the first place.

"Don't sound so guilty," she replied through a chuckle. "I have two teenagers, and if you think I'm off my phone all day, you're nuts."

That made me smile a little too. "I promise I'm getting work done."

"I know you are. Don't worry." The ease on her face shifted into something else then. "Do you maybe have a second to chat in my office?"

"Yeah, of course."

In the corporate life, having your boss come and find you usually meant you were getting some kind of news and it was usually either really bad or really good. No in-between. I had no idea what this was going to be, especially coming off another successful convention stop, albeit a convention stop where footage of me had surfaced on the internet.

Clearly, I was going to these things for more than just promoting Jackson's books.

Lynn had just reminded me that she had two teenagers. Had they seen one of the videos? Had they recognized me and told their mom? Lynn was a terrific boss, but she was also one of the most professional people I'd ever met in my life. Having a conversation about social media etiquette wasn't something she'd likely do in the open office. Not that I'd been doing anything *bad* at the convention.

Oh no. Had she found out about the wine night with Tori? I hadn't brushed up on the employee handbook in a while. Was that some sort of obscure HR violation?

My thoughts continued to race until we were in Lynn's office and she instructed me to shut the door.

"Take a seat, Jordi," Lynn said, gesturing to one of the seats on the opposite side of the desk from where she sat.

She took up a seat in her own larger leather desk chair, and I suddenly felt like a character in all those office comedy movies. The one that doesn't suspect a thing until—boom! Her life gets upended in the best/worst way with an announcement from her boss.

The Debby Downer mood that had overcome me lately made my mind wandered toward the latter option, obviously.

"So," Lynn started. She leaned forward, resting her arms on her desk and steepling her fingers. "I took a look at the file you asked me to pass along to Rahm." It took me a moment to realize she was talking about Mr. Singh.

I tried to still my face into some sort of neutral expression, but I couldn't help it falling when Lynn sighed. It had only taken a matter of seconds for me to go from nearly pissing myself in fright over what she would say to wanting to dig a hole in the floor and jump through it. Sighing was never good.

"First I need to ask why you kept such a talent from me."

Perhaps sighing actually wasn't that bad.

I tried to find some sort of strength through all my nerves in order to reply, "I didn't want it to seem like I was using this position for some sort of gain."

"What position?"

"My job at Starr," I said. "I've wanted to work here since I was a little girl, and I-I didn't want to hand anything over in case you thought I was just using you or anyone else."

The smallest hint of a smile curled up Lynn's lips. "Jordi, I interviewed you four years ago, remember?" I nodded. "When I'm in an interview, I look at the qualifications the person lists on paper, but I also look at the qualifications they show me. Do you want to know what you showed that day?" She undid her hands and held one up to count as she listed. "Drive. Passion. Love of this industry. And more than anything, authenticity. I've interviewed a lot of people, Jordi. I can call a bullshitter when I see one. Pardon my French, but you weren't a bullshitter."

I truly didn't know what to say to that, so in true, awkward fashion I asked, "Am I in trouble?"

Thankfully, Lynn chuckled. "Far from it. Well, except for the fact that you kept that work of art you wrote from me for all this time."

My eyes widened. "Work of art?"

Lynn's smile grew. "I was up all night reading it. It's *exactly* what I've been looking for in a book. The way you crafted that world and developed such nuanced but lovable characters?" Lynn made a sound like she'd just tasted the most delicious dessert on the planet. "I feel like *I* should be in trouble for taking so long to get to it. You gave that manuscript to me *ages* ago."

"Well, I know you're really busy so…"

"That's no excuse. You're a member of my team, and you made what, in hindsight, was a very simple—and surprisingly enjoyable—request."

The euphoria that had been brought about by Lynn's compliments of my work faded when she steepled her fingers again. She met my eyes head-on in a way that made me feel like I couldn't look away. I couldn't even blink.

"You've put me in a very difficult position, you know that?" she said.

Oh no. She'd only brought me up to let me down—

"On one hand, we usually don't push manuscripts of family and friends in front of Rahm. And I know you're an employee, but the sentiment is all the same." Lynn explained, brushing away the semantics with a few flicks of her wrist. "But I truly feel like I'd be doing him a disservice by not showing him what you've written."

"And the other hand?" I asked, my question clearly showing my nerves because my boss smiled.

"On the other hand, I don't want to show him because I'll be losing a great asset to my team when you're undoubtedly signed."

I couldn't help the half-relived, half-excited noise that came out of me then. *Signed?* Lynn actually thought my book had the potential to attract a publishing contract offer! And with her connections to Mr. Singh, I knew he'd take her opinion into high consideration.

"Now, don't get your hopes up right away," Lynn warned. "You saw how long it took me to get to the manuscript, and Rahm is dealing with all sorts of editors coming at him with projects they found on submission and want to put in bids for. I'll try to persuade him as best I can, but I can't promise any sort of immediate gratification."

"No, no, no—of course, not!" I assured her, sitting forward in my chair perhaps a little too eagerly. "I know these things don't happen overnight."

"It might go a little quicker than normal, though. Rahm listens to me, you know. I'm the one who makes sure all the authors he *does* sign get good sales through the work of my team."

Which I selfishly hoped would shrink by one soon enough.

"I'll let you know when I have updates, okay?" Lynn stood from her chair, and I mirrored her movements. "Otherwise keep up the good work, Jordi. For your job and for your writing."

"Yes," I said like an idiot. I was at a complete loss of words. "Yes, of course. Thank you so much, Lynn. I owe you."

"Just keep doing what you're doing," she repeated. "This tour idea of yours is turning into a big deal. Lots of people around the office are talking about how successful it's been."

"Oh, well that's just—"

I froze, mid-thought, like a deer in headlights. I'm pretty sure my sudden realization showed on my face because Lynn's smile dropped, any sign of comradery replaced by the look of a nervous boss.

"What?" she asked. "Is there something I should know about?"

"Um, no," I said. "No, no, I just, uh—I forgot about some of the data I realized I needed to include in my summary report. I'll probably need to redo part of it now."

"Oh, well, then you're free to get back to work. I just wanted to let you know the good news."

"Yes, I appreciate it so much," I replied, turning on my corporate charm once more. "I can't wait to hear what Mr. Singh thinks."

I left the office after that, acting like I needed to hurry back to my desk, when, in reality, I made it far enough away from where I thought I might be caught red-handed, ducked around a corner, and leaned back against the wall. My head hit a bit harder than I'd wanted it to, but I deserved it. How could I have been so stupid?

My timing couldn't have been worse with everything going on. Lynn had taken so long to read my manuscript that I hadn't thought of the possibility of her actually doing it, even with my repeated reminders. Now that she had and was planning on personally presenting it to Mr. Singh...

If I was presented with a book deal, I wouldn't be on Lynn's team anymore.

If I wasn't on Lynn's team anymore, I wouldn't be a part of Jackson's tour.

And if I wasn't on Jackson's tour, I wouldn't see Alfie.

I WAS TWO beers and half a jar of queso in when my phone chimed with the notification for a video call. It was Olivia in the group chat. Grace and I had learned long ago to let our mom friend choose when the calls happened.

"You look like you're having a good night," she greeted when I joined. I had just popped another cheese-covered tortilla chip in my mouth.

I don't know why I'd picked queso. Now melted cheese had even more emotions attached to it, dammit.

"It's been an interesting day," I replied.

"Let's give Grace another minute and then we can get going."

It took three minutes and two call-backs before Grace managed to join in.

"Sorry, I was listening to music and didn't hear my phone."

"Dance party?" I asked.

"Is there any other way to cook when you live alone?" Grace retorted. "But enough about me. You're the one with the gossip, Jords."

"We don't get to say that often," Liv added.

"Or at least we haven't in the last decade since she hung around with Alfie Fletcher."

"You don't have to keep using his full name, Grace," I chimed in. "How many Alfie's do we all actually know?"

"One, and he's hot and British and apparently back on your radar," Liv said. "Spill, Jordi."

I sighed quietly to myself. There was a reason I never had any gossip to deliver on these catch-up calls, and that was because I made sure to steer clear of anything that was even remotely considered dramatic. I preferred to be the innocent bystander, or the listening ear and voice of reason for my friends who found themselves in sticky situations. Meanwhile, I kept a calm life filled with books, comic con visits, and good food and drink. Nothing to see here.

Until now.

Come to think of it, I now had two things worthy of telling my friends: Alfie and the potential book deal. But not wanting to jinx the latter, I decided I'd only stick to the conversation that had initiated the call in the first place.

"What do you want to know?"

"You're making it sound like there's a lot to talk about?" Grace's question held too much enthusiasm.

"How long ago did you reconnect?" Liv asked.

"Remember when I was in Tulsa?"

My friends responded at the same time with "Yeah," and "Uh-huh."

I recounted how Alfie had shown up at the Starr booth, and how I hadn't realized his name had been on the guest roster for the weekend. I'd stopped looking at those a long time ago, once I realized I'd be too busy working to actually go stand in line and meet any of my favorite pop culture icons. Then again, work hadn't stopped me in Albuquerque.

The story continued with our reconnection over social media—which then made me realize that was still our primary form of communication—then to my grand tour plan after I realized Jackson's recent success might actually give me some leverage.

"Wait, is that the annoying author?" Olivia asked.

"Yeah, the diva," I confirmed. I didn't have much drama, but a girl was allowed to vent about her job to her friends from time to time.

Grace's eyes got all big and sappy on the screen. "Aw, Jords! You sacrificed a tour with The Diva just to see Alfie?"

"You're making it sound romantic," I said.

"Yeah, Grace. Even Jords knows she's bordering on sociopathic stalker with this one."

"Okay, I wouldn't go as far as sociopathic, but stalker is pretty accurate." I paused, not long enough for them to say anything but enough for me to decide that I wanted to admit, "He figured out what I was doing at the last con. He seemed excited about it though, which thank God, because anyone else probably would have written up a restraining order."

Grace smiled and Olivia laughed.

"You're like a silent killer," the former said. "Innocent until all your schemes come to light."

"Alfie knows exactly what he's getting into with me, so it's his own fault if he doesn't take necessary precautions."

Apparently, something about what I'd said hadn't struck as humorously as I'd wanted it to. Both my friends' faces fell, and I knew exactly what part of the conversation we'd come to.

"How has that been?" Liv asked.

"Has he, you know, brought up the past stuff at all?"

My stomach sank, knowing *past stuff* meant a messy break-up caused by fear of long-distance. Not even remotely close to the truth, but it was what had been easiest at the time. Now, a decade later, it was a bit late to change the narrative.

So I rolled with the story I'd started all those years ago.

"He did," I admitted, keeping my response as general as possible. "He tried to, anyway. I kinda swerved around it."

"Why?"

"We *will* talk about it," I clarified. "I just didn't think a diner as old as my great-grandparents at one in the morning was the right setting for it."

"Shut up." Grace's phone shook as she set it on her coffee

table then sat down on her couch, legs curled under her. She held what looked like an Asian noodle dish that she was starting to poke at with her chopsticks. "What were you there for?"

"French fries and a final chat before he took off for New York then London."

"Who initiated *that* meet up?"

"He did."

"So, he clearly learned his lesson about the distance stuff. Seems like he's making more time when you're together?" Olivia asked. I heard a child scream from somewhere in her home and she turned over her shoulder to assess the situation. We probably didn't have much longer on the call.

"As best he can, yeah."

"It sounds like you haven't, though," Grace pointed out through a mouthful of noodles.

Guilt bubbled inside me.

"I mean, it's still a pretty big obstacle?" I dipped another chip in the queso then curled up in a way similar to Grace as I brought it to my mouth. In a voice muffled by food, I tried to say, "We have history."

"That's putting it lightly."

Another kid screamed—or maybe it was the same one; a scream was a scream to me—and Olivia turned again before she faced her phone enough for me to see her eyes practically rolled into the back of her head in annoyance.

"I'm so sorry, but I think Derek's lost control of them."

"I've got enough nieces and nephews to know bedtime sucks," Grace said. "Go rally the troops, hot mama."

"Can we plan another call? Please? Maybe after you see Alfie again and have another update, Jords?"

"Yeah, I'll make sure to keep you guys updated," I said, noncommittally.

"Perfect." Another scream. "Love you ladies. Wish we could've talked longer."

Liv hung up after our quick goodbyes and Grace and I didn't last much longer after that. When I was sitting in my apartment alone again, the silence of the room was almost overbearing. My head, on the other hand, wouldn't shut up.

CHAPTER
NINE

"IF IT ISN'T the talented crew of Starr Publishing and Media."

By the third day of the latest convention, Alfie was basically a part of the team himself, what with how many times he'd stopped by. This morning, without any pesky pop-up banners or books to set out—we were running low on stock; Alfie had decided to give us a shoutout during his panel the day before, resulting in record sales—he arrived with a new excuse: a coffee.

"I'll take that," Tori said, swiping my pre-existing cup away and hiding it behind a box. "Go thank lover boy."

I'd already been on my way to do that, so I had to turn back over my shoulder to give my colleague the annoyed glare she deserved. Tori smirked, even though she knew Alfie and I hadn't gotten up to anything even remotely close to warranting the nickname "lover boy". I'd only told her because she hadn't stopped pestering me all weekend about seeing Little Alfie.

I had to admit, it'd been hard to look him in the eyes with that thought on my mind. I didn't remember there being anything "little" about him at all, but I also hadn't seen Alfie naked for almost a decade.

After the kiss at our last convention two weeks before, I'd thought I might eventually have the chance, but Alfie hadn't so much as acknowledged it, let alone pulled any further moves. The closest we'd come to intimate physical contact were hugs. Otherwise, it was all polite hands on my back or soft, joking squeezes of my hips.

Not that I didn't enjoy those small gestures too, but, well, I'd hoped we'd crossed some sort of bridge into normality again.

Apparently, that bridge was lifted, and no one but me had any sense of urgency when it came to making it to the other side. Probably because no one but me knew there was a potential ticking clock now.

Still, I couldn't help noting the look in Alfie's eyes after we pulled away from our greeting hug. He passed me the coffee he'd brought with a certain twinkle that made me think he wanted to whisk me away to the nearest secluded area. It was almost painful too, like he was exercising all the strength in his being not to do just that.

If he asked, I didn't know that I'd deny him. I'd been just as ravenous since our kiss. Went to show how exciting my love life was, if one kiss had me desperate to jump into bed with a man I'd only just rekindled my relationship with.

"What're you doing here so early?" I asked, even though I knew the answer.

"I wanted to bring you that," Alfie said. "And stop by my favorite booth."

"Your flattery is very much appreciated," Tori called out from the background, making Alfie smile.

The attention on her was short-lived before his hazel eyes wandered back to me again. "Busy today?"

"I feel like I should be asking you that," I said before bringing the coffee up to my lips to take a sip. It tasted like a vanilla latte. How Alfie remembered my order from almost a decade ago was beyond me. "They decided to keep you three days?"

"I have a panel this morning, Louie and Elliot have a duo photo-op, then April and I are closing out the day with another duo photo-op."

"They're smart, capitalizing off the fangirls and the most popular ships."

Alfie held up his hands. "I've never understood all of that. It's more your forte, wouldn't you say, fangirl?"

I rolled my eyes and gave his arm a punch so weak it would have been surprising if he'd even felt it. Alfie chuckled all the same.

"Hey," he said, his voice softer now. He reached out for one of those gentle touches, hooking a finger through the belt loop of my jeans and pulling me closer. "You look nice today. I like this."

A tingle went through my whole body when he brushed back a piece of chestnut hair that I'd left out of my ponytail.

"Thanks," I replied, hoping my voice didn't betray me. "This look is called day three of a convention, and I'm out of hotel shampoo."

Alfie chuckled louder that time, his lips splitting in a toothy smile, giving me a glimpse of the pointy canines that were probably part of the reason behind his casting in *Crimson Curse*. I tried not to remember where those canines had been—how much of my skin he'd dragged them across in the past—but our proximity was making it difficult. If not for my coffee—and our company—I would have thrown myself at him by now, but neither one of us could afford an outfit change with our day's schedules.

Maybe he'd brought it to me for just that reason. An excuse to keep us from going too far disguised as a kind gesture.

By now I knew plenty of people were watching us. I stole a glance past Alfie to the girls with colorful hair at the booth across from us. Maybe I'd buy one of their keychains later just to make sure they didn't put anything about Alfie and I on the internet.

He didn't seem to care, though. The usually very private Alfie still hadn't let go of his hold on my jeans, and his thumb had found its way under the hem of my shirt to stroke my skin there.

"You okay with meeting up for lunch again?" Alfie asked. "Maybe this time I can sneak you into the green room. My castmates have been asking about you."

That was enough to distract me from the hypnotizing pattern his thumb was moving in. "Really?"

"Does that surprise you?"

"A little bit, yeah." I'd only met them a few times while Alfie and I had been together, and a decade later, I'd assumed they didn't give two shits about seeing me again.

"If you're worried about April, you know we didn't actually date in real life, right? At any point," Alfie said. "All those bleeding gossip sites used us as clickbait."

"No, I know," I confirmed. Then I smirked. "Do you think she has reason to be jealous of me?"

A slow grin split Alfie's lips. "I don't know, Jordi. *Should* April be jealous?"

"Given the way we're standing right now…" I hummed as if contemplating something. "I'd say a lot of people have a reason to be jealous."

"I wouldn't want to be standing here like this holding anybody else."

I might have tried to kiss him then, forgetting my coffee altogether and dealing with the consequences later, had the voice of the comic con god not come over the loud speaker at that moment, announcing the floor was opening to VIP-ticket guests in approximately five minutes.

"I should go before the stampede comes," Alfie said. "I'll come find you later for lunch?"

I nodded. "I'll see you then."

My whole body was hit with a rush of cold when he walked away from me, leaving me standing just far enough away from the Starr booth for it to be awkward if I remained there.

"Now I know what romance authors mean when they mention feeling the radiation of sexual tension," Jackson said by way of greeting.

"I thought you didn't read romance?" Tori fired back.

"I said I don't read erotica. It's different."

Tori rolled her eyes, and when they stopped, they landed on me. "I'm starting to think you're lying to me when you say you two haven't slept together yet."

"When and where would that have happened?" I challenged.

"A bathroom. Behind the celebrity curtain. In the backseat of a car. I don't know."

"The answer is no."

"To those particular venues or in general?"

"All of the above," I replied. "Now can we please stop this conversation?"

"Jackson, leave," Tori commanded. "Go massage your signing hand or something. You're making Jordi uncomfortable."

"Yeah, I'm sure my one comment is the problem," Jackson

retorted, but walked away all the same.

"Seriously, Jords," Tori continued in a softer tone as we both got to work finishing set-up. "Is everything okay? Jackson wasn't wrong. I mean, it's clear your little plan of seeing Alfie all the time is working."

"Everything's fine," I assured her. "We just… we need to take things slow. There's a lot of other factors involved, you know?"

Tori shrugged in a semi-understanding way. Then, "Screw Dawn and Cain. I'm full-on shipping Alfie and Jordi."

I laughed, but didn't say anything more as the tidal wave of con-goers came flooding onto the floor and the daydreams were put on pause.

Time to work.

"THERE SHE IS!"

The greeting was far more enthusiastic than I'd imagined it'd be after a decade of not seeing Elliott and Louie. They stood from their seats in the green room where the other celebrity guests were enjoying a con-provided lunch. I tried to ignore the fact that I was now not only accompanied by Alfie and his castmates, but some of the biggest names in pop culture history. Instead, I kept the focus on the two coming towards me.

Elliott beamed as he pulled back from our hug. If Alfie hadn't been in the picture and Elliott was interested in women, I would have definitely tried to shoot my shot at a chance with him. He was easily one of the most handsome men I'd ever seen. Like a gay John Boyega—with the most stunning blue eyes I'd ever seen.

Many would have said the same about Louie, who took his turn to hug me next. But I knew too much about his past from Alfie for him to be attractive anymore, even if his shaggy brown hair, freckles, and brown eyes were definitely more my usual type. Looks only went so far, and last I'd heard, he'd been cheating on his son's mother with their nanny.

"I didn't think you guys would remember me," I admitted.

I smiled when Elliott put his hand up to his heart, his face one of someone who was truly offended by the statement I'd just made. Louie said, "Forget the girl who left our boy Alfie here absolutely smitten? Never!"

"How have you been, love?" Elliott asked. He grabbed hold of my hand, guiding me back to the table they'd been sitting at before. I glanced back over my shoulder to see if Alfie was following. It appeared Louie had stopped him, and they were talking in hushed tones. The smiles they wore were reassuring, though, and when Alfie noticed me, he gave me a quick wink.

"I've, uh, I've been good," I replied, trying to ignore the butterflies that had just taken flight in my stomach. "And what about you?" I fired back at Elliott. "I've seen you're doing a lot of new projects."

"Indie work mostly," he said. "I was connected with a few of the directors from *Curse*, and I'm one of the few who continued to act after the show ended."

"You'll have to give me the names of your favorite projects you've worked on, and I'll watch them."

Elliott grew very serious, one of his brows raised, before he held out his pinky to me. "I expect a full review when we see each other next."

I linked my pinky with his. "It'll be glowing, darling."

Elliott let out a squeal of excitement. "I've missed you so much. I'm going to have to yell at Alfie for taking so long—"

"Ugh, talk about poor timing. My bladder couldn't have given me five more minutes to be here to greet you."

Every head in the room turned, regardless of celebrity status, as April Evans made her return from the restroom. Even though I'd been most worried about seeing her—I couldn't quite shake the memory of the face she'd made when she saw me in Albuquerque—up until that point, I'd forgotten she was part of the roster.

Where the men of the cast were handsome, April couldn't be described as anything short of stunning. A decade hadn't seemed to age her a bit from the last time we'd seen each other. Her hair was still a beautiful caramel brown, styled in her signature loose curls, her lips tinted a subtle, beautiful pink. There was no way her skin wasn't coated in some sort of self-tanner, but it worked better than it did on most people. Less orange, and more natural. I had the pleasure of saying I'd known her when she *had* been orange.

Given the casual attire of her male castmates, I'd expected something similar from April, but I was pretty sure she was wearing something designer. My thrift-store-chic-styled self wouldn't know for sure.

"I was wondering when we'd finally have a chance to talk," April said, her lips spreading into a stunning smile. She reached out and took ahold of my hands and that's when I noticed the *massive* engagement ring. I'd forgotten she'd recently been proposed to by the photographer that did her infamous *Vogue* shoot. The one where she'd worn nothing but vampire fangs and rubies that had been glued to her lips and strategically over her bare body. Every article that had shared the announcement had used the pictures from that very same shoot as the featured image, making it hard for me to miss when they came across my various social feeds.

"Yeah, sorry I didn't stop by at the last show."

"Oh, don't worry, hun," April said. "I know you're busy. Alfie said you're doing fantastic in your little career."

If I hadn't known April, I might have taken offense, but I knew she meant well. She was one of those celebrities with good intentions, but also with no idea of how to talk to us non-famous folk.

"It has been so terribly long," April continued. That was

when her face softened. "How are you?"

It didn't take long for me to see it. That look in her eyes. That sympathy. She wasn't just offering me a polite *how are you*. It was a loaded question.

April Evans knew.

CHAPTER TEN

"JORDI, WAIT. PLEASE."

I'd tried to stick around and answer and many questions as possible with a smile on my face, but I was no actor. It felt forced, and I knew it probably looked like it too. April never said anything more after I replied with a casual, "Fine." Neither had Louie or Elliott, bless them. But Alfie had stuck closer by my side after he noticed my cheeriness fade, even though he didn't know why it had happened.

It wasn't like I could have told him in front of his castmates—hell, in front of an entire room full of celebrities!

I'd run—actually it was more of a brisk walk because I still had some level of awareness left in me—from the green room as soon as I realized I couldn't keep the tears at bay. The thoughts. The phantom touches that haunted me. That made my skin crawl the longer I stayed in that room, trying to ignore them like I had for the past ten years. They'd ruined so many—

"Jordi."

The intrusive thoughts I'd been lost in made me flinch more than I normally would have when Alfie grabbed my arm, trying to stop me. He pulled back instantly, the shame of what he'd done written clear across his face. I wanted to tell him he had nothing to be ashamed of. *Nothing* had been his fault. It had all been mine—for not seeing the signs and making sure I put an end to it before things went too far.

"Jordi…" he said again, his voice like a soft caress. He must have noticed the tears that had finally managed to spill over. At least he was the only witness now.

"She knows," I replied. "April knows. *How* does she know, Alfie?"

It wasn't something I wanted shouted from the rooftops. It had been my source of shame for so long—a shame that had resurfaced with Alfie reentering my life.

"How does April know?" I repeated when he didn't answer, my voice breaking halfway through.

Alfie continued to stare at me. Maybe not breeching this subject had been the right choice after all. Alfie clearly still had no idea how to handle it either, and we'd had almost a decade to figure it out. Given his insistence to bring it up the last time we'd seen each other, I assumed that meant he'd figured out what he wanted to say.

Apparently not, since he couldn't even admit to being the

one who told April that—

"She found you."

My whole body went loose. "What?"

"That night at the club? April was the one who found you. She came and got me, and that's how I saw everything," Alfie explained. "I would've been none the wiser had she not said something."

My mind went blank. April Evans had been the one to tell Alfie? I'd always wondered how he'd chosen that precise moment to come check up on me, but I'd never guessed it had been her who went to get him. Who got someone to help.

Alfie took a cautious step forward, and this time I didn't flinch. I was still too busy processing.

His voice remained soft as he said, "I'm guessing that time at the club wasn't the first time, was it?"

My face scrunched as I tried to ignore what he'd just said. No, of course the club hadn't been the first time. But it had been the time that mattered. The one that ended everything between us.

God, why had I been so *stupid*? Why had I ended up alone with him so many times? But even worse, why had I allowed him to think it was okay?

"Alfie, not now. We don't—"

"No, Jordi, we *are* talking about this because if not now, when? You and I both know this is what's been hanging over our heads. It's why you won't open up to me like you did before."

"What? You want me to tell you how many times you were cheated on?"

"Cheated?" Alfie looked appalled at what I'd said. "Jordi… you think that's what happened?"

"I could have said no," I said, my tears flowing hot and fresh down my cheeks with no sign of stopping. "I could have been more aggressive and stopped him and—"

Alfie stepped closer, and I swore in that moment he was more Cain Luther than I'd ever seen him off-screen: dangerous and fiercely protective. "Jordi, he *assaulted* you. *None* of what happened was your fault, and I'm asking so I know how many times that piece of shit actually laid a hand on you."

I supposed I knew, deep down, that what Alfie was saying was true. I'd tried to forget most of what had happened, but I did know that one minute, Josh and I had been talking. Then he'd gotten closer and his hand had been on my hip. That wasn't anything new; he'd snuck a few touches at other gatherings when no one else had been looking. This particular instance, I'd blamed the crowded club as I'd tried to ignore the way his hands stroked me over the fabric of my tight dress.

Each time it had happened, I hadn't wanted his hands on me, but he was Alfie's friend. I thought… I hadn't thought he'd do anything harmful.

But it hadn't taken long before his gentle touches turned into possessive grabbing, and despite my protests, he'd still kissed me. He'd kissed me and touched me in ways I'd only ever allowed Alfie to, but unlike with Alfie, I'd felt disgusting. I hadn't wanted Josh's tongue that still tasted like cigarettes from his last smoke in my mouth, or his hands on my inner thigh, sneaking higher and higher up my dress. He wouldn't stop. No matter how hard I'd squirmed, he wouldn't stop, so I'd just… succumbed. It had been easier than causing a scene.

"Mr. Fletcher?"

I sucked in a deep breath, trying to appear as put together as possible for the poor convention volunteer who had come to track down Alfie. We hadn't made it very far from the green room, but it was far enough where they'd apparently put out a search.

If I'd thought Alfie had turned into his on-screen alter ego before, I'd been poorly mistaken. I watched as his hands clenched into fists, his jaw tight.

"What?" he ground out.

"I-it's almost time for your autograph signing."

"Have them wait."

"But, Mr. Fletcher—"

"I'm clearly in the middle of something," Alfie said, voice dripping with ice as he turned on the volunteer. "Tell them I'll be late, and I'll pay the fucking fine if I need to."

I'd never seen this side of Alfie before. Not even then, on that night when he'd finally seen Josh and me. I hadn't even known he had it in him to become so angry.

And all of it was because of me.

"Go."

Alfie's eyes were filled with a mixture of surprise and worry when he turned back round to face me.

"Go to your signing," I repeated. "I-I have to go back to my booth too."

"Jordi…"

He said my name with so much reverence, so much concern, that I almost changed my mind. But I needed to leave. We needed to end this conversation that was bringing out the worst of us both.

It was exactly why I'd wanted to leave it in the past to begin with. To pretend that none of it existed and Alfie and I could start anew.

"Good luck at your signing—and the panel too, I guess," I said.

I offered a semi-polite smile to the volunteer who, to their credit, managed to give me one too as I walked past. I probably looked like a mess, but I refused to stop, even as Alfie called after me, trying to get me to do just that.

I kept my head down the whole way back to the Starr booth, not wanting too many con-goers to notice my appearance. Even amidst all the cosplay, a crying woman would still stand out as the most absurd thing in the room.

"There you are," Tori said when I ducked under the tables. "How was your time with—?"

She didn't even bother finishing her question when I lifted my head and she got a good look at my face.

"Oh no…"

Tori opened her arms to me and I went into them immediately. I needed comfort, and I would take it from anyone at that point. Even Jackson if he'd offered it.

"I don't know what happened," Tori went on, still hugging me, "but just know I'm here for you, okay? I promise I'm a great listener."

A strangled laugh escaped me, one of those disgusting I've-been-crying ones that also came with a saliva bubble when I opened my mouth.

"If you want to head back to the hotel, you can," Tori said. "I should be okay by myself for the rest of the day."

"Are you sure?" I asked.

"Yeah, I'm freaking sure," Tori replied, her own laugh finding its way out. "It's early close anyway since it's Sunday. Go wash your face and get some rest."

Normally, I might have argued more, but some of the con-goers circling the booth were giving me looks. I didn't want their pity if I ended up having to help them with anything. My eyes already hurt, which meant they'd be puffier than a blowfish soon enough.

Instead, I grabbed my purse from its hiding spot under the tablecloths and headed out.

CHAPTER ELEVEN

A BOTTLE OF wine from the hotel bar and streaming rom-coms on my laptop weren't doing the trick.

I didn't know what I'd been thinking, coming back to the hotel without any plan of distraction. My mind wandered at a sprint, and no matter how much I tried to flood it with some of my favorite flicks, nothing was distracting enough to make me forget what Alfie had said.

None of this is your fault.

If that was true, then why did I feel so guilty?

And like any guilty, half-drunk woman would, I texted my crush. Actually, I slid into his DMs, which sounded worse, but it was my only option.

Usually, unless he was busy, Alfie managed to respond pretty quickly. But as Jenna Rink got closer and closer to figuring out that being thirty wasn't all that great, I still hadn't heard back from him.

I hadn't thought that in running away from my problems I might have also given Alfie a great, bright neon sign that said I was running from him as well. That hadn't been my intention, of course, but was that how he'd taken it?

The next sip of wine was more like a gulp. Jenna and Matty argued on screen. Maybe I'd picked the wrong movie. It was stressing me out more than it was helping me.

Almost half an hour passed with no response, and if I didn't think Alfie was either sitting in his hotel room or out with Louie and Elliott, I might not have worried so much.

This felt a lot like ignoring, and I didn't want to catch my flight in the morning with us on that sort of basis.

It was a miracle I remembered to throw on a bra, because I didn't even bother changing out of my pajama pants and t-shirt before I grabbed my purse and headed out the door.

I REALIZED, IN hindsight, that showing up to Alfie's hotel in my pajamas with a bag of greasy food wasn't the most brilliant idea I'd ever had. He'd made the mistake of telling me where he was staying during our late-night get together on the first night of the convention, probably not thinking anything of it.

Given the look on the front desk attendant's face when I

approached him, it was clear that they must have been warned against visitors. I'm sure they'd been briefed on what celebrities were staying with them during the duration of the convention and to be wary of crazy fangirls. He probably assumed I fell into the latter category, and I couldn't say I blamed him.

"And how, exactly, do you know Mr. Fletcher, Miss…?"

"Miss Wright. Jordi Wright. You can call his room, and he'll know who I am."

"If you know him so well, why don't you contact him and ask for his room number directly?"

Touché, Mr. Sassypants.

"He's not answering my messages," I admitted.

"Well, I'm sorry, Miss Wright, but it's against hotel policy to give out our guests' room numbers. Even more so when those guests are of celebrity status."

I plopped my greasy bag on the counter, much to the attendant's obvious dismay. He would probably have to clean up the residue it left behind when I left.

"Listen,"—my eyes slid down to glance at the name on his badge—"Steve." I placed my palms on the desk and using my best serious-adult voice. "I'm not a crazy fan. I know Alfie. I'm trying to give him peace-offering food so that we don't leave this city hating each other."

This seemed to pique his interest a little. "Do you know the name Mr. Fletcher is actually under in our system?"

I fell back. Shit. I hadn't even thought that he might go

incognito. Made sense given the number of fans probably staying in the very same hotel. The ones who were *actually* crazy. Not me.

"I-I didn't know he—" My palms found the counter again. "Listen," I repeated. "You have to believe me. I'm not crazy. I'm not a fan. Well, I was, but now I'm a friend. Look!" I pulled out my phone and opened Instagram. "We message each other all the time, and as you can see, he didn't respond to the last one. But I swear we talk. We're friends. And I'm here to give my friend an apology burger and fries with ketchup and mayo."

In Steve's head, I was probably one of those people who would end up with their own *60 Minutes* specials. *Psycho Fan Believes She's Celebrity's Best Friend.* If he had a strait jacket behind the desk, I figured he'd trap me in it before calling the cops and shipping me off to Phoenix's finest mental establishment.

It didn't look like he had a strait jacket, but he did have a button he pressed. I had no idea what it was for, but I could guess it wasn't the fun kind from game shows that would end with me winning some money.

"Is the room under Archie Fletcher?" I asked, now in a panic. "That's his dad. What about his grandpa's name? Daniel?" From the corner of my eye, I saw a large man in a black uniform approaching. He put anyone the cons had hired to guard Alfie to shame.

"What about Cain Luther? Did the he use his fictional name?"

"Miss, please step away from the desk," the man in the uniform said.

"Steve, please," I said, not planning on obeying whatsoever. "I just want to give this to him. I fly back to Chicago first thing in the morning, and I won't be able to—no! Please! Sir, don't touch me! Let me go!"

Every single person in the hotel lobby was watching me as I tried to get out of the security guard's grip. He had my hands behind my back, and even though I'd never been handcuffed, this might have been worse.

"Jordi?"

A British accent had never sounded so beautiful.

Hurried footsteps echoed on the tiled floor of the lobby, then Alfie was there, grabbing hold of the guard.

"Hey, mate, she told you to get off her, so get off her," he said as he tried to pry me free.

"You know this girl?" the guard asked.

"Yeah, he's the one I was trying to come visit." I eyed Steve the whole time I spoke.

Thankfully, the guard believed it and let me go. The freedom of being able to move my arms again was incredible.

"Mr. Fletcher," my new enemy said, coming out from his hiding spot behind the front desk. "She was trying to ask for access to your room. You have to understand that with everyone here, I thought she was lying."

"I've known Jordi for years, and I've never once known her

as a liar," Alfie replied. Smart of him to omit the part about us not actually being in contact for most of those years.

"So, it's true?"

"Of course, it's true." Alfie's eyes slid past Steve to the bag on the counter. "Were you trying to bring me food?"

"The key word is *trying*."

Alfie eyed Steve, but at least this time the hotel staff member had the decency to look ashamed.

"I'll just grab that then." Alfie walked over to snatch the bag, and when he got back to me, he said, "Let's go up to my room and eat, shall we? It's a tad loud down here."

I made sure to give Steve a fun little smirk as Alfie led me away, his arm around my shoulders.

"CARE TO EXPLAIN why I came back to my hotel to find you almost getting yourself arrested?"

Alfie shut the door behind us, and I let him make the first move into the room. I lingered in the small entryway of the suite, watching as he carried the bag of food in his fist before setting it down on the coffee table and taking a seat on the couch. He draped his arm along the back, showing off the swells of his muscles, the fabric of his black t-shirt clinging to them.

I moved further into the room, but instead of sitting next to him, I chose to sit cross-legged on the floor. Not only had I managed to infuriate him that afternoon, but I'd also gotten him caught up in what hopefully wouldn't become a scandal. Given his nonchalance during the whole situation, I took that to mean he wasn't too concerned.

"I don't think you're the only one who thinks of food when they're stressed," I said. "Now, would you care to explain why you didn't answer the message that could have helped avoid that whole situation in the first place?"

Alfie lifted himself off the couch to get his phone out of his back jean pocket. He waved it in front of me. "My phone died. I thought I had enough of a charge to get through my walk, but it turns out I was mistaken."

Ah. So, my worst-case-scenario-oriented brain had lost the battle again.

"Why, uh, were you taking a walk?" I asked.

"To get out of this room," he replied. "And to clear my head. Like you said, it was a stressful day."

I deserved that one.

"I'm sorry I left," I said. "I just… I needed to get back to work."

"You weren't at the booth the rest of the afternoon."

My brows shot up. "You came to check?"

"You were crying, Jordi. Of course, I came to check on you. Tori said you went back to the hotel, but didn't offer me much else."

"You could have messaged me too."

"I'm sure you know that I don't do well with reaching out during these sorts of situations."

Yes. I was more aware of that than most people probably were.

I lowered my eyes, distracting myself by playing with a loose tuft in the carpet. "Now that you brought it up, I have to ask."

"I figured you would."

I lifted my eyes again, meeting his head on. "I-if you didn't think anything that happened was my fault…" I trailed off, fighting back the tears that were already trying to make their return. "*Why* didn't you reach out to me? This whole time I thought you hated me, Alfie."

The pain caused by my statement was evident, and I swore I saw Alfie's eyes well with his own tears, even from where I sat. It took him only a moment to compose himself.

"Truthfully?" he asked. When I met him with expectant eyes, he sighed. "I couldn't forgive myself. For any of it. And if *I* couldn't forgive myself, I couldn't imagine how *you* felt, Jords. I mean, Christ—how do you apologize to the woman you love for not being able to protect her? From one of your best mates, at that. I was stunned. Absolutely stunned that I'd even witnessed what I had, and… and I think it took me some time to get out of that state of shock and figure out what to do. By the time I did, it was too late."

Social media hadn't been what it was now. Neither were

international messaging plans. We'd never exchanged emails; our relationship had ended before we'd had the chance. Alfie had known as much as I had that the moment my plane took off, we'd lose touch. Anything left between us would remain unsaid.

"I saw it, you know," he said next.

"Saw what?"

"That last text you sent me."

My heart jumped. I'd hoped he'd gotten it, but hadn't held my breath, seeing as I'd sent it right before take-off on my flight from London back to the States.

I'm sorry. I love you.

"You had nothing to apologize for then, and you have nothing to apologize for now," Alfie continued. "And today when I heard you blaming yourself for everything that happened, I think I got so upset because it reminded me of that text. That had been my chance to tell you I wasn't mad, and I went almost ten fucking years holding that guilt with me."

You and me both, Alfred…

My eyes found the floor again. "I never said anything," I muttered.

"What?"

I chewed on my lower lip, buying some time as I tried to figure out how I wanted to say this. How I would finally admit aloud the secret I'd kept buried for so long. The secret only Alfie and I shared.

"I never said anything," I repeated. "About the…" I swallowed, still unable to say the word Alfie had used earlier to describe what I'd gone through. "No one knows."

The quick widening of his eyes was enough to show his shock, but Alfie regained his composure almost immediately. "No one?" he echoed. "Not even your parents?" I shook my head. "Grace? Olivia?"

"Not a soul." I raked my fingers through the carpet. "I felt so… so not myself, I guess? And I was so confused. Like, you hear stories, but you never think it will happen to you. And when it does…"

The silence that overcame us didn't feel tense. It felt necessary, as we both tried to process everything that had happened. It was the first time either of us was probably voicing any of these feelings. At least, I knew it was the first time for me.

"It was easy to play it off," I said, then sniffled. The tears weren't too far off now. "I told everyone we broke up because of distance, and when we didn't officially say goodbye, that we'd decided that would be easier. It was too upsetting." I shrugged off the old excuse before I sighed. "Everyone believed it."

I closed my eyes and the tears spilled over. I couldn't see him, but I heard the old hotel couch creak and the soft pad of feet on the plush carpet as Alfie made his way over to me. He wrapped me in his arms, and I sank into his embrace, soaking up the comfort I always felt with him.

He sat in silence while I let the emotions that had been bubbling inside me finally burst. A decade of doubts and guilt—he'd freed me of them all with one conversation I'd been dreading, convinced he hated me.

When I pulled back from his chest, I saw the wet mark my tears had left behind on his shirt, but Alfie didn't seem to care. His arms unwound from me, and his hands moved to cup my face. He brushed away the remaining tears with his thumbs.

"I want you to know," Alfie said in a voice as soft as his caress. "I wasn't at the Starr Publishing and Media booth by accident."

"W-were you stalking me too?" I asked.

I adored the smile that broke across his lips and felt the tremble of his body as he chuckled. Then, his face twisted into some mixture of contemplative and amused.

"I actually suppose I was," he admitted. "But I'd only hoped to find your name."

"My name?"

"On books," Alfie explained. "I knew how you loved writing and you held an interest in the publishing industry. I don't always get time to walk the convention floors, but when I found a few spare minutes, I'd go to where they hoard the authors and see if I could find your name on any of the books. I never in all my life imagined I'd actually find *you*."

His thumbs stroked my cheeks again.

"I wanted to know you were okay," he whispered. "Finding a book with your name on it would have been my way of knowing you made it past everything. That you were… safe, I suppose is the best word for it."

I had no words. Nothing in my entire life would have prepared me for what Alfie had just told me.

He'd spent nine years looking for any sign of me. Not only that, but he'd believed in my talent enough to think he'd actually find a book with my name on it. I didn't want to think about how close that reality might be for me now, and what that might mean for us.

"Alfie…" I finally managed.

"And I know what you're going to say," Alfie continued. He sounded worried, almost like he'd admitted his deepest, darkest secret and didn't know if he should have. "I know I hate reading, but I swear I would have bought the whole stock of anything with your name on it. And I promise I would have gotten around to reading them eventual—"

"Shhhh," I cut him off. A strangled laugh escaped me because dammit, this perfect man.

I placed my hands over his before I lowered my head. Alfie's eyes fluttered shut and mine followed just as our foreheads met. We sat like that in silence for I don't know how long. All I knew was I'd missed this. I'd missed *him*. So fucking much.

"Alfie," I whispered again, but neither of us moved. "I forgive you."

There was nothing to forgive, of course. Alfie had never done anything wrong, but I knew it was what he needed to hear. As much was confirmed when his breath shuddered out of him, relieved.

When I pulled back, he finally met me with his hazel stare.

"But I want you to know," I said and removed his hands from my face so I could lace our fingers together. "You never have to apologize. I'm always yours."

It was scary to admit, but it was true. Alfie Fletcher would always have my heart. As much had become evident in the short amount of time we'd spent rekindling what had once been. We'd fallen back into each other's lives in a whirlwind, but now that we'd finally put all our dirty laundry out to air, I knew it more than ever.

He seemed to enjoy what I'd said, his eyes glassing over with an intensity I hadn't seen in years.

"Did you only come here tonight to talk about this?" he asked, his voice still low, but it had taken on a new, huskier quality.

"For the most part," I said.

"And the other part?"

I leaned back, biting my lower lip. Alfie's eyes traced it, and his tongue slid out to wet his own. It was amazing how his simplest movements could be so damn sexy.

It was difficult to believe how hard I'd been crying not long before. All the tears had dried up, replaced with a sudden desire. Alfie's reactions and low tone caused reactions that started with my irregular heartbeat, traveled down to make an ache grow between my legs, and ended all the way at the tips of my toes.

We didn't need to voice the other intention of my visit. The casual touches and flirting we'd been engaged in all weekend had said enough. And now that we'd finally cleared the air between us as well…

Nothing was going to stop us from what we'd both been waiting for.

I shifted from my spot on the floor so I could crawl onto his lap, straddling him. His eyes never left mine while I situated myself.

Then, I lowered my lips to his.

CHAPTER TWELVE

ALFIE'S FINGERS TIGHTENED on my hips at first contact, and a low groan rumbled in his throat. Almost a decade stood between this moment and when we'd last been truly intimate with each other, but it was clear time had done nothing to diminish our chemistry.

His tongue brushed over my lower lip, and I opened for him. He tasted like scotch this time—like he'd had a drink at the hotel bar before he'd ventured out on his walk. I relished it. The feeling of being pressed so close to him after so long. I'd only been with a handful of men in our years away from one another, but none had come anywhere close to the level of pleasure I got from the man I was currently kissing. We'd barely gotten started, and I was already aching for him.

Alfie moaned against my mouth, biting my lower lip as he

pulled back. He watched with heavy-lidded eyes as I ground my hips against his in response, loving the feel of his hardness between my legs. It was so glorious that I couldn't help but moan myself.

"Fucking hell, Jordi," Alfie growled, his fingers digging into my hips.

He found my lips again, kissing me with a vengeance while his hands roamed my body, until finally they snuck up and under my shirt. My messy state wasn't lost on me. I was in a pair of old pajamas I used when I traveled. My face was probably swollen and splotchy from all the crying I'd done, but it didn't seem to matter to Alfie. He touched me like I was the most precious item in the world to him, regardless of my flaws.

He removed my t-shirt impatiently. His followed soon after.

I tilted my head back and let out a shuddered breath, my mouth hanging open, when Alfie shifted his attention from my lips to my neck. He kissed along my jaw, nibbling every so often like he knew I liked. I clutched his bare shoulders, gasping, when he found my sweet spot.

"Bedroom," I rasped, as I brought my head back down. "Now."

Alfie obeyed.

My legs wrapped around his torso as he rose off the floor and carried us the short distance to the bedroom of his suite. On the way, he unhooked my bra, taking advantage of the easy access to the clasp, and I shrugged it off. As soon as it hit the floor, Alfie's hands flattened on my bare back, pressing me against his chest.

Only seconds later, my back gingerly met the bed before he climbed on top of me.

I buried my fingers in the hair at the back of his head while we kissed. It didn't last long before his lips found my neck again. His ravishing went lower, lingering on my peaked breasts. One of his hands cupped me, his thumb circling my hardened nipple, while his mouth found the other, his tongue performing a similar task. I gasped, my back arching off the bed, as he took it in his teeth, tugging.

"Fuck," I moaned, fisting the duvet as he repeated the action on my other nipple. Was it possible to come just from this? If the growing ache between my legs was any indication, I was beginning to think it might be.

I never got the chance to find out, though, as Alfie moved lower, trailing kisses down my stomach until they ended at my pajama pants. I waited in impatient anticipation as Alfie took his time to hook his fingers in the elastic band. He pulled them down with agonizing slowness until I was able to kick them off, leaving me in nothing but my panties.

Alfie ran a finger over my center and moaned at what he found there.

"Look at you," he said in his lust-filled accent. He followed it with a kiss on either side of my inner thighs. "You're so wet for me already, Jords."

I squirmed when he kissed the spot his finger had just been stroking.

"Less talking," I instructed. "More doing."

Alfie chuckled as he followed my orders, pulling my underwear aside so that nothing stood between him and me.

His head disappeared between my legs, and his tongue made glorious strokes against my center. I writhed in the sheets, biting my lower lip to keep from crying out. We were in a hotel, after all. I didn't need any of the other guests knowing what the celebrity next door was getting into.

There was a reason the celebrity in question had been named one of young Hollywood's biggest sex symbols. Of course, that honor had come from his looks, but I knew how true the status actually was. I hadn't felt so much pleasure from foreplay since... well since I'd last been with Alfie.

I dug my fingers into his hair when he pushed one of his fingers into me. Another followed soon after. They moved in perfect rhythm with his tongue, working me in ways I hadn't thought I'd experience again, listening to my reactions to make sure he was giving me the most satisfaction possible.

It didn't take long before I hit my peak.

My body trembled as the orgasm rushed over me. Fighting against the effects of it, I sat up, grabbing Alfie's shoulders, turning him, and forcing him to lay on his back. A brief flicker of amusement overshadowed the lust in his eyes, and it only made me want him more.

I climbed atop him, straddling his hips as I ground myself against him. He was so fucking hard, and still wearing far too many clothes for me to truly enjoy it.

I gifted his lips with a brief kiss before I worked my way down his body the same way he'd gone down mine. His abs tensed with each brush of my lips, making them even more defined.

His jeans and briefs weren't on for much longer after that, and a new rush of yearning overcame me when his impressive erection sprang free. I'd forgotten what I'd been missing over the years—and was proud to report that I hadn't been mistaken in my assessment for Tori. There was in fact *nothing* little about Alfie.

My awe must have been evident because he chuckled. I watched him from under my lashes, where he lounged comfortably on the bed, one of his arms behind his head, the other reaching towards me. He grabbed my hair, brushing it away from my face. It was a not-so-subtle hint at what he wanted.

Lucky for him, I was happy to oblige.

I watched his head tilt back, eyes shut and mouth hanging open in pleasure, as I took him into my mouth. His grip on my hair tightened as I worked him, using my hand to stroke what wouldn't fit. When he lifted his head again to watch me, I made sure to make a show of it, running my tongue up the length of him before circling his tip and replacing him between my lips.

"Fuck, I can't take it," he finally moaned, giving my hair a gentle tug. "I won't last much longer if you keep using your pretty little mouth like that."

I grinned. "Do you have a condom?"

"Wallet. Small pocket in the middle."

Part of me wondered if he'd been expecting this at some point and had prepared ahead of time. Given the way we'd acted with each other all weekend—particularly Alfie—I wouldn't have doubted it. I was just grateful he'd thought so far ahead.

I hopped off the bed to retrieve the condom, but before I grabbed it, I lowered my panties, bending at the waist to give Alfie a good view of my ass. I found him stroking himself, watching with hungry eyes, when I glanced back to see if he'd enjoyed what he'd seen.

"Get back over here," he said, sitting up, hand still working his cock. "*Now.*"

He tore the foil open as soon as I returned to the bed, and I watched as he rolled the condom on before settling over him again. I bit my lower lip as his tip teased my entrance, then slowly lowered myself, allowing his length to fill me.

"Fucking hell," he mumbled as his hands found my hips, holding me steady as I rode him.

It was gentle at first, slow as we both adjusted to the feel of one another after so long. Even though we'd just participated in some of the hottest foreplay I'd ever experienced, sex was different. It had always been different. Alfie and I were both the kinds of people who took it seriously, not offering ourselves to just anyone. He'd come to be that way because of his fame and his fear of being taken advantage of. I'd decided long ago that I'd only offer myself in my most vulnerable state to men who deserved it.

Alfie had proven to me long ago he was one of the men who deserved me like this. Perhaps, he was the *only* one who did. I wouldn't have minded having Alfie be the only person I ever slept with. Hell, given his performance thus far, I wasn't sure I'd ever find pleasure with anyone else again.

A moan escaped me as we picked up the pace, falling into a steady rhythm. My oncoming orgasm was building, and if Alfie's hurried breaths and ravenous eyes were any indication, so was his.

Suddenly, he flipped us, and I found myself on my back. He hovered above me as he pumped in and out vigorously, chasing his release. My legs widened, giving him greater access to me. Allowing him to go deeper, deeper, deeper…

His hands tightened on my hips. "Come for me, Jords."

I bit my lower lip, and nodded. There was no doubt I'd be able to obey that command.

I reached out my hand to him, cupping the side of his face, and forced him to look at me. My other hand brushed his dark hair back before I pulled his head down to kiss him.

That's when I broke, finally soaring over the edge for the

second time that night. I moaned into Alfie's lips as I felt myself tighten around him, coaxing him to his own climax.

"Fuck, Jordi—"

He stilled inside me as he finished, his moan the only sound in the room. My breaths left me in heavy pants. If I tried to move, I wasn't sure I could trust my legs to keep me upright. Thankfully, Alfie made that move, pulling out and rolling onto his back to lay beside me. His chest rose and fell with breaths just as heavy as my own.

I stared at the ceiling as Alfie stood to go to the bathroom and dispose of the condom. I'd need to get up soon too, but I wasn't ready. Not yet.

When he returned, he took the same spot as before, both of us saying nothing. Until—

"You sure this convention ended today?"

I couldn't help the laugh that escaped me at his comment, but also couldn't deny that I'd been thinking the very same thing.

When I turned to face him, I found Alfie already watching me, a big, goofy grin on his face. Never mind that he'd just made me come twice. Gone was the man that fucked like a god, replaced by someone who looked as happy as a kid in a candy shop.

I reached out, turning onto my side so my bare breasts pressed up against him, and caressed the side of his stubble-covered face.

"We should probably make the most of what time we have left, huh?" I suggested.

"Probably," Alfie agreed.

I laughed again as he took me in his arms and dragged me on top of him, both of us content to enjoy each other as much as we could.

If I returned to work the next afternoon, post-flight, and found that Lynn had an answer from Mr. Singh, the time might be shorter than we'd thought.

I tried to push that notion aside, choosing to relish in the ecstasy that Alfie brought me instead.

CHAPTER THIRTEEN

WORK DRAGGED. AND not only for the usual because-it's-work reasons. I did my wrap-up reports. Went to meetings. Listened to Jackson's team rave about sales. Asked Lynn if she'd heard from Mr. Singh. (She hadn't.) She asked me if I'd started writing the sequel to the manuscript I'd given her. (I hadn't.) Sounded like my boss and I were both in slumps.

On and on and on. The monotony seemed more monotonous than usual. Even the follow-up call I'd had with Grace and Olivia had been lackluster, despite their dramatic enthusiasm when I announced my sex drought had ended. Olivia had actually thrown the bowl of pasta she'd been feeding her toddler.

Despite everyone else seeming to find some sort of excitement during the week, I knew mine wouldn't come until the weekend. Not until I flew to the next city on Jackson's record-breaking convention book tour and finally had the chance to see Alfie again.

Denver. Omaha. Boise. Minneapolis.

Every other weekend—at max, every three—we'd reconnect. We'd explore the city we found ourselves in, going full tourist. Sometimes Louie, Elliott or Tori joined us on our adventures, but eventually everyone caught on.

Alfie and I wanted to be alone. We wanted to cherish whatever time we were allowed so long as this little tour scheme of mine was still in play. We'd gotten lucky as it was. Even with the budget increase and two additional con attendances granted to us after yet another Alfie Effect moment caused sales to skyrocket, it would all come to an end eventually.

I'd told myself now that we'd talked everything out, we wouldn't have any other hurdles to overcome.

Wrong.

Distance. Distance was a massive hurdle that had been staring us in the face the whole time. I knew eventually we'd get used to it, but right now we were both in the dreaded honeymoon phase. And instead of being like every other fresh couple that could fuck like rabbits to get all that fresh lust out, we were in different countries for the majority of the month.

It didn't seem like a very big issue until I found myself recharging my vibrator twice as much as normal.

But when those glorious con weekends hit, it was like

nothing I'd ever experienced. Especially after the recent dreaded three-week break from seeing one another.

I was in the middle of straightening the books on display when two, strong arms wrapped around me from behind. A soft kiss was placed just behind my ear.

"Hello, beautiful," Alfie whispered.

I turned in his hold, smiling, partly because he was finally with me again, and partly because I knew he didn't need to be. His obligations weren't until the next day, but he'd been showing up at the convention centers a day earlier than necessary.

"Hi," I whispered back.

Then he kissed me.

Had this been a few cons ago, I might have been nervous about the owners of the surrounding booth spaces watching. I would have scoured the internet trying to make sure nothing incriminating was being written or shared. I might have even blushed when Tori wolf-whistled.

Now, I didn't care about any of it. For the first time in a long time, I was giving myself a break, allowing myself to live in the moment. I needed to stop worrying so much, dammit.

"Hello to you too, Victoria," he said over my shoulder.

"Morning, Alfred."

I chuckled and shook my head. She'd told him not to call her by her full name at the first con post Alfie and I getting back together, but he said it suited her. When she'd asked why and he'd said because Victoria was a great queen of England, she'd huffed, but let it go after he'd promised to let her call him by his full name too.

"Mind if I borrow this one just for a moment?" Alfie asked next, shifting positions so that he stood beside me, his arm still wrapped around me.

Tori shrugged. "Borrow her for as long as it takes. I'm not one to judge."

"Tori," I hissed, but Alfie chuckled.

"My intentions are innocent, I promise," he assured her. "I would never dare to upset her royal highness."

"I'm more upset that you *are* innocent," Tori countered. "Go have fun, lovebirds."

"Thanks, Tor," I said as Alfie ushered me away. Once we'd gone a respectable distance from the booth—and all the others too—I asked, "Is everything okay?"

Alfie grinned in that devilish way of his. He'd perfected it while playing a vampire bad-boy for seven years on TV, and I thankfully still got to reap the benefits.

"What if I told you I simply wanted to steal my girlfriend away from her work so I can kiss her in a corner of a convention hall?"

He took slow steps forward, forcing me to take equal steps back until I bumped into the wall behind me. Alfie placed his palms on either side of my head, caging me in.

Oh yes, he'd definitely learned many valuable lessons on that

TV show.

I grinned in return. "That sounds very okay to me."

He lowered his head so his lips could reach mine, gifting them with the tenderest kiss I'd ever experienced. He lingered for a moment, allowing me to take in the essence that was Alfie.

"I did actually come with a question," he said when he pulled away.

"Oh?"

"A few, actually."

"Even better."

"First, I heard that St. Louis is home to a restaurant that has over thirty types of ranch dressing, and my ranch-deprived British soul was wondering if you'd join me for dinner and try them all."

I couldn't help smiling. "Alfie Fletcher you know the true way to my midwestern heart."

"Good. I knew that would be the easy one."

My brows scrunched. "There's a hard one?"

"Well, it's one that requires a bit more commitment."

Color me intrigued. "Go on…"

"There's a gala happening in two months at the Natural History Museum. Be Positive," Alfie said, using air quotes around the name of the event. "It's supposed to be a pun—like the blood type. They ask a group of rich people to dress up and gather in a room to donate money and blood for sick children. It's a good cause with somewhat poor execution."

I nodded slowly, not quite understanding why I needed to know about it. Alfie had been to plenty of events since we'd reconnected and usually only told me about them right before he attended.

"The whole *Crimson Curse* cast is invited—at least the primary names, that is. I think the organizers find it humorous for us to attend, given the nature of the show," Alfie continued, rolling his eyes. "It's actually rather fun once the blood drive is over and everyone can eat and drink. And most years it's a nice little reunion for the *Curse* cast."

He meant except for this year when they'd already been spending months together for the convention tour.

"So do you not want to attend?" I asked, still trying to figure out where I fit into this puzzle. Was he expecting my advice? I'd been separated from Alfie the Celebrity for too long to feel like I could offer anything helpful in that department. "Who else is going?"

"I asked the lads if they were going and, as of right now, both Elliott and Louie said they were. Elliott had also heard that some of the other secondary cast members would be there."

"And April?"

"An excuse to dress up and be photographed?" Alfie huffed a laugh. "She'll be there."

No shocker there. "So everyone you like will be there and you said you enjoy the event. Why the cold feet?"

Alfie lowered his arms from the wall, letting his hands settle on my hips as he took a step closer. "Not *everyone* I like will be there."

It took me longer than it probably should have to realize what he was suggesting.

"*Me?*" I asked. "Are you asking me if I want to go to this blood drive?"

"In a very indirect way, yes."

I'd officially been stunned into silence. I stared at him with wide, incredulous eyes before I took my turn to let out a nervous laugh.

"Alfie… You want me to go to *London?*"

"That's why I pulled you away from Tori," he said. "I knew it would affect your work, so I didn't want to ask in front of her. But my publicist told me I need to confirm with my plus one so she can give the gala committee—"

"Wait, wait, wait," I interrupted. "You told your publicist you'd have a plus one?"

Embarrassment reddened Alfie's cheeks. "I was hopeful I would."

I tilted my head and shook it, a small smile curling the corners of my lips. He'd gone from sexy to adorable with the flip of a switch.

"I'll ask my boss about it."

Alfie's brows rose in surprise. "Really?"

"Yeah," I said. I rarely took vacations, so I had time saved up. It was just a matter of skipping out on these weekend events that *I'd* planned. "But are you open to a trade off?"

The surprise shifted into something like worry. "Oh?"

"You're only signed on for obligations tomorrow and Saturday, right?"

"Yeah."

"What time is your flight on Sunday?"

"I'm taking an overnight flight back to London," Alfie said. "Why?"

My smile widened in a mischievously playful way. "Since we're in St. Louis, I talked with Tori about her handling Sunday's duties so I can go visit my parents." Surprisingly, she hadn't protested the prospect of being left on Jackson patrol by herself. "I got a rental car this weekend, and I'm going to drive to them on Sunday morning."

It took Alfie a lot less time to figure out what I was hinting at, and to his credit, he looked less nervous than before. "You want me to come with you?" he asked. "Meet your parents?"

I nodded. "I just figured since, well—since we're kinda… you know."

Alfie's body shook with a silent chuckle as he smiled down at me. "Since we're what, Jordi?" His index finger found my belt loop like it so often did and gently tugged me closer.

I tried to ignore the wobbly feeling in my legs as I replied, "Since we're… together again."

"Still getting used to it?"

"A little," I admitted. "It still feels surreal."

"We've been *together* before," he reminded me.

"I know, but this time feels different."

"Yeah, it's *meet the parents* different," Alfie agreed.

"I've met *your* parents," I countered.

The laugh that burst from me at the look on Alfie's face was unavoidable.

"You had no choice but to meet them," he said, sounding half amused and half mortified. "They walked in on us!"

"You're the one who chose to give them a key!"

"You know how my mum is," he said then shook his head. "I'm not letting that happen with your father. He's going to be impressed, I swear. In fact, I'll go buy a new shirt. With a collar."

"Alfie, we're going to southern Illinois, not the Met Gala," I said through a chuckle. "Even if we go out to eat, it'll be a local dive. Nothing fancy." I pulled at the dark fabric of the shirt he'd chosen to wear. "The usual clothes will do."

DESPITE MY ASSURANCES, he did, in fact, go buy a new shirt, which in turn left me feeling very underdressed two days later. Not that *I* needed to impress my parents, but still. It was the principle.

We ambled up the cement walkway that led to my parents' home. I noticed Alfie eying the hydrangeas and daisies that lined the path, his own bouquet of flowers for my mom in his hand. The man had attended more red carpets than I'd probably seen on TV, yet here he was, practically sweating through his new black collared shirt, at the prospect of meeting my parents.

"Breathe," I whispered. "They're gonna love you."

I'd never rang the doorbell or knocked at my parents' house. We operated on an understanding that even though I'd moved out six years ago, I could still act like I lived there too. And that meant barging in unannounced.

I knew they were both home, given their cars were parked in the driveway.

"Mom?" I called once I opened the door to the humble ranch-style home. "Dad?"

I ushered Alfie in as I listened to the clanging in the kitchen, followed by a gasp from my mom. The Sunday paper rustled from where my dad was more than likely sitting in his recliner, watching some pre-game special for whatever sport was currently in season.

"Is that our Jordi girl?" Mom shouted.

"I've brought a guest too."

Alfie paused, half-way through removing his shoes like I'd silently instructed, to stare at me wide-eyed. "You didn't tell them I was coming?" he whispered.

I shrugged. "I thought this would be fun. Like one of those TV shows where celebrities show up and say they're giving away a free home makeover or something."

In all honesty, I'd forgotten to mention it. I'd been so excited about seeing my parents on a day other than Thanksgiving or Christmas that the idea of warning them they'd have two guests instead of one had slipped my mind.

And technically, now I *had* told them.

"Is it that crazy coworker of yours?"

I chuckled. "No, it's not Tori."

I heard the soft footsteps on the creaking floor and knew Mom was on her way down the hall from the kitchen.

"Who'd you bring with you, sweetie—oh."

She dropped the towel she'd been using to dry her hands. My petite mom with her brown bob and eyes stood stunned in the entry hall of her home, staring at Alfie like I'd brought someone with four heads.

I hindsight, maybe I should have given them more than two-minute's warning that my ex-boyfriend who was now my boyfriend again would be joining us for lunch.

"Hi, Mrs. Wright," Alfie said. He gave my mom a shy wave. "You have a lovely home. And, uh, these are for you."

Mom took the bouquet Alfie offered her while she quietly assessed the situation. She didn't usually find herself at a loss of words, but given our history, I'm sure Alfie was the last person she'd expected to see. Even after we broke up, I'd never once painted him in a bad light, so I knew she wasn't judging him negatively. I figured she was just confused.

The floor groaned under my dad's footsteps as he came to join us.

"Hey," he said. "You're that vampire guy, aren't you?"

Dad thought he was *so* subtle.

"I am, sir." Alfie stepped forward and extended his hand. "Alfie Fletcher. It's nice to finally meet you both."

Dad nodded in reply to Alfie, then to me said, "Good thing you took down all those posters, Jords. Not that I'd let him in your room anyway."

"*Dad!*" I knew my face was red as a tomato. I could feel the heat of embarrassment rushing through my body. Alfie knew I'd been a *Crimson Curse* fangirl, but he didn't need to know *that* many details.

"I need to get these in water," Mom finally managed. "They're absolutely beautiful, Alfie. Thank you."

"Of course. I'm sorry I was such a surprise."

"Oh, don't worry, son," Dad said. "Kim has enough food here for a whole party. We could use the extra mouths."

"Aren't we going out to eat?" I asked.

"I wanted to make sure you had some of your favorites while you were home since I know you aren't making them for yourself up in Chicago." Ah, classic midwestern hospitality. "The buffalo chicken dip only has a few more minutes in the oven, but there's also the loaded ranch dip in the fridge."

Alfie perked up beside me. "Ranch?" I couldn't stop myself from chuckling.

"C'mon, c'mon." Dad gestured for Alfie to join him, using the food as an excuse to cover the real reason he wanted to get out of the entryway. He was missing valuable pre-game analysis. "There's plenty to go around, but hey—do you watch sports at all?"

"Probably not the same ones you do, sir," Alfie's fading voice said. I smiled at his continued use of formalities, knowing my dad probably didn't give two shits about how he was addressed.

"Football season's just starting up. The *real* football, not soccer like you Brits call it. Big day too with the Bears playing the Packers for the season opener. It'll be interesting to see how…"

Alfie peeked back around the corner to give me one last wide-eyed look before he disappeared with Dad, their conversation muffled by the sports broadcasters on the TV. Mom and I laughed to ourselves before she continued her inspection of the flowers.

"He really didn't need to bring anything," she said then tsked. "How sweet of him."

"He's wonderful," I agreed.

That's when my mom finally paid me her full attention. If Alfie hadn't been there, I knew that was how it would have been from the moment I walked in the door, being the only child and all. Mom liked to dote on me, even though I was more than capable of taking care of myself—for the most part—at twenty-eight years old.

Her free hand grabbed hold of my fingers. "How are you, sweetheart?"

We'd catch up in earnest later, but for now, I offered my mom a soft smile and squeezed her hand once. Twice.

"I'm good," I said. "It's been insanely busy with all the travel, but... Alfie's made it better."

"I didn't even know you'd reconnected with him."

"I didn't want to say anything until I knew it was going to last," I admitted.

Mom offered me an understanding smile. "It's okay, honey. He's..." She huffed a laugh. "I knew he was handsome from that show you used to watch, but—"

She mouthed the word *wow*, her eyes wide and impressed by the looks of the man I'd brought home.

"He's very nervous," I said. "So try to be nice."

"Honey," Mom said, shaking her head. "Your dad's got him trapped now. I'd be surprised if I get a word in otherwise."

When we joined the men in the other portion of the house that consisted of the open kitchen and connecting living room, my mom went to find a vase for her flowers. I insisted on helping get all the dips prepared, but she gave *those* eyes that told me to go join Alfie and Dad.

I followed orders after I retrieved the loaded ranch dip and a bag of chips.

"Eat up, boys." I moved aside some ten-year-old magazines—I would actually bet that Alfie was in at least one of them—and set the food on the coffee table before I took a seat on the armrest nearest Alfie on the couch.

His hand found my leg, rubbing up and down over my athletic leggings before I finally looked away from the TV to him.

"Hi," I whispered.

"Hello."

I leaned down and gave him a quick kiss.

"Hey, hey, hey—he's got to learn, Jord!" Dad interjected. "Stop distracting him. Now, Alfie, that guy they're highlighting now? He's a future hall of famer, no doubt about it."

"I have no idea what he's talking about," Alfie muttered out the side of his mouth as Dad continued his explanations.

"Just smile and nod," I replied. "That's how I've managed for most of my life."

Alfie did just that, schooling his face into an expression of undivided interest before his hand moved off my leg and to intertwine our fingers. He brought my knuckles up to his lips to kiss before asking Dad what qualities made a star quarterback.

Picking up on vocab words. Nice. It was clear Dad was impressed, too, as he dove into his answer.

I looked over at the kitchen where Mom was setting the flowers, now in a vase, in the center of the table. She met my eyes and gave me a thumbs up.

Alfie had passed the parent test in less than thirty minutes.

CHAPTER FOURTEEN

LYNN DIDN'T USUALLY schedule multiple one-on-one meetings with me during the week, so when I saw one appear on my calendar a week and a half after the St. Louis Comic Convention, I couldn't help but feel a small jolt of excitement. It also came with some nerves, since I needed to ask her if I could take off for the Be Positive Gala. Seeing as how Alfie had passed with flying colors with my parents, I couldn't go back on my promise of attending with him.

Not to mention I'd already procrastinated having the conversation. More than a week had passed since the initial invitation had been presented to me, and I'd felt awful telling Alfie that I hadn't requested the time off yet. But now I needed to if I wanted any chance of finding a last-minute flight that would be semi-affordable. Alfie had offered to help pay, but I'd insisted I could handle it.

Though the more I refreshed my browser, the more I felt like a liar.

I sighed. I should have been preparing for whatever it was Lynn wanted extra time to talk about. I could venture a few guesses, but that also meant getting my hopes up. I'd been trying to keep a positive attitude about what Mr. Singh might say about my manuscript, but I also had a hard time ignoring my realist tendencies. As much as I hoped he would offer me a deal, I knew how high the possibility of rejection was too. This was an extremely competitive industry I was trying to enter—or re-enter in a different way, I supposed. He needed to be picky about who Starr signed with.

Although, a nice advance would take away some of the pressure for how I would afford to get to London. Being a stowaway on a barge was becoming more and more likely.

"Ahem."

I turned in my swivel chair to find Jeff from IT leaning on the wall of my cubicle. Jeff was a nice guy, and he helped me more than I'd like to admit when my technologically challenged ass ran into computer issues.

Right now, he didn't look very happy, though.

"Hi, Jeff." I smiled. "I think everything's working today."

Jeff returned the smile half-heartedly, but his eyes slid to my computer screen—where my airline ticket search was in plain view.

Whoops.

"We just got the network report for the last month," he explained. "I just wanted to stop by and give a friendly reminder that personal searches should be left for personal time."

"I know," I replied, playing it off like I hadn't been the top culprit on that report.

Jeff didn't fall for it. He nodded slowly as his eyes drifted to my screen again. This time, though, he squinted, getting a clearer look at what, exactly, I'd been searching for.

"That big tour taking you across the pond?" he asked.

"Big tour? You mean with Jackson Albrecht?"

Jeff nodded. "Yeah. Searches for his profile on the Starr website were up big-time over the last few months too. You're doing a lot of good work when it comes to driving traffic."

"Oh, um, an international stop is a possibility," I lied. Anything to make it seem like I wasn't slacking off. "It takes a lot more planning and logistics, though. We have to connect with our international divisions and stuff."

"Makes sense," Jeff said. "You ever been to London before? My wife and I went… geez, probably fifteen years ago now? Time flies."

"I studied there in college."

"Lucky girl. I would go back if I could."

Same, Jeff. Same.

He left my cubicle after some more small talk and another

reminder to use the work-provided computer for work-related functions. I stared at the ticket prices for a few more seconds before I closed the tab. I couldn't buy anything without confirming with my boss that this trip was allowed anyway.

I shut the troublesome laptop, unplugged the charger, and made my way to Lynn's surprise meeting. On the way to her office, I scrolled through Instagram, only to see that Alfie had posted a picture of an airplane on his story. I'd begun to recognize the many terminals of Heathrow from the other tidbits he shared with his followers, but I had no idea where he was traveling so early in the week. In fact, he hadn't mentioned traveling at all.

I'd never expected Alfie to give me an hour-by-hour update. That would have been insane, and I wasn't that kind of partner. I respected boundaries and trusted that Alfie would tell me what I should know. But, still. Not getting the update that he was going off somewhere to do his celebrity thing hurt a little.

I hadn't exactly been one-hundred percent honest with him either, I supposed. My own secrets had been kept, but with good reason. Hopefully when I left Lynn's office, I'd finally be able to disclose everything. I'd never seen the point of building everyone up to potentially let them all down. No one outside of the small trio of Lynn, Mr. Singh, and myself even knew this manuscript existed, and no one ever would unless I left with positive news.

I tucked my laptop under my armpit then swiped up on the

story to send him a quick *"Have a safe flight!"* before I knocked on Lynn's door, only entering when I heard the muffled call for me to come in.

"I would tell you to sit, but it would be a waste of your time," she said by way of greeting. I startled when she slapped her palms on her desk and aimed a giant, beaming smile at me. "I *will* tell you to start planning out that sequel I so desperately want, though, because you're gonna need it."

"Shut up." Screw professionalism. My excitement had reverted me back to a college sorority girl on bid day. "Mr. Singh like the manuscript?"

Lynn nodded. "I told you he would. He would have been an idiot not to—"

"An idiot, huh?"

The professionalism switch turned right back on.

I straightened my posture, putting on my best I-mean-business face when Mr. Singh appeared at Lynn's door. I hugged my laptop to my chest with one arm and made sure the massive amounts of emotion coursing through me didn't mix too much with the caffeine I'd ingesting that morning.

In comparison to Lynn and I, who had both opted for jeans and casual blouses, the Publishing Board Director of Starr Publishing and Media looked the part, donning a fresh-pressed navy suit and white button-down shirt that stood out against his umber brown skin. He'd chosen not to wear a tie, but perhaps that was normal. I'd never had the chance to meet him before, despite my four-year tenure at Starr.

Lynn smiled at our new meeting guest. "You weren't supposed to hear that," she said. "I told you to come ten minutes later so that I could have some time with Jordi beforehand."

"And you know I'm always ten minutes early," Mr. Singh countered. He turned on me, and my customer service smile popped onto my lips. "You must be the budding author in question. Jordi Wright."

"I am, sir," I said.

"To think you've been hiding under our noses this whole time," Mr. Singh commented as we shook hands. "Should we sit?"

I followed the orders, taking one of the chairs opposite Lynn while Mr. Singh took the other. Normally, Lynn broke down the hierarchy wall when we spoke with one another. She never failed to make Tori and I forget that she was the one leading the team, but she didn't make us feel inferior or afraid to approach her, either.

Something about sitting beside Mr. Singh made me realize how lucky I was to have a boss that had that kind of leadership style. I was sure he was a nice man; he'd come into the room with a sarcastic remark, after all. Clearly, he knew how to joke around. But I also knew he held the fate of my career—or rather, my career change—in his hands.

"Now, Miss Wright," Mr. Singh started. He crossed an ankle

over his knee and steepled his fingers in his lap. "You know what got us to this point. You passed your manuscript off to Lynn who took the time to read it and passed it along to me with raving reviews."

I eyed my boss sidelong and found her waiting to give me an encouraging smile. "Yes, sir."

"You have to understand this isn't typically how this process works," he continued. "Usually, I only see agented manuscripts that have been found by one of the many editors here at Starr, and it's from there that we decide whom we wish to make offers to. It's all based on budgets and quotas. Do you understand?"

"I do, sir," I said. "And I'm honored you considered my novel at all."

"Lynn and I have worked together for a long time, and I know firsthand she won't vouch for something she's not passionate about." He unfolded his hands and pointed at me. "*You* seem to be one of those things, Miss Wright. You and your novel."

"Jordi has been a wonderful part of the Starr team for so many years," Lynn jumped in. "As much as she's been a benefit to the work of the marketing department, I'd love to see what she can bring to the table as an author."

Mr. Singh nodded along to Lynn's statement. "Which is exactly why I want to offer her a deal."

I clenched my jaw, trying to avoid another outburst like the one I'd given Lynn earlier. I was sure Mr. Singh had heard it, but I still wanted to appear a bit more professional.

My book. It was finally being given a chance. The dream I'd had all those years ago, which Starr had inspired by allowing me to meet my idols and see it was actually possible for my name to be on a bookshelf, was finally coming true.

I wanted to run out of the room. Call my parents. Alfie. Grace and Olivia. Even Jackson S. Albrecht to tell him he wasn't as special as he thought. Me—little old me—would be taking over the booths now.

"I truly have no words to describe how grateful I am for this opportunity, Mr. Singh," I said. "Thank you so much."

"Of course, of course," he said, smiling. "And when I learned you came with a pre-packed celebrity endorsement, I couldn't help but move this one up the—"

"Wait," Lynn interrupted, holding up her hand to Mr. Singh. "Celebrity endorsement?"

"Do you mean Alfie, sir?" I added, my brows creased.

Mr. Singh nodded. "That's the one. The one from that old vampire TV show. I heard vampires are making a comeback, you know. It could be very beneficial during your initial launch to—"

"Rahm, I'm going to have to stop you again." Lynn shook her head. "Regardless of Jordi's connections, she's written a wonderful book. She shouldn't have to exploit people in her personal life to get sales. I'm confident she can do that on her own."

"I'm very sure Miss Wright can, yes," Mr. Singh said, but something in his tone told me he didn't quite believe what he was saying. "But you've seen the numbers, Lynn. That new Albrecht series is flying off shelves—or off the tables, I suppose, since most sales are occurring at these cross-country events."

"And?"

In that moment, it became very clear that Rahm Singh was not used to getting any form of pushback.

"*And*," he repeated, sitting up straighter in his chair. "You know as well as I do, Lynn, that no author is offered a deal with Starr if we cannot justify profitability." I shrank in my chair when he turned his attention to me. "Your story was good, Miss Wright, but I have many similar ones land on my desk each month. What differentiated you was Lynn's backing and your connections with this Alfie fellow who seems very keen on marketing books our house releases."

So, Mr. Singh hadn't cared about my story at all. Not in the way Lynn had. She'd been passionate about the characters and what came next for them. Mr. Singh only wanted something that he considered entertaining enough, but came with guaranteed sales dollars.

My relationship with Alfie was that guarantee.

I knew he would have happily done anything to help promote the book. Hell, he'd admitted he'd been searching for a cover with my name on it for the better part of the last ten years. Now that one would actually exist? I couldn't see him passing on the opportunity to tell anyone and everyone about it. As much as I was his fan, he was also mine. My biggest cheerleader. He always had been, encouraging me to follow this dream that everyone else thought was so easy to accomplish.

It wasn't. Not even close. I was being given a chance that people worked years for. Decades. Some never even saw it to fruition, no matter how hard they tried.

"You should be grateful," Mr. Singh continued, as if trying to start an argument with my thoughts. I eyed Lynn again, hoping to get a read on if my emotions were obvious, but she gave me nothing. She, quite frankly, looked pissed off and was doing nothing to hide it. "We rarely offer opportunities like this to Starr employees."

I knew they rarely offered opportunities at all. I was on the events marketing team. That meant I saw the list of all titles that needed some sort of promotional tour attached to it, whether it was a collection of small, independent bookstore events or something on the scale of Jackson's current convention tour.

"I am grateful," I said. "I know I'm being quiet right now, but I'm just trying to take everything in."

Mr. Singh grinned. "It's not every day a girl gets offered a book deal, is it?" He placed his hands on the arm rests of the chair, preparing to stand as he continued, "I'll get a member of my team to start drafting up a contract and we can—"

"Sorry to interrupt, sir, but I won't be accepting the deal."

His shock was apparent. I didn't blame him. I'd surprised myself by voicing aloud what my subconscious had been screaming ever since Alfie was brought into the conversation.

"I'm sorry?"

"I've dreamed of being published ever since I was a little girl, so I've read every blog post and advice article on the matter. Every single one of them says to never sign with someone who doesn't believe in your story."

"I just told you—"

"You told me that you see stories exactly like mine land on your desk all the time," I reminded him. "If you believed in my story, you'd tell me how unique it was or how you connected with it. Instead, you showed more belief in my partner's ability to use celebrity influence than you did my work."

Once again, Mr. Singh's surprise at being given pushback was obvious. I wouldn't have doubted if he told me I was the first author he'd given an offer to that denied it. But since I'd skipped the agent phase of the plan, I needed to be picky with the publisher.

I never thought I'd reject the one that employed me.

"I'm sure you're busy, Rahm," Lynn interjected, "so why don't you go back to your work and allow Jordi and I some time to discuss this further?"

"Yes, I believe that would be best." Mr. Singh stood. "We

wouldn't want Miss Wright making any brash decisions. I'll talk with you later, Lynn."

Silence followed him out. It wasn't until the office door clicked shut behind him that Lynn and I finally breathed.

"Jordi, I'm so sorry," she said. "I had no idea that was his motive. Frankly, I didn't know you were seeing anyone—not that that's any of my business."

"It's okay, it's kind of complicated."

"But he's a celebrity?" Lynn asked with a raised brow. I nodded. "Would I know him?"

"Did you watch *Crimson Curse*? It's that British vampire drama from a while back."

"Not back enough, apparently, for someone my age."

I smiled at Lynn's attempt at soothing the energy in the room. "His name's Alfie Fletcher. You can look him up if you want."

"I'm going to have to, now that I know how big of an influence he's been. I mean, I've seen the sales reports, but I didn't think this person was the *only* cause of that." Lynn leaned back in her chair, staring off into the distance and shaking her head, before she met my eyes again. "Have you been telling him to promote Jackson's books?"

I shook my head. "No, he's doing it on his own. But that's the thing. I know he would do it for my books too, and I don't want that to be the reason I get a book deal. I've wanted this for so long, and this whole time I've wanted to do it on the merits of my story. I don't want any of my connections to influence anyone's decision to give me an offer."

A slow smile curled Lynn's lip. "You remind me a lot of myself, Jordi," she said. "I admire what you just told Rahm. I know it must have been very difficult to do. So, you know what? I'm going to help you get that deal you deserve."

I couldn't stop my brows from shooting up, my eyes widening. "What?"

"I've been in this industry a long time, so I have plenty of connections at various publishing houses. I'm going to see what I can do to get you in with someone on their publishing boards. Or at the very least with one of their editors."

I couldn't believe what I was hearing. "Is that even allowed?" The last thing I wanted was for Lynn to get in trouble for breaking some sort of non-compete or fine print clause in her employment contract.

"As a manager, I'm supposed to vouch for my team members. That's all I'd be doing."

"But it would be going against Starr."

Lynn shrugged. "That's Starr's fault for not giving you and your story the respect that's deserved."

I could have cried in that moment. Just when I'd thought everything I'd been working toward had been lost, there was Lynn again, going to bat for my work.

I didn't have the chance to say anything before the door to Lynn's office burst open and a frantic Tori was standing there.

"Jesus Christ," she said, panting. "You." She aimed her index finger at me. "Sam has been calling your desk for the last thirty minutes."

Why would the office receptionist need to get ahold of me? "Is everything okay?" I asked, half standing from my seat.

"You're going to want to come to the front desk. *Now*."

CHAPTER FIFTEEN

TORI LED LYNN and I to the front of the Starr office. Curiosity had gotten the better of our boss, and she'd invited herself along. I couldn't say I blamed her. My heart was beating a million miles a minute as I tried to guess what in the hell could have made Tori so eager to find me. She definitely had her dramatic moments, but even this was a lot for her.

My eyes narrowed in confusion as we grew closer to the front lobby. A whole gaggle of female Starr employees were gathered by the glass doors that separated our main office from the space where my mystery waited. They were giggling and whispering like schoolgirls, while the ones in the front of the group reported their findings back to the others.

"Don't you all have work to do?" Tori asked as we passed right through them all.

As soon as we entered the lobby, I froze.

Standing there, chatting with Receptionist Sam, his hand resting on the handle of his suitcase, was Alfie.

Sam noticed my posse and I first. "Ope, there she is."

The young receptionist pointed our direction, and Alfie turned to greet us with a beaming smile. His movement allowed me to see the bouquet of flowers that had previously been hidden.

"Surprise," was all he said.

He released his hold on his suitcase and opened his arms to me. Ignoring that not only my boss but a whole crew of female Starr employees were watching, I accepted and jogged as quickly as my heeled booties would allow.

His laughter vibrated through the length of my body as he enveloped me in his strong hold, and I melted. The stress from the previous meeting instantly vanished, my whole body overcome with a sense of calm relief.

I hadn't realized how much I'd needed this. To be with him. To rest my head on his chest and take in his woodsy yet sweet scent. To feel the beat of his heart.

Alfie's embrace had always been, and always would be, my safe space.

His lips found the top of my head before he said, "If you don't let go, I can't give you your flowers."

"One more minute," I replied, hugging him a little tighter.

He chuckled again before he lifted his chin from where it rested on the top of my head. "Thanks for finding her, Your

Highness."

"Oh, my dearest Alfred, it was nothing."

Finally, I pulled away from his chest and tilted my head back to look up at him. "What are you doing in Chicago?"

"It's part of my press tour," he replied, making my brows crease in confusion. "I was surprised when you said Starr wasn't attending, and I knew that meant I needed to get here earlier than usual to get some time with you."

How could I have forgotten? Well, actually, there were a million reasons why my brain had probably decided to neglect that little detail. I purposely hadn't scheduled the Chicago stop since we were local to the area. We preferred doing events with smaller bookshops and venues to give back to the community while we were in town. That wasn't to say we avoided conventions, but our involvement with them was rare.

"How did you find Starr's building?"

"The internet?"

Duh, Jordi.

"I wanted to surprise you at your desk," Alfie continued, "but this nice young lady was doing her job a bit too well."

My eyes slid to Sam just in time to watch her face fill with red. "I'm sorry I ever called you a liar."

"At least you got your selfie with me, right?" Alfie said with a wink. "All's well that ends well." His attention strayed over my shoulder. "And can I guess that you are the infamous Lynn?"

I managed to release him from my death grip. We shifted so one of his arms remained around my waist and the other was used to shake my boss's hand.

"Lynn Hauser," she greeted. For someone who hadn't known who he was until about fifteen minutes ago, she sure looked starstruck. "It's a pleasure to meet you Mr. Fletcher. Welcome to Starr Publishing."

"And media," Alfie corrected. His dorkiness made my heart flutter.

"You've been teaching him well," Lynn said to me.

"It's hard not to learn when he's reading the pop-up banners all the time."

Lynn made a *pft* noise. "That's hardly learning. Would you like a full tour, Mr. Fletcher? I'm sure Jordi could spare a little of her time. We just got out of a pretty big meeting and break times are necessary."

"Big meeting, huh?" Alfie teased, squeezing my side. "Are you more important than you're letting on, Jords?"

"Hardly," I replied, eying Lynn, hopefully passing along the silent message that I hadn't told him anything about Mr. Singh yet. "It's just… don't you hate books? We could maybe go to lunch instead?"

"Hate books?" Alfie repeated. "Are you kidding? I *love* books. What do you have to show me?"

His smile only spread when I leveled something just short of a glare at him. I knew Lynn and Tori were probably looking at me funny, but at least the latter probably understood what I was going for—unlike Alfie. I wanted him as far away from here as possible, not only because the possibility of him running into Mr. Singh was much higher, but because that hug had made me crave Alfie. I needed him alone.

And preferably naked.

"Uh, Lynn? Can I talk to you about some post-mortem stuff from that meeting really quick?" When she joined me just out of earshot from where Tori and Alfie had taken up their own conversation, I continued. "Do you think it's a good idea to have him here given how that meeting ended?"

"I'll keep Rahm busy," Lynn said. Bless her for acting as the sacrificial lamb. "He'll probably hear about the visit later, but by that point, Alfie will be gone." She put a comforting hand on my arm. "After you give him the tour, take the rest of the day. I'm sure with everything going on, your head won't be in work today as it is. Besides, you deserve the break."

I gave her a soft smile. "Thank you, Lynn."

She returned it. "Not a problem. Oh, and by the way, I heard Alfie mention something about a tour?" Her brow raised suspiciously, and I knew what was coming next. "This tour with Jackson wouldn't have anything to do with that, would it?"

A blush heated my cheeks. "I was going to tell you eventually."

She chuckled. "I have no qualms. Besides, it worked out, didn't it?" Lynn's eyes drifted over to Alfie. "In more ways than one it looks like."

"SO, THIS IS the headquarters of the infamous Starr Publishing and Media," Alfie said, his head turning to take in the colorful walls with quotes about books and reading painted onto them. "The very place where *the* Jordi Wright works her magic in the world of literature."

I snorted. "Yeah, right. You're giving me too much credit."

"Where do you sit?" Alfie asked. He smiled at a girl from sales who did little to hide her awe over his presence. She must have missed the memo from the group that had gathered by the front doors earlier. We'd been stuck taking selfies (Alfie) and answering questions (me) for ten minutes. "Do you have an office?"

"No, just a cubicle. Managers and executives get the office rights."

"What about the authors? They probably need quiet."

I smiled at that. "The authors don't work in the office. They come in on occasion for progress updates regarding their book—you know, like sales reports and plans for any future work—but everyone here is part of the business side of publishing. Not the talent side."

Alfie nodded as we continued our walk. Sam had allowed him to leave his suitcase by her, so he wasn't dragging it around, drawing even more attention. She'd even volunteered to find a vase for my flowers, so we had as much time as possible. I wasn't giving much of tour, though, since I wasn't really pointing anything out. I didn't think Alfie cared much about where sales sat versus IT versus marketing, though. He seemed to have his own questions—that were venturing dangerously close to a path I didn't want them to go down.

"You should be on the talent side."

There it was.

"That's easier said than done," I replied.

"You said you're still writing, though?"

"Slowly but surely. Why?" I needed this conversation to go in a different direction. Immediately. But I also couldn't be obvious about it. This was Alfie. He'd notice any sort of diversion I threw his way with maybe a little too much ease. It was a blessing and a curse having a partner that knew me so well.

"Well," he drawled as his hand found mine. "Do you remember all those years ago when I first discovered your hidden talent?"

"By opening my manuscripts when I thought you were looking over a media communications paper?" I replied, making him chuckle. "How can I forget?"

"I don't regret it for one second," Alfie said. "Those were the best fifty words I've ever read—before I got caught."

I smiled. "Why are you bringing it up?"

"You promised me I could star in the film adaptation."

I stopped walking, using our joined hands to force Alfie to halt as well. "You still remember that?"

"It's become my life's ambition. How could I forget?"

I chuckled and shook my head. "Well before that happens, I have to continue with this career." I pulled Alfie along for a short distance before I dropped his hand and gestured in a very Vanna White way to the cubicle I called home between the hours of nine to five. "Allow me to show you my desk."

Alfie humored me by walking into the entry of the five-foot-by-five-foot space and acting like he'd just walked into a mansion. I'd decorated with a few potted plants, pictures, and some thank you notes from authors, attempting to make it feel a little more personal, but it wasn't anything that deserved that sort of reaction.

"This is nice." He ambled in and immediately took an interest in the few pictures that I had tacked up. "Parents, friends, I'm assuming some vacation scenery."

"You'd be correct."

He turned back over his shoulder. "Someone's missing."

I rolled my eyes. "Relax. You'll make the wall in time. Besides, I don't need pictures when I've got the real thing standing here."

"That's bloody right." He sat down in my chair with a groan the proceeded to take a little spin. "This isn't half bad."

"Coming from someone who's never worked a desk job a

day in his life."

"Hey." He pointed a finger at me, suddenly serious. "I came very close to it."

"When?"

"Remember that time Cain Luther was trying to impress Dawn after going on a blood bender and attempted to hold down an office job in pursuit of a normal life?"

"Before he murdered half the office?" I said, then smiled. "Yeah, I remember, and I can't believe you actually just used a fictional TV show as a comparison."

"It's all I've got." He shrugged, smirking. "But, hey…"

He scooted close enough to grab onto my hips. I laughed as I was pulled into his lap, one of his arms keeping me balanced while the other brushed some hair back behind my ear. My arms found their way around his neck.

"How was your flight?" I whispered. I didn't have any direct neighbors, but I was sure most of the office was trying to eavesdrop by now. Word spread fast around here.

"It was long, and made even longer with the knowledge that I'd get to see you at the end of it."

"That eager, huh?" I teased.

"Unbearably."

I chuckled. "Well, you're here now, and you've seen where I work. What else were you hoping to do during your visit?"

Mischief shone in his eyes as he asked, "Where does human resources sit in relation to your desk?"

"The other side of the building," I informed.

"So, there should be no problems when I talk about *all* the things I want to accomplish on this trip, or even better, show you…"

I dipped my head down so my lips could meet his, and at the precise moment we touched, I heard the pointed "Ahem" behind me.

I practically jumped off Alfie—and might have caused him a little pain, given the grunt that escaped him. But for as embarrassed as I felt in that moment, Lynn looked equally as amused.

"You left this in my office," she said, handing me my laptop and mug.

My eyes slid sidelong to Alfie who watched me with a proud grin. He'd definitely noticed the *Crimson Curse* show logo that decorated my drinkware. At least he couldn't complain about not being represented in my cubicle anymore.

"I'd also suggest taking that half day sooner rather than later," Lynn continued, and it didn't take me long to realize what she meant.

If she was here, that meant nothing was keeping Mr. Singh trapped in his office and he was therefore susceptible to the wildfire that was word of Alfie being in the office.

"Got it," I said with a curt nod.

Alfie watched with wonder as I moved around the cubicle at rapid speed, gathering everything that I needed before heading home for the day. When I grabbed his hand and yanked him from my chair, his eyes grew even wider.

"I'll see you tomorrow, Lynn," I said as I rushed past with Alfie in tow.

"It was a pleasure," he added.

I only allowed us to stop so that Alfie could pick up his bag from behind Sam's desk. While he did that, I pulled out my phone and started calling a car. Normally, I used public transportation, but there was no way I was taking Alfie through that, given what had just happened in the office. Not that the majority of the Chicagoland population would care, but I wasn't going to take the chance.

Alfie's warm presence sidled up beside me, the *click-clack* of his suitcase wheels on the tile floor going silent. "Oh, I think my hotel is only a few blocks away," he said, apparently having read my phone screen.

Truth be told, I hadn't even thought about him at a hotel. I turned my head up to him.

"Does it have a cancellation policy?" I asked.

Alfie grinned. "I'm sure I missed the cutoff if it does." The grin became more mischievous. "Why?"

"It's completely up to you," I prefaced. "But, well, since you're only in town a few days, I just—" I huffed a laugh, suddenly embarrassed, even though I knew he knew what was coming. Maybe that's what made it worse. "I assumed you would stay with me at my apartment."

"You mean I have to choose between staying alone in a hotel suite again, or getting to spend uninterrupted quality time with you in your flat?" Alfie took my phone out of my hand and hit the button to confirm our ride. "I'll pay you back for that later to make up for the free room and board."

I shook my head, smiling. "I'm getting something out of this little arrangement too, you know."

Now, the grin was nothing but devilish. "Oh? What's that?"

"We're a little bit closer to HR now so I can't say, but trust me." I inched closer, and both of us turned so Sam wouldn't be able to see as my hand found Alfie's belt buckle and slid teasingly lower. In a whisper, I said, "My apartment will have much better service than *any* hotel around here."

CHAPTER SIXTEEN

AMID THE HUSTLE and bustle that came with maneuvering his suitcase up the three short flights of stairs to get to my apartment, it was amazing how much Alfie could talk. He'd asked questions the whole way, and it made me pathetically aware of the fact that I couldn't have done the same. I clambered up the stairs every weekend with my carry-on to find myself out of breath when I reached my floor. That was without holding a conversation.

After leading us down the hall to my front door, I stuck my key in the hole then paused.

"I just want to warn you that I don't remember what's waiting on the other side of this door," I said. "I wasn't expecting a guest, so I didn't clean."

Alfie chuckled. "I'm sure it's wonderful."

His reaction when I pushed open the door and allowed him

to enter ahead me hinted that he believed it actually was.

I tried to ignore the way his movements had slowed as he took in the details of my apartment. He discarded his suitcase in the corner before he took a few more steps inside, his head on a swivel.

I supposed I hadn't realized that this was the first time Alfie was in my space. When we'd spent time together in London, we'd always gone to his place. Mine had been nothing more than a glorified dorm room with hardly enough space for Olivia, Grace, and I to share. And it hadn't actually been *ours*. Even if Alfie had visited me there, he would've been greeted with an environment that looked perfectly staged for a virtual tour.

My home in Chicago, on the other hand, screamed, "Jordi lives here!"

It wasn't a large space since I couldn't afford that, but it was enough for me. One bedroom. One bath. A living space lined with bookshelves. A kitchen that made the mini bar of a hotel room look luxurious.

Most of my decorations were thrifted and refurbished, the finished products creating somewhat of an eclectic feel when paired with the old building. The exposed brick wall behind my TV stand gave it that true Chicago feel, often reminding me how old this place actually was despite the collection of twenty- and thirty-somethings that lived in it.

Alfie had moved to the bay window on the wall opposite my

front door, eying my plants. Many of them had grown so much that I'd needed to tack up their vines along the walls to keep them from taking over my floor.

When he moved over to my record player stand, I saw a cute smile curl up his lips. It had been him, after all, that had gotten me into buying records. I now boasted a humble collection of somewhere close to one hundred and fifty. Having the music taste that was a cross between my eighty-year-old grandfather and a K-pop fan really came in handy. It meant there wasn't much I'd pass up, and most of my collection had been bought for cheap resale.

I let my guest go through them as I started to do what I could about picking up. I didn't leave a lot of clutter around, but sometimes putting away a box of cereal or cleaning a pot was just too much of an inconvenience. Not to mention I wanted to give Alfie his time. I loved that even though he'd never been in my private space before, he already felt comfortable enough to make himself at home.

A few minutes later, the sounds of Earth, Wind, & Fire's greatest hits were coming out of the speakers.

"This is nice," Alfie finally commented. He was still moving around the living room, his head bopping to the beat of the current song, until his eyes landed on the stray papers I'd left on the coffee table.

Shit.

I didn't say anything, not wanting to seem suspicious, as Alfie picked up a sheet and began to read what I'd written on it. I knew it wouldn't take him long to figure out what the random notes were.

"Is this a novel in the works?" he asked.

I nodded. "A sequel. I, uh, wanted to start working on it soon. Before I get pulled too far away from the world. It's only messy ideas right now."

"I want more," Alfie said, holding up the paper. "How do read more? Where's book one?"

"Book one is in the deep depths of my laptop, which is staying far away from you because I know how you operate." Thankfully that made him chuckle. "You have to wait just like everyone else."

I tried not to think about how short that wait would have been had I only said yes to the offer a few hours before.

"You're killing me, Jords," Alfie said, putting a hand over his heart as though he were truly wounded.

I shook my head at him as I hung up a fresh hand towel on the bar of the oven then went into the living room to join him. I took a seat on the small sectional couch, and he plopped down right next to me, his arm draping across the back behind me.

"To round out the tour," I began, "the bathroom is down that hall and on the left. There's extra soap and shampoo under the sink if you need it, and I promise it doesn't smell like flowers."

"And the bedroom?" When I raised a brow at his question, Alfie held up the hand still in my vision. "I ask with purely jet-lagged intentions."

I grinned. "Same hallway on the right," I said. "And I don't know if I believe you."

"My dearest Jordi, haven't you learned by now?" His arm curved around me drawing me closer to him. His other hand found my face, his thumb brushing across my cheek. "I don't need a bedroom in order to ravish you."

For a moment, I'd believed him when he claimed he wanted sleep, but Alfie disproved his previous statement the moment his lips met mine. All the tension that had been building since he'd first arrived at the office poured out, the two of us clinging to each other in hungry passion.

I'd gotten selfish, knowing that I was able to be in his arms again, feel his skin on mine, share in these intimate moments as well as the tender ones that followed. The ones where we got lost in conversation, our legs tangled and skin sticky with sweat under the covers of the hotel beds.

But that's all they'd been. The most time we'd gotten so far were four-day stints in hotel rooms across the continental U.S. Now, he was here, in my apartment, on my couch. We had almost a full week together, and the excitement at knowing that energized me as much as his touch did.

His arms snaked around me as he leaned me back. I would never get over how simple it had been to fall back into sync with Alfie in every way possible. For starters it made it easier to get comfortable on the narrow couch while we explored one another, hands sneaking under clothing, craving the contact of skin-on-skin wherever possible.

It also made it much smoother as that clothing was removed.

Alfie rolled off the couch and pushed my coffee table back to get on his knees in front of me. His hands found my hips and pulled me closer to the edge of my seat. I bit my lower lip as I watched him, staring at me like I was the greatest prize he could ever win in life.

He spread my legs apart, giving each of my inner thighs a kiss before he began working me with his tongue and fingers, each stroke sending a fresh wave of fire through my body.

I curled in my lips, trying to muffle my moan. Old building. Thin walls. That did continue to be a problem when Alfie and I were together, to a point where I was having trouble holding back at all. The man worked miracles with his touch.

My back arched as I came much sooner than I would have liked, and while I was still coming down, I watched Alfie fumble with his discarded jeans to find his wallet. He produced a foil square, and I smiled as he tore it open.

He moaned as he teased my slick core with his length, the sound of it making me crave him even more.

My head rolled back as soon as he entered me, my body adjusting to the way he filled me. Alfie knew this—knew how my body worked, what I needed from him. We'd fallen back into our rhythm, yet no matter how many times we'd had sex, it never ceased to amaze me how wonderful he felt inside me.

Alfie eased in and out with slow, tantalizing strokes before picking up the pace. I spread my legs further, urging him to go deeper…deeper…

"Fuck, Jordi," Alfie ground out. When I caught sight of his eyes, I saw they were completely clouded over, his pupils dilated with lust.

I was already building again when Alfie suddenly pulled out. My hand instantly found where he'd just vacated, still chasing the feel of the release I craved. I swore I heard Alfie growl before he sat down on the couch beside me then guided me atop his impressive length.

His hands braced my hips as I rode him, enjoying the new control I had over our pleasure. I watched him stare at where we joined, his expression nothing short of ravenous.

I sated my own growing hunger by capturing his mouth with mine while I continued to move on his cock.

It didn't take much longer for the two of us to reach our peak.

Our chests rose and fell with heavy pants as we tried to regain our breath. I rested my head against Alfie's.

"I don't want to move," I said, grabbing his face with both my hands before I dragged my lips across his cheek, down his neck. "You feel so fucking good."

"I'm happy to stay here all day," Alfie replied. "Keep at it until daybreak."

I might have allowed it, had he not finished saying it through a yawn.

I chuckled as I finally got off him and grabbed the sweater I'd worn to work, tossing it over my head without bothering to find my pants.

"I'm going to use the restroom," I announced. "Meet you in the bedroom?"

"With innocent or devious intentions?"

"I told you," I said as I walked away. Turning back over my shoulder, I winked. "Hotel Jordi offers only the best service."

THAT SERVICE ENDED up being a body to cuddle while Alfie took the world's most aggressive power nap. I didn't mind. With all the hustle of our usual con weekends, we hadn't enjoyed this kind of time together. Pillow talk, yes. Actually spending the night with one another, no. We always needed to be at different places at different times, our reasons for attending the conventions being vastly different.

It brought me back to the nights I'd shared at Alfie's apartment in London. The ones where I'd stayed too late watching a movie or studying in his company. He'd refused to let me use the Tube too late at night by myself, even though I assured him I'd be fine. With *Crimson Curse* having still been on the air during our first attempt at dating, him taking public transportation was also out of the question. Not without his trusted bodyguard, Harry, that was.

That meant sleepovers—and very early mornings to make sure I made it to class on time.

Now, I didn't even need to worry about making it to work, the sun sinking below the beautiful city skyline instead of rising to greet it by the time Alfie finally started to stir.

Eyelashes that would make any girl jealous fluttered as he blinked the sleep away, arching his body to stretch.

"How long was I out?" he asked groggily, looking around as if trying to figure out where he was.

"A few hours," I said.

"Christ," he muttered. "Really?"

"Yeah, but it's fine. I was able to answer some emails on my phone and start a new audiobook."

Alfie ran his hand down his face and groaned. "I feel awful. I surprised you only to steal your bed and sleep."

"You more than made up for it before you crashed," I assured him, leaning down to kiss his forehead.

Alfie groaned again as he shifted, turning onto his side and enveloping me in his hold. He'd never put a shirt on, opting to sleep in a pair of grey sweat pants he'd packed, so the natural heat of his body radiated onto me. My big spoon placed a kiss to my head, and his hold tightened the slightest bit more, ensuring nothing separated my body from him.

I was overcome with an overwhelming sense that very few people in my life could provide me.

Safety.

I allowed my eyes to shut, relishing in the quiet, normal moment. Because if there was anything our relationship wasn't, it was normal.

Here, I was able to forget about work, that my partner was a celebrity from my favorite TV show, that if he walked out on the crowded street of Chicago, he'd be recognized at least once. Probably more.

Instead, here, he was just Alfie. *My* Alfie.

I placed my hand atop his and laced our fingers together. "I'm perfectly content here," I whispered.

Then, my stomach betrayed me. I felt the vibration of Alfie's chuckle through my back.

"Liar," he whispered.

I admit, I'd forgotten about food. And Alfie's last meal was probably something served to him by an airline.

"I have pizza bites," I offered, trying to remember what food I owned that could be turned into an actual meal. Not just a bunch of random ingredients I hoped would work together. "And bagel bites. Or there's a wing place down the street we can order carry out from."

"All of the above, except can we replace the takeaway with delivery?"

"Of course."

"And eat all these delicious treats right here like this?"

Normally, I wasn't an eat-in-bed kind of girl, but I'd need to do my sheets probably a minimum of three times during Alfie's stay anyway. "That would be preferable."

"Then I'm in."

"And as a bonus we can throw on re-runs of *Crimson Curse*."

"I'm out," Alfie replied, pretending to pull away, the light hold I had on his hand supposedly being the only thing keeping him trapped. He chuckled as he settled back in and kissed my head again.

"Re-runs of *Friends*?" I amended.

"Sold." He sighed contentedly. "You were right. I'm starting to really like the Hotel Jordi."

CHAPTER SEVENTEEN

ONE THING THE Hotel Jordi hadn't put into consideration was her actual career.

Alfie knew I needed to work the next day and promised he'd find something to entertain himself with while I was gone, but I still felt bad as I snuck out from under the covers to quietly dress and head out. I made sure to leave the espresso pods that were normally tucked away in a cabinet out on the counter by the machine as well as a note to let Alfie know where to find the rest of the coffee fixings. I removed a pound of bacon from my freezer, hoping it would thaw enough for him to cook it by the time he woke up and added that to the note as well. Hopefully eggs and granola bars would also do. I wasn't much of a breakfast person.

Or a make-meals-at-home person at all, really.

If I really wanted to put a positive spin on my lack of

preparation—not that I'd been given any warning before Alfie's arrival—I was giving him the perfect excuse to go out and explore. Man had to eat, after all.

"Morning, Jordi," Receptionist Sam greeted when I walked in. I nodded at her as I went past her. Up until yesterday, I was pretty sure she hadn't bothered to learn my name.

The same surprise came at me when I entered the primary office space.

"Hi, Jordi."

"Jordi! What's up?"

"Hey, Jordi."

I'd never interacted with some of the people that were calling out to me—most of them females. I recognized some from the gawking gaggle that had gathered for Alfie, but the rest must have simply known me from office gossip.

That was a terrifying thought.

"Good morning, sunshine."

I'd hardly managed to log onto my laptop when Tori snuck into my cubicle, using the far end of my desk that I never utilized—mostly because I couldn't easily reach it—as a seat. She admired the fresh bouquet of flowers beside her then hummed as she sipped on her morning coffee. Not even the cup could hide her mischievous smirk.

"Just ask," I said.

"How many times?"

"Only three."

"*Only?*" she repeated. "Do you know how much money most of these nosy busybodies in the office would have paid to have the night you did?"

"As the person asking me outright, aren't you also a nosy busybody?"

Tori scoffed. "I'm asking for your well-being. I wanted to make sure I wasn't mistaking that post-sex glow you're wearing as something else."

"Keep it down," I hissed, peeking my head up just enough to see if anyone else might be within earshot. "There's actual co-workers around now. It's a miracle Jackson hasn't said anything yet."

"Jackson would never."

My eyes slid to Tori. I swore I noticed a hint of blush on her cheeks, but she brought her coffee up to her lips again before I could get a good look. She was probably just flushed from the heat of her drink.

"Is everyone here really talking about it?"

Tori lifted a brow. "Talking about your sex life?" She shrugged. "A little."

So that's how it was. All those cheery *hellos* I'd received had been laced with guilt.

I groaned and leaned back in my chair. "Really?"

"How can they not when Alfred fucking Fletcher strolled into the office to surprise you?"

"You're still calling him Alfred?"

"I'm committed," Tori said. "Besides, at least I've moved on from calling him Cain."

That was true. "Is Lynn pissed off?"

"Why would she be?"

"Because I'm being disruptive to the office?"

Tori shook her head. "She thought it was sweet. I have to admit we also talked about you in our meeting yesterday afternoon, but all good things, I swear. No sex life talk. She just wanted the details of the tour that we've been on." Her head tilted in curiosity. "I take it you told her?"

"She asked me directly, so I couldn't lie."

Tori nodded. "She did seem a little moody for the rest of the day." I tensed. "But it didn't seem to have anything to do with you and your tour antics."

I sighed. "It did have to do with me, though."

Genuine worry was not something I saw often from my favorite colleague, but in that moment, she was presenting a whole lot of it. She even managed to almost spill her coffee.

"Did you quit?" This time Tori did a quick check to see who might be around to listen. "Please tell me you didn't quit. They'll move Alexis up from social media and you know I hate Alexis from social media."

"You only hate her because she makes fun of your pictures from the conventions."

"I'm *sorry* I was raised with disposable cameras and don't know how to do all those fancy angles," Tori complained. "But

seriously, you didn't quit, did you?"

"I didn't quit."

If Tori hadn't believed in any higher being before, she certainly looked like she did now as she raised her eyes to the ceiling and lifted her free hand in praise.

The relief was quickly replaced with confusion.

"Then why would Lynn be upset with you?"

"I don't think she's upset with me. It's more of a situation I've found myself in, and she just so happens to be involved." When Tori's brows raised, urging me to stop beating around the bush, I sighed. "I was offered a book deal."

"You write?"

Looked like I'd done just as good a job as I'd thought about keeping my hobby a secret.

I nodded. "For years," I admitted. "I finally had something I thought might land me a deal, so I asked Lynn if she would take a look, and she did. She passed it along to Mr. Singh a few months ago, and he offered me the deal yesterday."

"So you *did* quit," Tori said. "Not officially, but by default when you took the deal."

I knew my expression had turned as somber as I felt by the way Tori's face shifted back into her version of concern.

"I turned it down, Tor."

"*What?*"

Then I went into it. How Mr. Singh had wanted Alfie more than he'd wanted me. The deal wasn't a result of my talent but

of the celebrity endorsement that would come along with me. The sales that would follow.

"That prick," Tori spat, careful to keep her voice down. "You know, I've heard that everyone who works for him is scared of him."

Now that I'd spent a little more time with him, that didn't surprise me. "It's fine. Everything will work out the way it's supposed to."

"Does Alfie know?"

"You're the first person I've told."

Tori's eyes widened then narrowed again. "While I'm honored to hold a level of importance above Alfred the Great, I'm afraid I have to say *what the fuck*. Does *he* know you write?"

"He does, and I didn't want to tell him for exactly this reason. I knew he'd probably be more disappointed than my parents."

"Why?"

I leaned forward in my chair, resting my elbows on my knees. "Tor, the reason he was at the Starr booth that first time we saw each other was because he was looking for a book."

"Makes sense. We have lots of those."

"With my name on it."

Tori set her mug down on my desk before she tilted her face up to the ceiling again. Good thing, too, because she definitely would have spilled it that time as she slid off her makeshift seat and onto the floor, like an emotional human puddle, where she pulled her knees up to her chest and hugged them there.

She rested her chin on her knees, her eyes on me again, as she said, "Are you fucking kidding me?"

"Dead serious."

"Remember how I started in marketing for the romance division?"

"Yeah."

"None—absolutely zero—of the stories come anywhere close to that. I mean, looking for *your* book? C'mon!"

"But do you see why I can't tell him?" I asked. "It would break his heart to know the reason that dream didn't come true was because of him."

"Well, you have to tell him eventually, Jords," Tori said, uncurling her legs now that the moment had passed. "You're gonna marry the guy, after all."

"We just got back together a few months ago. I don't think either one of us is ready to talk marriage yet." But that didn't mean I hadn't thought about it a few times after nights of particularly good sex and the following sentimental pillow talk.

"There's a lot of stuff we're still working on overcoming," I continued. "I don't want to get into it, but maybe once we're all good there, I can bring up the book stuff. I'm still waiting to hear about some final details as it is, so I don't want to announce any good or bad news prematurely."

And there was a lot. Namely me needing to talk to Lynn about taking a weekend away from Jackson's book tour to go to London. Not only was the previous day's conversation still

lingering with me, making it that much harder to build up the courage to do so, but I'd also realized I liked having Alfie in my world for a change. Going back to his world… I was worried it would bring back some of the challenges we were just starting to overcome.

I knew the chances of running into Josh in London were slim. More than slim. In a city of nine million, it was practically miniscule, especially since Alfie had cut off contact. But I also knew the chances were much smaller if we stayed in America.

It was self-serving, and I knew it. I was getting too used to being in this little bubble of Alfie where we had a whole ocean separating us from the place where our problems first began. But by trying to pretend like we could survive together like this forever, I was cutting out the whole of Alfie's life.

I knew he would do anything to make sure I was happy and comfortable, but I also knew how close he was with his parents. His little sister. I couldn't take that away from him, no matter how much my past made me selfishly want to.

"Do you actually know if Lynn's in yet?" I asked. "I need to ask her something and want to catch her before we both get distracted for the day."

"I thought I saw the light on in her office," Tori said.

That was my sign. I needed to do this. I'd tried to use every excuse in the book to avoid it, but there was no more hiding. I needed to show I was in this just as much as Alfie was showing me.

I told Tori that we would get lunch together so I could update her on the rest of the night—and hopefully some plans I'd be able to confirm after speaking with Lynn.

When I knocked on her door, her presence was confirmed by a muffled, "Come in."

Despite having been warned that my boss might be in a bad mood, she greeted me with a polite smile.

"I was expecting an email from you this morning asking for another day off," she said. "Did you leave your visitor at home?"

"Alfie's an independent soul," I said. "I think he'll be excited to explore by himself for a bit. But would it be okay if I left a little early today? He said he wants Chicago-style pizza and all the good places are always packed with tourists."

Lynn nodded, still smiling. "I don't see why that would be a problem. Just make sure I have that list of bookstores that are willing to participate in the charity event in the spring by end of day."

"Got it," I said.

Lynn raised a brow. "Is that it?"

"Well… no," I admitted.

My boss sat back in her chair. "I'm afraid I haven't heard back from any of my connections yet," she said. "It's still early, so one or two might reply by end of day, but it might take longer."

"Oh, I'm not worried about that," I said, and I wasn't. Just

like it had taken Mr. Singh some time, I knew it would likely take Lynn's industry network just as long. "I actually wanted to talk to you about the tour with Jackson Albrecht."

"If you're worried about getting in trouble, don't," Lynn assured me. "If it weren't so successful, I might be telling you differently, but there's no reason to worry. Just try not to make this a habit. There are other ways to see your boyfriend that aren't on the company's dime."

Point taken. And it was only going to make what I was asking that much harder.

Do it, Jordi. The worst she can say is no.

"Actually, I need to talk to you about that…"

CHAPTER EIGHTEEN

"SORRY I'M LATE."

I looked up from my phone just as Alfie hurried up to the table. He sighed as he removed his light jacket and placed it on the back of the chair opposite me before taking a seat.

"You're fine," I assured him. "I'm sorry we're stuck in the middle of the room. I tried to ask for a booth."

Alfie waved it off. "It's no bother," he said, but I wasn't sure if he'd be saying the same within a few minutes. Already, some of the nearby patrons were staring, probably questioning how they recognized him, while others had retrieved their phones and were taking photos or videos outright.

I tried to ignore it as well as Alfie was—if he'd even noticed yet. He'd probably gotten pretty good at blocking it all out.

"How was work? Continuing to change the world of

publishing?"

"Again, way too much credit being given," I replied, just as the server came up to us to ask what we'd like to drink. I ordered a glass of wine while Alfie ordered an IPA from a local brewery.

"It smells delicious in here," he said once the server left us.

I narrowed my eyes at him. Even for Alfie, he was too excited. He always talked a lot when that was the case, beating around the bush to avoid talking about something. *Building suspense* is what he liked to call it.

"What happened today?" I asked, ignoring his previous comment.

"What do you mean?"

"Did your agent call you with a new job or something?" I had no idea what could have possibly changed between last night in my bed and now. "Were you cast in your dream role?"

"Don't you think I would have led with that yesterday?"

"You're building suspense."

The accusation seemed to impress him, and Alfie leaned back in his chair, his toned arms crossed over his chest. A smirk grew on his lips. "Can't I simply be excited to finally see you? I've been waiting rather impatiently all day."

"You can," I agreed. "But I don't think that's the *whole* reason."

"You know me so well, Jords."

"Out with it, Alfred."

He chuckled at the use of his full name.

"I want to start off by saying that if we're going to be successful this second time around, we need to start with being open and honest," he said, making worry dance around in my stomach. "I haven't exactly been honest."

My heart sank and had the server not chosen that moment to bring our drinks, I would have questioned him immediately. Instead, I needed to tell the oblivious teenager tasked with making sure we had a fabulous dining experience that we needed more time with the menu. Hopefully his teenage attention span would ensure he'd disappear for a very long time.

"What do you mean you haven't been honest?"

A million scenarios ran through my head, starting with him having a secret sex tape, landing on him having an affair, and eventually settling on him not actually being out of contact with Josh.

No—Alfie was Alfie. He wouldn't do or lie about any of those things. He was more loyal than a golden retriever.

So what could he have possibly been dishonest about?

Compared to everything I was also being dishonest about, it probably wasn't as bad as my worst-case-scenario-oriented brain was thinking.

"I told you I came here to surprise you, and I did," Alfie said. He reached across the table, palm up, inviting my hand. I did as he wanted, taking note of the not-so-subtle patrons around us, examining our every move. If he felt comfortable talking about whatever he was about to bring up in public, I supposed I should too. "But I came here for another reason as well." Alfie sighed, then aimed a large smile at me. "I'm going to move to Chicago."

"*What?*"

If they hadn't been paying attention before, I'd just made sure everyone sitting around us was now.

"It's not official yet," Alfie continued. "But I spoke with my real estate agent and he put me in contact with a wonderful woman here in the area who I met with today."

I blinked in response, not sure what to say to any of this.

"We looked at a few different places in a few neighborhoods, and I didn't really find anything that was my style. We're going out again tomorrow, though."

"Alfie…" I finally managed to squeak out. "*Why* are you moving to Chicago?"

"You and your career are here," he explained. "My career can be from anywhere, and quite frankly it will probably take a me away from wherever I locate myself anyway. Besides, you know how I love to move around."

"Yeah, move around London. Not across an ocean."

His face fell. His whole body went lose. "Do you not want us to be closer to one another?"

My heart sank for a whole new reason at the dejection in his voice. I squeezed his hand.

"I do," I said. "More than anything. But I don't want you making any brash decisions. Your whole family is over in England. I'm the only one here."

"That's enough for me. More than enough. Think about it." Alfie leaned forward in his seat. "Think of how much time this year alone I've spent away from my family. All my obligations have been here in America."

When he put it that way…

I sighed, closing my eyes to compose myself before I opened them again, "I haven't been exactly honest with you either."

"If you're pregnant, we'll make it work."

I chuckled, amused that his head went to the same place mine did for these kinds of scenarios. "I'm not pregnant." That time I smiled at his reaction, a mix of relief and mild disappointment. "But do you remember those book notes you found yesterday? For the sequel I'm planning?"

He nodded. "I might have stolen another peek at them today."

I tilted my head at him, giving him a half-hearted look of betrayal before I said, "I turned the first book into Lynn."

Alfie was quiet for a moment, probably trying to figure out what that meant before he decided it was better to ask.

"It means absolutely nothing that Lynn read it," I explained. "But she passed it along to our publishing board director."

"That sounds important."

I nodded. "He offered me a deal."

Alfie's eyes widened. "You're going to be published?"

I swallowed the fear of telling him the truth. "Not exactly…"

"I'm confused."

"I turned it down."

"What?" Once again, everyone sitting near us turned our way to see what the commotion was about. Alfie seemed to notice this time and leaned in closer, keeping his voice low, as he said, "What do you mean you turned it down."

"This is loaded, so I don't want you to take it the wrong way, okay?" I began. "This is a personal choice that I made and I believe it's best for me."

"Okay…"

"The only reason they offered it to me is because they saw the numbers that are coming in for Jackson's book tour."

"What does that wanker have to do with you?"

I lifted my brow at him, letting him piece it together for himself—mostly because I was too much of a coward to say it out loud myself.

It didn't take long.

Alfie sat back in his seat again as understanding dawned.

The server reappeared at our table, the fear he'd interrupted something monumental clear on his face.

"Um, should I come back?" the boy asked.

"We'll take a medium cheese deep dish and the house salad," I said. "Thanks."

Taking the hint, the boy walked away. Alfie still hadn't come out of his stupor.

"I feel like you're reacting more to this than you would have if I said I *was* pregnant."

"You were offered the deal because they thought *I* would sell your books?"

"Pretty much. And I couldn't, in good conscious, take a deal that I didn't earn on my own. It wouldn't have been fair to myself or my book."

Just like I'd told Tori it would, the truth crushed Alfie.

"I don't want you to take it the wrong way," I repeated. "This is one step on a really long journey, and quite frankly I had it easy, skipping a few steps in the process. Lynn's already working to put me in contact with some other people she knows to see if any of them are looking for new clients or if they're taking submissions from un-agented authors."

Alfie nodded slowly. "So there's still a chance your book will be published?"

"Yes." That seemed to cause him at least a little bit of relief. "It might not be right away, but there's still a chance. All this to say"—I offered a small smile—"let's not make quick decisions about moving to Chicago because I'm not even sure *I'll* be here."

"Where would you go?"

"Maybe New York," I said. "That's where all the big publishers are located. Or maybe London." Alfie smiled at that. "Maybe you can show me around again in a few weeks. Remind me of all your favorite places you've lived."

"Hold on," he said quickly, the smile growing wider than a kid in a candy store. "You got permission?"

"A full week off, plus one weekend where a con was scheduled," I informed him. "Lynn and I ran it past Tori and she seemed to think she'd be fine handling Jackson on her own. So I'll officially be joining you at your blood gala."

"Let me buy your plane ticket," he said quickly. "Please. As repayment for allowing me to stay with you this week."

I raised a brow. "Will I not be staying with *you* in London?"

"Darling." He smirked. "Hotel Alfie, I'm afraid to say, will put Hotel Jordi to absolute shame."

I laughed at that, throwing my head back and feeling at ease for the first time since we'd gotten to this dinner. I had to admit that telling Alfie the truth hadn't been as bad as I'd chalked it up to be. Apparently, nothing I'd been dreading talking to him about had been.

Per usual, I was worrying for no reason. I wouldn't have been surprised if I started getting gray hairs by my next birthday at this rate. But when I looked across the table again and saw Alfie beaming, I remembered why I had every reason to be at ease.

He reached across the table again, asking for my hand back. I gave it to him.

"We'll make this work," he said. "I think it's obvious that whatever feelings we held for each other a decade ago haven't faded. I think we need to stop trying to find excuses and just admit to the fact that, well…" His thumb stroked the back of my hand. "We're worth the challenges."

He was right. All I'd been doing since we'd started talking again was making excuse after excuse as to why we wouldn't work out. Josh, my book, the tour, distance. We'd been met with many of the same issues before, but our decision to end things hadn't been made by us. This time *we* had the choice. And I'd been ignoring it because I'd been too afraid to admit that we might actually stand a chance.

I nodded. "I know we can make this work."

WE STOPPED AT a convenience store on our way home and picked up a cheap bottle of wine. Alfie carried the brown-bag-clad bottle in his fist, while his other hand held onto mine, keeping me grounded in the busy city. He hadn't had a proper chance to see Chicago yet, given his day with the real estate agent, so instead of ordering a ride home right after dinner, we took a detour.

Even though he'd grown up in one of the world's largest cities, Alfie's wonder over Chicago was evident. The sun was just finishing its descent over the lake, and it was clear that we weren't the only ones who'd decided to stay out and enjoy what would probably be one of the few nice days left in the year. The city was alive as ever.

Its beauty managed to disguise the uglier parts: the occasional wafts of sewage, the blaring horns of angry drivers, the flocks of pigeons that refused to move out of the way, the not-so-scenic passes under the elevated train tracks.

None of that seemed to matter to Alfie. I didn't know if he'd ever been here before—and I'd actually never thought to ask—but I imagined he hadn't gotten to play tourist very much, if at all. Most of Alfie's trips were duty-bound, so it was nice that this one was different. That he'd taken time out of his schedule to see, in earnest, the place I lived.

But nothing entertained the man like chaos. He liked being uprooted, surprised. Thrived on it even. I think that was why he liked acting so much. He constantly got to try out new lives. It made me realize that if it came down to it, maybe this wouldn't be the worst place for us to settle down.

By the time we made it to the lakefront, the sky was painted pink and navy. We could barely see enough to find a decent spot on the lawn overlooking the water, but, with the help of our phone flashlights, managed to find one free of dog and goose poop.

"We're going to have to do this the old-fashioned way," Alfie said as he extracted the bottle from the bag. It was so cheap we didn't even need a bottle opener. He twisted the cap off, took a swig, then passed it to me. "If anyone comes to yell at us, we'll blame it on my lacking knowledge of American drinking laws."

"And what's my excuse?" I asked before I followed his lead.

"I'm a bad influence."

I almost spit out my wine when I laughed. It definitely almost came out my nose, given the burning. I passed the bottle back to Alfie, but he was too busy watching everyone around us to notice.

A group of women powerwalked past us on the lakefront path. Some boys who looked like they attended one of the universities in the city were playing flag football. A couple was playing a game of fetch with their dog. All of us holding onto the last dregs of sunlight as was Chicago tradition this time of year.

"It all seems so normal," Alfie finally said. "No one's even paying attention to anyone else."

"You mean they aren't paying attention to you?"

"No." He turned to me. "I doubt anyone here can see shit directly in front of them, let alone my face. I'm only soaking it in, is all. I don't get a lot of moments like this where I'm not flying to one place or another."

I realized as he said it that this would have been the day he normally flew in for a convention. He'd gotten two extra days to do whatever he'd wanted—more now, since he only flew in early to see me anyway.

I reached across him to grab the cap to the wine bottle and screwed it back on before I laid it down in the grass. I took advantage of my position and wrapped my arms around Alfie, easing him backwards so we were both laying down, my head on his chest. We stared up at the sky. With all the light pollution, it was almost impossible to see the stars, but some managed to shine through. Mostly, I was watching the clouds pass.

"Do you know what this reminds me of?" Alfie whispered. His hand trailed up and down the curve in my side.

"What?"

"One of our first dates. The one where we went to The Globe to see Macbeth then walked along the Thames."

"I loved that night."

"So did I," Alfie said and kissed my head. "It felt as normal as this, until those bloody photos showed up online the next day."

I'd almost forgotten. That was the first time I'd ever been photographed by the paparazzi. We'd been on the home page of every teen news site known to mankind, everyone wondering who Alfie's mystery girl was.

They'd never learned my name; his team made sure of that. But it had been odd, having such a private moment broadcast to the public like that. We hadn't even determined that we wanted to be in a relationship at that point. It was only our second date.

"There's no one here this time," I assured him. "This moment is all ours."

"Our redo."

"Yeah. Our redo."

He kissed my head again before we settled into silence. I listened to the beat of his heart in my ear, so steady. So sure.

We'd truly never had a moment like this.

"I could get used to this," Alfie said as if he'd been reading my thoughts.

"Yeah," I said, holding him tighter. "Me too."

CHAPTER NINETEEN

THE NORMALCY DISAPPEARED by the weekend. It didn't matter how much Chinese carryout eaten directly from the containers or leftover deep dish we'd had. It didn't matter how many square feet of the seven hundred I rented that we'd managed to have sex on. It didn't matter that Alfie farted in front of me for the first time. And it didn't matter that his embarrassment was the cutest damn thing I'd ever seen in my life.

Normalcy was shot the second he walked into O'Hare Airport with the promise of seeing me in two weeks.

I hadn't been prepared for the routine we'd fallen into. After we'd cleared the air and set the standard for how our relationship would succeed—no more excuses and no more hiding the truth—we'd actually managed to act like a real couple. One that shared bedrooms and bathrooms and living spaces for more than two days at a time.

I just didn't feel right going to bed that first night without Alfie there beside me, or brushing my teeth without another toothbrush sharing the little cup. I missed having a set of arms that would wrap around me from behind while I was doing dishes, the soft kiss I'd receive to my jaw, then have a companion to dry everything while we sang along or provided commentary to the album that he'd selected for us.

So when my plane finally touched down at Heathrow, knowing all those parts that had been missing from my life would be back again—albeit in a different city—made my excitement outweigh my nerves.

I hadn't been back in London in a decade, yet the moment I set foot in the airport, it felt like I hadn't done this very same thing for the first time all that long ago. Maybe because it was, in fact, only an airport. I was in those all the time. Once I went outside, however, my opinion might change.

Alfie texted me while I was in line for customs to let me know he was held up and couldn't pick me up like we'd originally planned. It was fine, but I couldn't deny the little pang of disappointment that hit me. I'd been so looking forward to my movie moment—when I'd burst through the doors and my love would be waiting to sweep me off my feet.

Instead, I exited the door and grew excited for a different reason.

"No way," I said, smiling the moment I saw who alternately awaited me, holding a sign with my name on it.

"Come here and give me a hug, sweetheart," Harry replied, smiling just as wide.

He lowered his sign as I rolled my suitcase over, opening his arms in the same way I imagined he did for his grandchildren. He'd always greeted me this way, making me feel like I had a back-up dad across the ocean, there to watch out for me while I was thousands of miles away from my actual dad.

They didn't even particularly look alike, but there was something about Harry that had instantly made me feel comfortable—once I got to know him, that was. At first, he'd intimidated the hell out of me, lurking nearby on my dates with Alfie. He was a bodyguard, after all. Even at his age, the signs of his strength were still there. If asked, I would have guessed he was a retired boxer. Maybe a wrestler. The hug he crushed me in was further proof of that.

Unlike the last time we'd seen each other, however, his hair had greyed and he had more wrinkles. Most of them were around his eyes, as if he'd gotten them from smiling too much.

A hearty laugh escaped him as he swayed me back and forth, giving me no choice but to join in.

"You haven't changed a bit," he said. Harry pushed me away, his hands on my shoulders, to get a good look at me. "Beautiful as ever."

"What are you doing here? Alfie said you retired."

"I did. But I've come out of retirement for the weekend. I've been over the moon since he told me you kids have reunited, and I couldn't miss the chance to see you."

I felt the tears welling up as I gave Harry another smile.

"Oh, come here, you," he said pulling me into another hug.

"I'm so glad to see you," I said. "It means so much that you're here." I pulled back. "I hear you have some very adorable grandchildren."

Harry's face swelled with pride. We finally released each other in full so that he could retrieve his phone, swiping through pictures with more force than necessary to find the one he wanted.

"See here?" he said, tilting the screen my way. "This one's the eldest. Hazel. She's about to turn four. Then there's Henry—named after his grandad, of course."

"Of course."

"He's a little ball of energy, this one. And finally, Freya's the youngest. Not even one yet, but she's got even more personality than her big siblings."

"They're adorable," I said. "You'll have to show me all your pictures while I'm here."

"I'd be happy to. But right now, I believe it's best we get you where you need to be. I'm pretty sure there's a young lad who's been anxiously awaiting your arrival."

"He said he got held up with something."

"Load of shit that was." Harry grabbed the handle of my

suitcase and began to roll it as we headed to his car. "I told him I wanted to surprise you since I knew he'd be hogging your time the rest of your trip—and rightfully so. But I wanted a chance to talk with you like the old times before that happened."

I smiled, trying to ignore that fresh pang of tears that were threatening to break free again. I was a jet-lagged mess with more emotions running through me than I wanted to acknowledge. I needed to keep it together for at least a day if I wanted to make it through this trip in one piece.

"We've got the whole car ride to catch up," I said. "I don't want you to spare any details. There's a decade to account for."

ALFIE BUZZED HARRY and I through the gate to his property in Kensington. He'd upgraded since the last time I'd been here, from an apartment to a townhome, though he still hadn't bit the bullet and bought anything yet. He was moving too frequently for that. And he always said he hated the idea of home-owner responsibilities while he couldn't be at the home.

I was still fighting off some residual laughter from a story Harry had been telling me when we walked through the front door. It echoed in the foyer, which didn't seem to hold much of anything other than a small table and the bottom of a staircase.

"Special delivery, Alf," Harry called up. He lowered the handle on my suitcase and tucked it into the corner. To me, he added, "I'll see you soon."

"You aren't staying?"

Harry let out a huffed laugh. "I think he's already debating if he wants to fire me after my request to escort you back here. I don't want to test my luck."

I didn't bother arguing that Alfie would never do such a thing, and instead opted to say, "I'll see you soon then."

Harry pointed up the staircase. "Head up there. He's probably hiding somewhere."

With one more goodbye hug, Harry left and I did as he'd instructed, heading up the stairs to what I assumed was the main floor of Alfie's home.

I'd assumed correct.

Where my home was the definition of eclectic, Alfie's was dark and modern. Everything had its place, and it was just the perfect amount of edgy, where anyone who walked in would immediately assume Alfie Fletcher lives here.

I'd entered straight into the kitchen and dining area, complete with a floating wall that hovered above an electric fireplace. On the other side was a living space, complete with a couch, decorative rug, and some arm chairs. Not much else.

Then, from another room down the hall, I heard the bang of a drawer shutting, a few muttered curses, and suddenly Alfie was coming around the corner at a half-jog to greet me.

I finally got my movie moment as he grabbed me around the waist and picked me up, only setting me down again to kiss me like he was a soldier being shipped off to war and I was his love left behind.

"I can't believe I let Harry talk me out of meeting you at Heathrow," he said. "The bloke knows I have a soft spot for him."

Ah, how I'd missed Alfie in his natural element. America did nothing for him. Here in London, I was getting the full-on Brit, slang and all. Thankfully, I'd learned most of it long ago.

"He had nothing but good things to say about you," I replied then nodded toward where he'd just come from. "What were you doing?"

A blush heated Alfie's cheeks. "It was actually, perhaps, a good thing Harry was available because I was finishing cleaning."

My head swiveled from side to side. Nothing about this apartment hinted that it was ever, at any point, even slightly messy. I was pretty sure if I ran my finger along any surface, it would come back free of dust.

"I have to admit," I said. "I think Hotel Alfie might have me beat."

He chuckled as his hands pressed flat against my back, rubbing up and down soothingly. After spending eight hours in a plane, it felt wonderful. "In Hotel Jordi's defense, I didn't allow for much time to prepare. Look."

His hands left my back, drifting down until they met my own. Alfie tugged lightly, pulling me with him into the kitchen where he opened the fridge. I hadn't noticed it before, but suddenly I was overcome with the scent of… something. I couldn't tell what it was, but it was oddly familiar.

"I've bought all your favorites," he said, gesturing to the various alcoholic beverages (mostly white wine) that filled the bottom shelf. When he opened the freezer, he added, "And only the best from the Tesco frozen foods section. Oh, let's not forget the cabinets."

When he opened them, I couldn't help but laugh at the amount of Pringles tubes I saw. Front and center were buffalo ranch, of course. But beside them—

"Oh my gosh." I released Alfie's hand to retrieve the goods. "Cadbury." Even though I could technically get the chocolate in the States, it wasn't the same. I squealed when I saw what he'd hidden behind the bar. "And Percy Pigs!"

Damn him, knowing my weakness for the fruit-flavored, pig-shaped gummies. I'd missed out on a decade of deliciousness.

Alfie smiled. "I knew you'd like those."

I tore the bag open and popped one in my mouth, moaning as I sucked on the gummy, getting the most out of the flavor before I started chewing.

"If you keep making sounds like that, I'm not going to be able to finish the tour."

"I'm happy to go see the bedroom next," I said before

popping another one of the candy pigs in my mouth.

"You haven't seen the true work of art yet," Alfie said, then threw open the oven. That's when the full force of whatever scent I'd caught before hit me.

He was cooking.

"A traditional shepherd's pie," he announced, then tilted his head, eying me with a proud grin. "I'll start heating the gravy soon. I knew you'd want some."

I shook my head at him. I'd always added gravy to everything I could during my first trip to England all those years ago. I found myself loving the food after a certain time, but I'd never consider it the most flavorful cuisine in the world. The gravy helped. I was pretty sure it—and ranch—ran in my veins.

"I figured we could get you some food then possibly take a nap," Alfie said. "Then we can head out, if you'd like. I can see what shows are playing. Or we can go sight-seeing."

"Food sounds amazing," I said, reaching up to grab his face in my hands before bringing his lips down to mine. In a whisper I added, "Thank you for doing this. For inviting me and hosting and being wonderful."

"I didn't know cooking and cleaning were held in such high regard," he replied. "I considered it the bare minimum."

"Well then I'm the luckiest woman in the world because your bare minimum is most men's utmost effort."

Alfie smiled as he leaned down to kiss me again, this time lingering. I melted into it like I always did, finding myself smiling against his lips.

"You know," he said when he pulled back. "That shepherd's pie probably has about twenty more minutes, and as you mentioned, I still haven't shown you the bedrooms."

I raised a brow. "Multiple?"

Alfie shrugged one shoulder. "I like having guests." My lips pursed and eyes narrowed, I regarded him with mischief that he picked up on instantly. "What?"

"Have you ever tested out the other rooms?"

He must have started getting my drift because a grin spread slowly across his lips. "I can't say that I have."

"Maybe we can do that this week?"

"Jordi, love," Alfie said, grabbing me around my waist and pulling me close. "I hope we test out many more spaces of this home than simply the bedrooms."

I couldn't stop the laughter that escaped me as he dipped his head down and showered my neck with kisses.

I didn't know why I'd been so worried about this trip. London was already proving to be oh-so amazing.

CHAPTER TWENTY

ALFIE AND I were seated at his kitchen table, him in nothing but his grey sweatpants and me in nothing but my underwear and the shirt that he'd been wearing when I arrived. Soft alternative music played from the Bluetooth speakers in the ceiling when his phone rang. I don't think we would have noticed had it not turned off the current song. We were too engrossed in planning what we'd do with our days (I did, in fact, want to do a little sight-seeing, despite Alfie's hard argument that staying in bed would be nice too) and the shepherd's pie. I'd also brought out the bag of Percy Pigs as an after-lunch dessert.

"Sorry," he muttered. "This shouldn't take long."

He picked up the call, and I watched from under my lashes as I shoveled another bite of gravy-covered mashed potato, meat, and veggie goodness into my mouth. The volume for the call was low enough where I couldn't pin-point the voice from the other end, but I could tell it was a woman. A member of his team maybe?

Suddenly, Alfie's eyes widened, shifting to me before they pointedly watched the fire he'd turned on. I set down my fork and leaned back in my chair, watching with a bit more intensity—and curiosity.

"That's today," he said, not so much a question as much as confirmation, though it was now clear that he'd forgotten something. The voice on the other line spoke again before Alfie continued, "No, no, that's uh—no I didn't forget!"

His eyes slid to me again and I raised my brows at him, silently calling him out. Alfie quickly hit the mute button before he said, "You shush."

"I've said nothing."

He unmuted himself. "No, I can come. It's only… can I bring a guest?"

My eyes widened and I sat up straighter in my seat when a younger voice shouted, loud and clear, "Shut up! She's here?"

"I told you she was coming, Iz."

Iz, also known as Isabella. Also known as Alfie's little sister.

So it hadn't been a member of his team, after all, but his mother. Which meant…

Oh no.

His mom said something else, and Alfie eyed me as he replied, "She just got in today. I think a nap is on the agenda, so… No she's sat right across from me… Yes we're eating lunch. I cooked for her, believe it or not." Whatever his mom said next, he clearly took offense to. "Of course she's not been poisoned. I've managed to keep myself alive for thirty-one years—yes, fine. You get credit for most of them, Mum."

I smiled. I'd always liked Alfie's mom. Having a career as a model in the seventies and eighties had taught her a whole lot about standing up for herself against men. Even if Alfie was her son and he would never show her disrespect, she talked back to him all the same.

I didn't know, however, how Alfie's mom liked *me*.

We'd never had any issues, his whole family welcoming me with open arms the first time we'd met. That might have been because they'd caught Alfie and I in a rather compromising situation, which required Izzy to be escorted from the room *immediately* while we made ourselves decent. But I liked to think it was because his parents had genuinely enjoyed me.

However, ten years did a lot to reputations. If they'd painted me in the same shade I'd painted myself in the time after Alfie and I had ended things…

I might not be starting in such a bright light this time around.

"I'll check train times, or maybe I can see if we can call a car… No, I'm not making Harry drive out to Surrey when he's gotten a place here in London. He's doing me a large enough favor as it is… I'm sorry, I forgot. I'll check with Jordi, but I might need to take a raincheck."

"No!"

Alfie jumped at my outburst, and even the other line went quiet. I knew he'd warned them that I was there, but maybe they hadn't realized I was sitting two feet away, listening to the whole conversation as best I could.

"Hold on, Mum." Alfie pressed the mute button again and turned to me. "No?"

"No, let's go. See your family, I mean."

"I thought you wanted to go to that restaurant along the river tonight?"

"We can do that another night," I said. "What's your family doing?"

"We get together one Friday evening a month for dinner. Mum cooks, Iz comes home from school, and we catch up. I didn't realize we'd planned for tonight."

"Next Friday is the last one of the month, and we have the gala that evening," I reminded him.

"I realize how pretentious this is going to sound," he began, "but I normally have people to remind me of these things."

I rolled my eyes while I grinned. Personal matters remained personal matters in the world of Alfie Fletcher. No team involvement. Which explained why the introduction of me into the gala and the dinner with his family had slipped his mind. He'd had no one to remind him of both.

"Let's go see your family," I said, deciding for both of us. "We have a full week to enjoy together. One night where we aren't entirely on our own isn't the end of the world."

Alfie didn't appear convinced of that, but he unmuted the phone and told his mom he would keep her updated on our arrival time. I heard Isabella squeal on the other side of the line.

Step one of convincing his family I wasn't a harlot, complete.

I WISHED I could have said I shared Isabella's enthusiasm as I stood outside the Fletcher family home.

Given Nicole Fletcher's luxurious background, it wasn't at all where I'd expected them to land once they'd moved out of London. It was, however, exactly what I would use as an example when describing the difference of homes in England to those in America.

The red brick was covered in ivy, and the roof looked like it belonged on a cottage. A worn, wood fence surrounded the property, so I couldn't see anything in the back, but I swore I heard water running. It wouldn't have surprised me to find some sort of creek back there.

Alfie, taking the same approach with his family's home that I had with mine, led us through the front door without knocking. That's when I saw more of how Mrs. Fletcher had gotten a hold on the place. While still quaint, she'd modernized the space with what looked like new floors and paint. I could just barely glimpse the kitchen from our spot in the foyer, but I thought I saw new appliances too.

A brand-new home was disguised by an exterior that had probably been built at least a hundred years before. The perfect mix of Alfie's laid-back British father and trendy Italian mother.

"Is that you, Alfie?" I heard the latter call from the kitchen's direction.

"Sure is," he called back, then in a whisper to me added, "Shoes off. Mum's crazy about the new floors."

So I'd been correct.

Alfie and I were still working on removing our shoes when Mrs. Fletcher came down the hall, dressed to the nines, just as I'd always remembered. You could take the woman off the runway, but you couldn't take the runway off the woman, I supposed.

I made sure my head was lifted, a smile aimed her way as I placed my shoes beside Alfie's. She did the same for me, but she hadn't said anything yet. That worried me. Nicole Fletcher was never short on words.

Alfie didn't miss a beat. He blissfully ignored any potential tension between his family and I and approached his mother, one of his winning smiles plastered on his face. Even while they hugged, Nicole never took her attention from me.

Another set of footsteps bounded down the staircase in front of us, and I moved my eyes in their direction, knowing exactly who I'd find.

"Holy shit," Isabella said. Well, that was much different from the last time I'd seen her. Of course, she'd been eight-years-old back then. Now she was a full-blown adult, complete with dark hair that had seen too many styling tools, tanned skin, and make-up that would make even the most talented stylists jealous. "I can't believe you're actually here!"

"Isabella. Language, young lady," Nicole scolded as her daughter ran up to me and wrapped me in a big hug.

My eyes widened in surprise. I'd never expected Isabella to know the full extent of what had happened between her big brother and me. Actually, I wouldn't have been surprised if Alfie hadn't told her anything at all. I could totally see him thinking that keeping her in the dark was a way to protect her innocence.

"I'm so glad you're here," Isabella said when she pulled back. "Alfie said you were coming to visit, but we didn't know when."

"Apparently neither did Alfie," Nicole muttered, eying her son. Then her attention returned to me, her eyes warm, welcoming. Not as cautious as before. Maybe Izzy's hug had been the sign she'd needed. The one that showed her I wasn't going to shy away. "It's been so long, sweetheart. Come in. Come on now. Leave it to my son to not even invite you in past the foyer."

"She was too busy being mauled by this little gremlin," Alfie commented as he walked up to Izzy and ruffled her hair. She quickly swatted him away, but didn't put up much more fight when he wrapped his arm around her shoulders and pulled her into his side for a hug.

"Asshole," she muttered, probably trying to avoid more of her mother's reprimanding. Izzy put her hand on her hip and turned on me with a look I think was supposed to be mature. Her brother was old news with me in the room, apparently. "Want me to make you a cocktail, Jordi?"

"Cocktail?" Alfie asked. "You're not eighteen yet. How do you know how to make a cocktail?"

Izzy rolled her eyes. "I'm two months short. And you weren't an angel either."

"No, but I *was* a vampire," Alfie countered, eliciting soft laughter from his mom and I. "And how would you know? You weren't even out of nappies yet."

"Enough you two!" Nicole rushed over to her children and pulled them apart. "We have a guest. Archie! Will you help me tame them?"

Mrs. Fletcher marched back into the kitchen with Izzy on her tail, arguing about how they let her big brother have all the fun and were way too strict with her. They'd all but forgotten said big brother and I in the foyer.

Alfie wrapped his arm around me. "See why I was a little hesitant about bringing you?"

"She grew up," I commented. "Like, majorly."

"I know." He rolled his eyes. "At least she's wearing a shirt that covers most of her stomach."

"Hey," I said, lightly hitting his chest with the back of my hand. "Her body, her choice."

He brought his other hand up to my face and gently caressed my cheek, the playful glow that had been in his eyes since we'd entered the home finally dimming.

"Do you blame me for being protective of the women in my life?"

I leaned into his touch to let him know I understood before I turned to kiss his palm.

"Jordi, come on!" Izzy called from the kitchen.

"We'd better go," Alfie said. "She gets vicious when she's kept waiting."

WE STAYED AT the Fletchers' home well past when I'd thought we would. It started out like all the dinners I'd been a part of ten years ago, full of laughter and poking fun at one another. They were a feisty bunch for the most part. Poor Archie Fletcher usually sat back, reining his family in when he deemed things were getting out of hand.

That was often since I was under the impression Izzy was trying to use smart remarks to make me laugh.

I hated to admit it worked more often than not. She could fire jabs at her brother like no one else could. And poor Archie dealt with it all, even though I saw him stealing longing glances at the glass-covered sunroom where his precious Persian cat,

Sugar, waited. I'd learned he was trying to train her like a dog, and was actually managing quite well.

Otherwise, I'd been the center of the questions just as I'd expected. I figured it was fair, since Alfie had endured the same with my parents. Worse, if my dad's football history lessons were considered.

They were particularly impressed to hear that I'd landed a job in my area of study. Even more impressed when Alfie interjected that I was working on publishing a book. But that quickly turned into them chastising him for never having any upper education, as if his acting career wasn't impressive.

More than anything, I learned Alfie was the butt of a lot of jokes, but he took it all like a champ. I guessed he was just happy to have everyone he cared about together again, like old times.

After dinner, we moved into the reception room, fresh glasses of wine in Nicole and I's hands, a soda in Izzy's, and scotch on the rocks for the gentlemen. Each member of the Fletcher family went to the seats that had been predetermined as theirs, and it was made apparent very quickly that I needed to figure out where I fit into the puzzle.

Izzy must have noticed my hesitation because she gave up her seat beside her brother on the couch. Despite their bickering over dinner, I caught the appreciative nod the siblings exchanged as I settled in beside Alfie. His arm instantly wrapped around my shoulders, pulling me close.

Cuddled next to Alfie, his body keeping me nice and warm, the wine relaxing me, the jet lag taking its toll, it wasn't long before I rested my head on Alfie's shoulder and closed my eyes. Just for a minute—

"Jordi's falling asleep," I heard Izzy say at some point.

Maybe I had actually dozed off, because when I opened my eyes, there was Alfie, leaning down to check if his sister's claim was true.

"I'm awake." I smiled sheepishly and he chuckled before he kissed my head.

"We should get going," Alfie announced.

He stood up before helping me. I was thankful for his sturdy body as I got to my feet and realized how the wine and exhaustion had made my legs wobbly.

"At this hour?" Nicole asked. "Alfie, by the time you two get home it will practically be morning."

"Jordi can sleep on the train. It'll be fine." But by the time he finished speaking, he was yawning.

"Stay, Alf," Archie insisted. "It'll give your mum some peace of mind."

"Jordi, you can borrow some of my pajamas," Izzy added.

Alfie turned his head down to me. At that point, I was using him for full support. My eyelids bounced back up the second I knew all attention was on me, my eyeballs probably red as tomatoes.

"That alright with you?" he asked. "We can catch a train

home first thing in the morning?"

I nodded. Finding a place to sleep immediately sounded much better than commuting back to Alfie's townhome so late at night, drifting in and out of sleep. Even if the solution was sleeping at Alfie's parents' house.

"Yes!" Izzy exclaimed. She hopped out of her seat and came at me with the energy of someone who hadn't started paying bills yet. "I have a pajama set I know you'll love."

Alfie tried to protest as his little sister grabbed ahold of my hand and pulled me away upstairs to her bedroom. It was just what I would have expected of little Isabella Fletcher—even if she wasn't so little anymore. Her room was the perfect blend of young, but attempting to transition into adulthood. I could tell she was trying to hide the childish parts she'd kept around, namely the large pile of stuffed animals that were shoved on or around a decorative armchair in the corner.

Izzy let go of me and ran to her dresser to grab the pair of pajamas she'd had in mind. When she emerged with a cotton set with cartoon avocados all over them, I smiled.

"These are very cute," I complimented, taking them from her."

"I knew you'd think so. I remember you being more fun than Alfie's other girlfriends." Her face fell then. "I meant… that is if you and Alfie are…" Her head tilted. "I've seen the pictures online, but I suppose I never asked if it was official again."

My smile widened. I'd seen the pictures too. Some more

videos as well, taken by nosy fans that had mostly been posted with the intention of sharing an Alfie Spotting, if the captions were at all honest. But just like the first one I'd spotted post-reuniting, they'd stirred questions of who I was.

Alfie had answered that with a few posts on his social media accounts. None had been directly of me, but I'd been included in the black-and-white photo carousel that kept his fans updated on what he'd been doing.

My personal favorite had been the silly selfie we'd taken in front of The Bean during his trip to Chicago. I was smiling like a fool, and he'd opted for puffed up cheeks and crossed eyes. It was blurry due the laughter we'd been fighting against while taking it, but that made it all the better.

I supposed while I'd considered that as much of an official announcement as anything, it was probably best we clarified.

"Yeah," I replied. "We are."

"Good. You've always been my favorite."

I was thankful Alfie chose that moment to appear at his sister's bedroom door, since I didn't know what to say to her admission. I noticed him right away, my eyes drawn to him like a magnet to metal. He needed to knock softly on the door before my companion took similar notice.

"Ugh, Alfie!" She scoffed. "Get out of my room! Jordi and I could have been changing!"

He didn't respond to his sister, and instead aimed suggestive eyes at me. I returned it with a look that told him not to go there in front of innocent ears.

"Meet me in the guest room when you ladies are done," Alfie told me, and I nodded. "Have fun."

I saw the sparkle in Alfie's eyes before he left us. Something told me he was excited to see us getting along so well, but Izzy had always clung to me. Maybe he was more excited to see all the years hadn't changed anything.

Even though my eyes were now almost completely dry and probably on the verge of falling out of my head, I stayed in Izzy's room with her, talking about anything and everything a seventeen-year-old girl might be interested in. As I offered my advice, I never thought that maybe it was hard for her, having only one sibling who was thirteen years older than her. I'd grown up without siblings, but this seemed like a close second to that. It meant the only person she could go to for things was her mom. Not that that was bad, since I'd been in the same predicament, but I knew she probably didn't want to tell Nicole about things like experimenting with alcohol and the story she'd told me about almost getting caught with weed. I sure as hell hadn't wanted to tell *my* mom any of that stuff.

So, I listened and gave advice where I knew I should—no alcohol until she was legal, stay in school—until Izzy showed the first signs of tiring.

I gave her a big hug before I left her room, shutting the door behind me and heading down the hall to find Alfie. He'd thankfully left the door open and a light on, so it was easy to figure out which room we'd be in for the night. The last thing I wanted was to accidently curl up in bed with his parents.

Funnily enough, even though I'd been the most tired, it looked like I was also the last one in the house still awake.

I pulled back the covers on my side of the bed and climbed under. As soon as I was settled, Alfie turned, his arm wrapping around me. He kissed my avocado-pajama-covered shoulder. Izzy had been right. They were super comfortable.

"I'm sure this isn't how you expected your first night in London to pan out," he whispered.

"Is it how *you* expected my first night in London to pan out?"

"Seeing as I forgot about my plans with my family?" he countered and I chuckled. His arm tightened around me. "As cute as these pajamas are on you, I'd pictured us both wearing nothing on your first night here."

I grinned. "There's plenty of time for that this week."

Then we were quiet, and when I was certain that Alfie had actually fallen asleep this time, he surprised me by saying, "Thank you."

"For what?"

"For talking with her. She adores you. Always has."

I smiled, even though I knew Alfie couldn't see it.

"Of course."

CHAPTER TWENTY-ONE

WE WOKE TO the smell of breakfast cooking downstairs, rare English sunlight leaking in past the curtains of the Fletchers' guest bedroom. Alfie's arm was still wrapped around me, my head on his chest.

I stretched my legs, trying to keep my movements as subtle as possible so I didn't wake my partner. Even with eye crust and morning breath, he was still the most perfect sight in the world.

I'd learned I loved watching him sleep. Not in a creepy Edward Cullen way, but in the way where I got to appreciate him without him noticing. Where I got to pinch myself and think that this was really my life.

And maybe... maybe we'd been on to something when we'd talked in Chicago. Maybe this time things would actually work out for us in the way we both knew they should.

Unfortunately, the moment didn't last long. Alfie stirred, his body going tense as he arched his body, groaning when he stretched. His eyes settled on me as soon as they opened, a soft smile curling up the corners of his lips.

I knew just from the shine in his eyes that he was thinking the same thing.

My hand went to his stubble-covered cheek and I leaned over him, kissing him tenderly. The arm that had held me through the night tightened around my waist, holding me close.

When I pulled back, I met his eyes again and said, "I love you."

Being half on top of him made it easy to feel the excited beat of his heart. Once upon a time, we'd said those three words to each other often. We'd been young, and even then, I wasn't sure if I understood what being in love meant, exactly. I'd thought that maybe I was confusing my feelings for infatuation, but in hindsight knew I'd spoken true.

I loved Alfie Fletcher—in more than a fangirl way. I loved the way he held me close and asked permission to touch me in even the smallest ways when we weren't alone. I loved his smile and that mischievous gleam in his eyes when he knew he was going to say or do something that might rile me up. I loved how he was constantly surprising me. I loved how he knew my coffee order and treated the people I cared about with kindness.

I loved him. Every part.

Alfie flipped me onto my back, his sturdy frame hovering over me. He leaned down to kiss me and I wrapped my arms around his neck. Even beyond the desire I felt in his kiss was something else.

An echoed reply to my admission.

His hand worked diligently with the large white buttons of my pajama top before his lips left mine to trail kisses on my jaw, my neck, down my chest. Alfie watched me as he pulled the shirt back and took each of my peaked nipples into his mouth, one after the other, swirling his tongue around each one before he released me with a soft pop.

I squirmed beneath him, pressing my legs together as my aching grew. Alfie didn't like that. His hand reached past the elastic band of my pants, working circles on my slick clit, as he continued his journey down under the covers.

He'd just gotten hold of my waistband, ready to remove my pants entirely, when his forehead landed on my stomach, and I heard him laugh.

"What?" I asked.

His head popped back up, tenting the sheet he'd disappeared under. "I can't believe I'm about to make you come while you're covered in smiling avocados."

I put my hand over my mouth to stifle my own laugh, but Alfie said nothing further before he shook his head, removed my pants, and disappeared between my legs.

"I WAS WONDERING when you two would join us."

Alfie and I walked into the kitchen, hand-in-hand to find his mom at the stove, Izzy at the espresso maker, and Archie at the kitchen table, reading the paper. Sugar the Cat waltzed along the counter, coming precariously close to the cup of frothed milk Izzy had prepared and was shooed away before it spilled. When Archie called her, she went obediently, probably knowing he would never turn her away.

"We told you last night we were tired," Alfie said. He dropped my hand to go greet his mom with a side-hug and his sister with a gentle punch to her shoulder—which she eagerly returned.

I used the moment to learn that Alfie's ass looked fabulous in flannel pajama pants. Maybe I'd buy him his own pair, since these had been borrowed from his dad.

The dad in question was watching me when I turned his way, and, upon realizing I'd been caught, blush heated my cheeks.

I quickly looked away. "What, uh, are you making there, Izzy?"

When I glanced back at Mr. Fletcher, he was grinning into his newspaper.

"A latte. Do you want one too, Jordi?" Izzy asked. "I have other flavors if you don't like caramel."

"She likes vanilla," Alfie answered.

"If you have that available," I added, well aware I was in his family's kitchen not an actual coffeeshop. "I'm sure whatever you make will be great, Iz."

She got to work on that while Alfie started helping his mom with some of the cooking. I offered my assistance too, but was quickly shot down by Nicole with the reasoning that I was a guest. So, I took a seat on one of the stools by the kitchen island while I waited and watched.

"Here you go," Izzy said as she slid my latte over to me. "Let me know what you think—wait!"

I stopped with the foam just barely brushing my top lip, eyes wide. I eyed the drink then its creator. "What?" I asked, sightly panicked.

Izzy rushed over to the counter to retrieve her phone and shoved it at Alfie.

"Take a picture of us," she demanded. "Look how cute we are with our coffees and matching pajamas."

The redness crept back up into my face when Alfie smirked, more than likely due to the pajama comment. I'd never be able to look at smiling cartoon avocados the same way again.

But Izzy was right. We did look pretty cute, all things considered. At nine in the morning, she wasn't exactly dolled up for the day either, which made me feel better about my messy hair and the minimal make up that was left over from the day before.

Impromptu sleepovers had never been beauty's friend.

Izzy rushed around the island and guided me on how to pose

for the picture. I hadn't realized it was such an art form, but having a model for a mom and actor for a brother had probably taught her a thing or two about photography. She'd at least been to some of Alfie's photoshoots, even if she hadn't been born while Nicole was on magazine covers.

"So cute," she gushed when Alfie handed her phone back. I didn't bother checking to see if I agreed. She was almost eighteen, so the odds of her adding enough filters to make us look flawless was high. "I'm posting more pictures of Jordi than you are, Alf."

"We've got a whole week ahead of us," he retorted. "Besides I'm cherishing being in the present instead of making sure I have every moment documented."

Izzy's face twisted as she said, "Ew. That was disgustingly poetic."

Alfie shrugged before he reached for one of the plates from the stack on the counter and started to scoop some scrambled eggs onto it, followed by some sausage links, and finally some potatoes. He slid it across the counter to me before he started on his own plate. When that and a cup of black coffee poured from the pre-brewed pot were in hand, he came to sit on the stool beside me.

"By the way," he said, taking advantage of his family's distraction while they, too, got their fixings and settled down at the kitchen table. "If it hadn't already been made obvious, I love you too."

I grinned at him before he leaned in to kiss me. When I pulled back, the first thing I saw was Archie, his wife now seated beside him, both of them staring pointedly at their breakfasts. Both of them smiling in silence.

CHAPTER
TWENTY-TWO

"I DON'T KNOW why you're freaking out so much."

Freaking out was putting what I was doing mildly. I was in full-blown panic mode, and I had a feeling I'd never get Alfie to understand. Why would he? He was a guy. Even worse, he was a guy who looked good in quite literally everything he wore.

I, on the other hand, was a very average woman with a very average figure, and no amount of arguing from Alfie that I was, in fact, well above average would help me out of this situation. He might see me as his own personal Aphrodite, but the cameras would not.

"Hush, it's different for us," Nicole Fletcher commented from her seat beside her son. There was just enough of a gap in the changing room curtain where I could see her smack his leg lightly with the back of her hand. "Jordi, sweetheart, do you have the mulberry one on?"

What in the fresh fuck was mulberry? "Um, I'm wearing purple?"

"Close enough. Come on out, dear. Let's see it."

I opened the curtain and Gemma, the sales associate that had been assigned to help us, held it back while I walked out to my entourage. The whole day had felt oddly like wedding dress shopping, which was made even worse by Alfie being one of the people offering opinions.

Not that he'd *said* anything negative, but considering his profession, I'd have thought he would hide his expressions better.

Though for the current dress selection, I couldn't say I disagreed with his not-so-subtle silent review.

"Oh goodness, that's lovely."

Nicole stood from the couch where she'd been waiting and walked over to me, champagne flute in hand. I twisted from side to side, making the too-many ruffles of the purple monstrosity that had been pulled for me move.

I realized I should have been more respectful of the gown that I was wearing. I'd never in a million years thought I'd have the chance to try on anything by a luxury designer, let alone know at the end of the day, I'd be going home with one of them.

When we'd been at the Fletchers' home, Izzy had brought up Be Positive which led to a discussion about the evening and, of course, what I'd be wearing.

Apparently, *cocktail dress* had been the wrong answer.

I didn't know what I'd been thinking when I'd packed. Actually, I did. I'd been thinking about Alfie and exploring London with him, not the *one* commitment I'd agreed to while in town. Besides, he'd told me it was a charity event. Since I'd never been to one of those, I dressed like I would have for a regular blood drive. Even then, I'd gone overboard with my outfit choice.

I guess I should have considered the venue and guest list. I mean, had I really thought April Evans would show up in a freaking cocktail dress?

In order to remedy the situation, Nicole had taken me under her fashionable wing and invited me to Harrod's. With only a few days before the event, it was apparently the best option we had, despite being swarmed with tourists. Not many were in the sections that we'd chosen to occupy, though. Probably because most of the luxury clothing and jewels that surrounded us cost double-to-triple the cost of my overseas flight.

I'd needed to dip into my savings for that flight.

We'd visited three floors so far, trying on dress after designer dress only to come up with duds.

I knew part of the problem was that Nicole was the one making the selections, not me. Not that I didn't trust her; she'd made quite the name for herself in this world back in the day. It was just that where Nicole wore leather leggings, I wore athletic ones. She wore a sweater, I wore a hoodie. Jeans versus sweatpants. Hair styled versus thrown up.

We weren't good matches for this.

I watched Alfie in the mirror's reflection before my gaze shifted to the third—and admittedly my favorite—member of the entourage: Harry. He'd driven us here and retaken up the role of bodyguard for the day, calling it practice for the gala. For the most part, he'd surprisingly left Alfie and I to do our own thing. But if there was ever a time for him to decide he wanted to join, I was glad it was this one.

Out of both the men present, he was giving me the most honesty—vocally and with his face.

"You don't think it's too much? All this stuff?" I asked, grabbing at the ruffles.

"I think it's lovely," Nicole countered. "So flattering on your figure. Don't you think, Alf?"

"I liked the last one better, I think," Alfie said.

"We all know why…" Harry added, referring to the dress that had come with a neckline that ended practically at my bellybutton.

Alfie, completely shameless, shrugged and sat back on the couch to sip his champagne.

"Miss, if you'd like, we can always have a tailor remove some of the details here," Gemma said, reaching for the dress to show me her vision.

"Unfortunately, we need this dress by Saturday," I said. "I'm not sure there's time for alterations."

For a moment, Gemma seemed to share in my panic before she regained her professional composure.

"What about a dress like the one you wore to that premiere?" Harry suggested. "I remember you looked lovely in green."

"We do have a green dress pulled for you," Gemma said. "Would you like my help unzipping?"

"Please," I said, eager to get the poofs off.

"Is it the one with sleeves?" Nicole asked. "She's going to a blood drive. Why did we think sleeves were a good choice?"

My body sagged with disappointment. Just when I'd thought I'd found my escape…

"Alfie, what are you wearing?" Nicole asked next.

"Fluorescent pink," he replied, earning a snicker from Harry. When his mom eyed him, not appreciating the sass, he said, "Black. When have I ever worn anything other than black?"

"Do you have any black in there? Perhaps matching would look nice."

"We pulled one," Gemma confirmed. It had actually been one of the three dresses I'd pulled myself. Black was always a safe choice, and I'd picked it in desperation when I saw the other options joining me in the fitting room with.

"Maybe we can try the red one first, actually. It might work well with the theme of the—"

"Mum," Alfie said, rising off the couch. "How about we let Jordi pick what she wants to wear?" He turned to me. "You want to try on the black one, love?" I nodded vigorously in reply and he turned to Gemma. "Can you help her into that one, if you don't mind?"

"Certainly, Mr. Fletcher. Miss, if you will."

I widened my eyes at Alfie, silently communicating my thanks and he nodded once before he guided his mom back to the couch. I could hear her complaining about needing to stand out at an event like this, especially since it would be our first public appearance together. That's when Harry politely reminded her that it actually wasn't.

"She's been away from this world for nearly a decade," he said. "It's best to let her ease back into it."

Thank God for Harry.

"Do you mind me asking what you do for a living, Miss?" Gemma whispered to me as she helped me out of the purple dress.

"Publishing," I replied. "Events specifically."

"So one of us regular folk." She smiled up at me. "I know Nicole Fletcher fairly well. I'm sure you can imagine she's a regular at the high-end retailers across the city, and I work part-time over on Sloane Street as well. You're doing great humoring her, but remember fashion is about being comfortable. You're going to look the best when you're most confident, and that won't happen in any of these."

I laughed when she grabbed at the rainbow of sequined, fluffy messes that had been pulled for me. From behind them all, she rescued the one dress I thought might actually stand a chance. I only hoped it fit.

"I've been waiting for someone to try this one," Gemma said as she helped me step into it. "It only arrived last week."

I ran my hands gently down the shimmering polyester skirt. There was no mirror in the room, so I could only judge the gown from what I could see when I looked down. So far, the minimalism was winning.

Gemma finished tying two strands of fabric together behind my back, holding the off-the-shoulder neckline in place. The gentle brush of the loose ends grazed the bare skin above the top of the otherwise sleeveless bodice.

"I know he's not your husband," she said to me, her hand going to the curtain, preparing for the big reveal, "but if he doesn't cry like it's your wedding day, I'll be so disappointed."

I didn't know if it was because I was still smiling from her comment or if the dress was truly that beautiful, but all bickering from my shopping entourage ceased the moment the curtain opened, and I was helped out of the fitting room.

Harry let out a low whistle, while Nicole had been stunned into silence, perhaps because her beloved embellishments had failed her. Alfie leaned forward, elbows on his knees, looking nowhere but at me. Just when I thought he might finally offer some sort of verbal opinion, he shook his head and ran his hand down the lower half of his face.

"Wow," was all he managed to get out.

That's when I knew it was finally time to put a stop to the

suspense.

The moment I turned to the mirror, I knew why Alfie had been left nearly speechless.

The dress was the most stunning piece of clothing I'd ever worn. Simple, yet luxurious. It was a dress that stood out on its own, without all the pomp and circumstance that other gowns might use to earn attention.

The synched waist fell into a glorious A-line skirt, complete with a slit that went up to my mid-thigh, and a small train. Unlike the dress with the deep V, this one accentuated my boobs in the perfect way, while the off-the-shoulder neckline hid the parts of my arms I was most nervous about.

It was like liquid metal had been poured over me, sticking and molding just where it needed to in order to hide all my insecurities while also bringing out the best my pear-shaped body had to offer.

"Well," Nicole said. She grunted as she pushed herself off the couch and came to stand beside me. "I stand corrected. This is stunning." She turned to Gemma. "You didn't pin this anywhere?"

Our sales associate shook her head while she donned a proud smile. "Not at all. Fits her like a glove."

"I'll say…"

Alfie made an *oof* noise when Harry knocked him upside the head. I watched in the mirror as he rubbed it and turned on his bodyguard with a look of betrayal.

"Mind yourself," Harry warned. "You've hit your limit for the day."

"It's a compliment," Alfie defended. His eyes returned to me. "You look beautiful, Jords."

"Enough to outshine April?" I replied.

"I'm the wrong person to ask since I've always thought you've outshone her."

I watched Harry's smile grow. "That's better."

"I'll go to the checkout while you change, dear."

"Oh, Mrs. Fletcher, I can't let you pay for this."

Gemma leaned over to me. "You said you work in events?" she muttered, hardly moving her lips. I nodded. "Let her pay for it."

When I eyed her sidelong, the sales associate gave me a single nod. Point taken.

"Now that that's taken care of…" Alfie downed the rest of his champagne in one gulp and set the flute on one of the decorate tables. "I'm going to run to the little boy's room."

"Want me to come with you?" Harry asked.

"I should be fine. I'd rather you watch over the ladies." Alfie walked over to me and grabbed hold of my hand, bringing it up to his lips to kiss my knuckles. "Beautiful," he repeated, then he was off.

HARRY WAS VISIBLY anxious, tapping his foot and checking his watch every few seconds as though multiple minutes had passed since the last glance. I didn't blame him. Alfie was like a son he'd spent the better part of his career protecting.

If Alfie didn't show up soon, I could see myself joining him in his panic.

"I've texted him," Nicole said for the third time. "And he's not picking up my calls."

"That doesn't mean there's trouble," I interjected, half to calm my own thoughts. "He keeps his phone on silent a lot. He might not have seen them."

Harry lifted his wrist to check his watch one more time, then threw his arms down in frustration. "I knew I shouldn't have let him wander off alone."

"Could we go look for him?" I suggested. I imagined the worse that could have happened was he'd been stopped by fans and didn't know how to get out of it.

"Looking for him in that crowd will be like looking for a needle in a haystack," Harry argued. Another watch check. "I suppose I could run in and see—"

That's when Nicole gasped. Harry and I followed her line of vision to see Alfie bounding out of the doors closest to where our car was parked, my dress laid nicely in the trunk.

Turning the mom switch on, Nicole was quick to reprimand her son. "Where were you? You just about gave us all a heart attack!"

"I'm sorry," Alfie said, half-breathless. At least it seemed like he'd made an attempt to hurry out. "I got held up."

"Fans?" Harry asked.

Alfie shook his head. "No, nothing like that. Well, there were a few selfies, but I had to run a personal errand."

"You could have told us."

Alfie shrugged one shoulder, then turned on me, beaming. "Now that that's settled, I was thinking about drinks. Celebrate a successful shopping day."

I narrowed my eyes at him, trying to coax him into admitting where he'd been. He had his *building suspense* face on, which meant whatever he'd done he was excited about. It was also clear he was trying to divert the attention by suggesting a completely unrelated activity.

"Okay," I agreed. I'd get it out of him eventually, I supposed. "Let's go."

CHAPTER TWENTY-THREE

I'D NEVER CONSIDERED myself a particularly swanky person. For starters, dressing up usually felt like a chore and consisted of putting on a pair of jeans instead of leggings. Even at work, I could get away with business casual. The only time my job ever required formal was at the annual holiday party, where we all got dressed up in glittery cocktail dresses and enjoyed the luxury of an open bar and one of the many rooftop views of Chicago.

That was a lot for me, given a flannel shirt had been considered high-fashion in the small town I'd grown up in. I'd never needed to worry about keeping up with fashion trends or if someone would notice if my hair was in a ponytail for consecutive days.

Fancy, for most of my life, had been defined as a birthday dinner at Olive Garden while you sported your latest thrifting finds.

Currently, however, fancy was defined as having my hair and makeup done in Alfie's second bedroom by a styling team his mom had recommended, my gown pressed and hanging from the curtain rod like it was my wedding day, not the afternoon before a charity gala.

Not counting the Starr holiday parties, I'd been to exactly three events that came remotely close to the caliber of this one over the course of my twenty-eight years. First, was my Uncle John's wedding. Even though it was his third, it was his bride's first, so she'd done everything in her power to make that barnyard shindig the best it could be. The second was Olivia's wedding, which had been a fairytale-like outdoor event in the forests of Maine. The third was the season four premiere of *Crimson Curse* where I'd stayed dutifully by Alfie's side until he was called over by his team to take pictures. That's when I moved dutifully over to Harry's side, intent to avoid the cameras at all costs.

I wasn't sure how lucky I'd be tonight, but I wanted to try to keep my avoidance streak alive as best I could.

A soft knock sounded on the cracked bedroom door, and I half opened an eye to get a look at Alfie. It didn't last long as the make-up artist told me to close it again. Right when I did, I heard the hiss of the hairspray bottle and Alfie's following cough.

"You ladies should open a window," he said. "How are you

all breathing?"

"Beauty is pain," the hair stylist said in her thick Scandinavian accent.

"Pain, maybe, but suffocating?"

I smiled softly, careful not to move too much out of fear of upsetting the make-up artist, and heard Alfie push open the bedroom window. His footsteps grew closer, and he whispered a kind, "Excuse me," before his hand landed on mine.

"I'm working with touch and sound only right now," I said. "Are you ready? What time is it?"

Alfie chuckled. "Don't worry, there's still plenty of time. I was just coming to let you know I'm about to hop in the shower, so if you need me—"

"She's not getting anywhere near water," the hair stylist said. My make-up artist grunted her agreement.

"Understood," Alfie said. His hand left mine, and I pouted. "I'll come back after and hopefully you'll be able to open your eyes."

"I hope so. I'm about to fall asleep here soon."

His chuckle faded as he walked out of the room, the door dragging along the carpet just enough for me to know he'd shut it again.

I was serious, though. We'd packed anything and everything into my trip. From tourist attractions that I'd missed out on due to classes to some of Alfie's favorite spots, we'd accomplished more in a week than I'd ever thought possible.

Now the primary reason for my coming here had finally arrived, and I would fly home on Sunday morning, the time change making it possible for me to arrive in Chicago by Sunday afternoon.

Then we'd be back to our routine of bi-weekly visits at comic cons, but even those would be ending soon.

We'd been spoiled with these longer trips, the extended time we'd gotten to spend together. Now that they were coming to an end, that original ember of panic was starting to rise again. The one where I didn't know how everything would pan out and my realist traits were starting to make me a pessimist.

I'd promised Alfie I wouldn't worry. That we'd figure out a way to make it work. But as I sat in my styling chair, being doted on by hired professionals instead of simply using my drug store brand products, waiting for the moment when I'd put on a gown that cost almost a full year's worth of rent…

I wanted answers. I wanted a sure answer that everything would work after I got on my flight back to Chicago. I didn't want to question when I'd see the person I loved next or worry about any lingering fears created by our past or if I even fit into this glamorous space that was his world.

I didn't want to think that I might never move up in my own career of my own volition. That everyone would only want to work with me because of my connections to various stars through Alfie.

No matter what I'd promised, worrying was a part of who I

was, just like optimism was a part of Alfie. Naturally, he wouldn't see the same issues I did because he'd never experienced them.

I kept going back to what Gemma had said at my dress fitting.

So one of us regular folk.

Not a retired supermodel. Not an actor on a hit TV show. A regular person that even the most devoted fangirls couldn't figure out the name of.

"Okay," I heard the make-up artist say. One final hiss of the hairspray can let me know the hairstylist was putting together the finishing touches. "Open."

It took severe effort to open my eyes after having them shut for so long. I blinked a few times, making my vision come back clear, before I gasped and gaped at myself in the mirror.

They'd taken away all my flaws. The look wasn't too over-the-top, my make-up definitely still natural and my hair in a messy-yet-styled bun. I'd shown them both pictures of my everyday style, and the tag-team had gone, by some miracle, and made it look glamorous. Like I could wear my gown, but I could also wear the cocktail I'd originally packed and pull off both.

"Wow," I said.

"I'll say."

I turned to find Alfie standing in the doorway. He was wearing his usual grey sweatpants and a black t-shirt, his hair still damp from the shower. He'd missed a few droplets on his neck and hairline when he'd dried himself off.

"You really like it?" I asked. As much as he was involved in the world of stardom, I knew Alfie wasn't for the glitz and glam in the way other celebrities were. He preferred lowkey events. Ones where he wouldn't have to pretend to want to talk to people or put on a tie.

His eyes drifted to the stylists who were still lingering in the room, not doing anything other than listening in on our conversation. They didn't move, failing to pick up on Alfie's silent request to leave.

He was a celebrity, not royalty. And if there was anything I'd learned from these ladies it was that they gave the orders. The rest of us were merely peasants.

"Yes," was all Alfie finally replied, and I smiled, knowing that if there hadn't been prying ears, he would have said more.

He was ushered from the room under the pretense that I needed to get into my gown. Alfie waggled his eyebrows at me, and I wasn't sure if it was excitement or another attempt at silently communicating one of any number of naughty comments I was sure he'd come up with.

Using the arm of the hairstylist for balance, I made my way into the black fabric. I'd put on shapewear to give myself more of an hourglass figure, but had opted to go braless. These women were seeing more of me than I usually showed to anyone other than Alfie, but I couldn't have managed without them. They zipped up the back of the bodice, tied the fabric that hung off my shoulders into place, and helped me put on my classic black strappy, open-toed heels. Before I knew it, I was walking out into the open as I put my diamond-stud earrings in. I could already hear the newly arrived Harry chatting with Alfie.

The men stopped their conversation when the *click-clack* of my steps on the hardwood floor announced my entrance. Alfie was dressed too, donning exactly what he'd told his mom he would be: a black tuxedo with a thin black tie. He'd used some form of gel on his hair to keep it tamed, and had trimmed his facial hair so that he sported a nice five o'clock shadow as compared to the usual slightly longer stubble.

The stylists followed after me, their rolling cases of products in hand. I offered them a quick thank you, Alfie doing the same, before they headed out.

I did a slow twirl for the men when they'd gone, showing off all angles of the finished look. "What do we think?"

"As lovely as ever," Harry complimented.

I'd expected something similar from Alfie, but instead I found him watching me with scrutinizing eyes.

"Is something wrong?" I asked, then instantly turned my attention down to the dress. If something was wrong with it…

"Something's missing," Alfie finally said. He shoved his hands in the pockets of his tuxedo's trousers and walked over to me, offering closer evaluation.

I had no idea what he was seeing. I'd done or bought everything that he and Nicole had suggested after giving me a history of the event. There had only been so much I could accomplish in the five days I'd been allotted.

He removed one of his hands to snap after figuring out whatever it was he thought I needed.

That's when his other hand followed, a long rectangular box in it.

I gasped. "Alfie, what is that?"

I figured I already knew the answer, and he didn't bother verbally responding before he opened the lid to reveal the most stunning diamond necklace I'd ever seen.

Three layers of small marquee-cut diamonds made up the portion that would wrap around my neck before they cascaded down into an elegant cluster. Each strand was finished off with a circle-cut, all of them sparkling brilliantly from the warm glow that the setting sun cast into the room.

"Wha…" I tried before I closed my mouth, hoping real words might come out when I opened it again. "When did you get this?"

"Remember when I had a little bit of a delay at Harrod's?" he asked, and my jaw dropped.

The little liar hadn't gone to the bathroom at all. He'd been buying me jewelry.

Absolutely *stunning* jewelry.

"Would you mind if I put it on you?" he asked.

I nodded and turned, still slightly as a loss. Alfie's hands brushed delicately against the exposed skin of my neck, sending a shiver down my spine. Goosebumps rose on my arms. When the clasp clicked shut and Alfie leaned forward to press a kiss to the underside of my jaw, I shuddered.

My hand reached up instinctively to the new weight resting on my chest. I couldn't see myself in any reflective surfaces, but I didn't need to in order to know that Alfie's finishing touch guaranteed I was prepared for a night among the elite.

When I turned to him again, I knew my mouth was hanging just slightly ajar, my eyes filled with wonder—and probably some tears. Those needed to stay away, though. I didn't want to ruin the make-up that had taken the better part of an hour to complete.

Alfie didn't seem to care, though, as his hand reached up to caress my face and all of a sudden, I was in a fairytale. My prince charming and I the only ones in the room.

Harry cleared his throat, reminding me that wasn't really the case.

"How about we head out?" he suggested. "There's sure to be traffic with some of the streets closed for the event arrivals."

Alfie helped me down the stairs and into the car, which barely fit all the fabric of my dress. And even though most of our trips with Harry back in the day had been much more casual, there was something about this moment that felt so familiar. This was the first time it had only been the three of us, I realized.

We'd always had an additional companion—Mrs. Fletcher—or Alfie and I had taken public transportation.

This was just like old times, except at the end of the weekend Harry would return to his countryside cottage and Alfie and I would go on however long-distance couples went on.

That thought made my legs go weak with anxious anticipation. Even more so than the sight I caught when I looked ahead through the windshield.

Cameras flashed in rapid succession, the cluster of them lighting up the miniature red carpet and backdrop that was decorated with the gala's logo. I couldn't help it as I gazed out the window, unabashedly drawn in by the glamor of it all, as our car moved forward in the drop-off line.

"We can skip it if you want," Alfie said. I turned to him and found him staring as well. I wondered when the last time he'd walked a red carpet had been. "There's a separate drop-off for guests who want to avoid all this."

I bit my lower lip, contemplating the pros and cons of walking out of this car with Alfie Fletcher. I was sure there were plenty of other celebrities here with a higher status, but the cameras would show him love all the same. And there I would be, on his arm, smiling like the obedient partners I always saw on award show carpets.

I'd avoided it before, and I knew, deep down, I should avoid it now too. They hadn't learned my name yet, but the press might after this. And if I'd thought it had been bad with Mr.

Singh, once my name was out in the public, there was no telling what issues I'd run into while trying to find a home for my book.

Still, I tried to push the doubts and fears aside. I needed to. I'd been doing enough of that while getting ready. If I wanted to even humor the idea of Alfie and I making it long-term, I needed to enter into his world. Fully.

And that meant going beyond fancy gowns and diamond jewelry.

"No," I said. "Let's do it."

Alfie's eyes widened, and I saw Harry steal a peek in the rearview mirror. "You sure?"

I nodded as I slid my hand toward one of Alfie's that rested in his lap. "We're being totally honest, remember?"

No more hiding. No more secrets. No more dwelling on the past.

It was time to show the world us: Alfie and Jordi.

Alfie's slow smile made it clear he understood what I'd meant. He squeezed my hand. "Everyone's going to fall in love with you the same way I have."

Harry stopped the car at the curb. The shouts of the photographers penetrated through the still-closed door of the car, calling for Alfie before they'd even seen us.

The moment the door opened, we were bombarded with camera flashes and the roar of the paparazzi. I moved my hand in front of my eyes, shielding myself from the bright lights while Alfie got out then proceeded to help me do the same. He guided us calmly and confidently toward the miniature red carpet, my arm hooked through his, an additional group now in tow behind us. I recognized a few as members of Alfie's team from ten years before. The rest of them must have been new.

I tried to keep my head from darting around, attempting to take in all the sights and sounds. It was overwhelming, and I had no idea how Alfie managed to keep his focus intact, trained ahead of us the whole time. He was completely at ease, despite his resentment of these sorts of affairs, a true testament to what all his years in the spotlight had taught him.

"Just smile," he muttered to me, keeping his own in place while he spoke. "Don't answer anything or react too dramatically. A few minutes of posing and we can head inside."

I nodded before we positioned ourselves in the line of celebrities and personnel awaiting their time on the carpet. It didn't take long before a man wearing a suit and wired earpiece ushered us forward.

Alfie helped me, letting me continue to use his arm for balance before we settled ourselves and he slipped it around my waist. At first, I wasn't sure what to do in return. The throngs of photographers were making me forget how to perform basic functions like taking pictures with my partner, even though we'd been doing it throughout my entire trip.

So that's what I pretended was happening. It wasn't a man desperate to sell whatever picture he took to a tabloid pointing his lens at us. It was Izzy or Mrs. Fletcher, telling Alfie and I to angle ourselves certain ways or smile bigger.

Alfie beamed down at me, noticing the sudden change in my disposition. I tilted my face up, meeting his eyes.

The cameras ate it up.

They didn't know who I was, only that Alfie Fletcher's arm was around my waist, his eyes watching no one but me. His smile was no longer for their lenses, but this mystery girl at his side. And any one of them would try to become the person who captured the best shot.

By the time we were escorted away from the cameras and into the museum, my cheeks hurt.

"Are you sure you've never done that before?" Alfie asked. I smiled and shook my head. "Very impressive."

We ventured further into the museum, descending the staircase that made me feel even more like a girl who'd suddenly found out she was a princess. I still managed to hear the train of my gown glide down behind me, even amongst the chatter and polite laughter of the guests.

Above us, a giant whale skeleton hung suspended in the air, but otherwise, the museum had transformed into a true event venue.

Tables covered by white linens filled the backmost section of the spacious area. Multiple carving stations had been set up throughout the space, the white-clad servers behind them prepared to plate the preferred cuts for the guests. Along the left-hand side of the room, nurses sat opposite the gala attendees that had chosen to donate their blood. White curtains separated each station, but from the current vantage point, I saw the bags filling with blood that would later be donated to a children's hospital.

Otherwise, everyone not busy donating mingled around the venue, the ones without bandages on their arms taking drinks from passing servers carrying silver trays. Those that did wear the badge of charitable honor opted for the many hors d'evours that were also being handed out.

Aside from the fact that I knew most of these people were probably part of the London elite or had some sort of connection to the entertainment industry, I felt like Alfie and I could have simply been attending a black-tie wedding—if I kept my eyes off the blood bags.

Alfie turned to me just before we reached the end of the stairs. "You ready?"

I turned up to him. If I'd survived the cameras, I could survive this.

I nodded my reply, then allowed him to take me into a night in his world.

CHAPTER
TWENTY-FOUR

"THERE THEY ARE!"

Louie approached Alfie the second we came into sight, the two ex-costars embracing in the manliest way possible. A woman hovered behind him, likely his date. I wondered if she was his son's nanny. That would have been a bold move, even for Louie, to invite the center of a scandal to an event like this. I gave her a smile in greeting, regardless, before Louie opened his arms to me.

"I was wondering if you'd be able to make it," he said. "How long've you been in town?"

"A week now," I said. "I fly out on Sunday."

Alfie handed me a champagne flute he'd grabbed off a passing tray, and Louie waggled his eyebrows. I took a sip as he said, "Plenty of time for Alf to tap that a few more times, eh?"

I spit the champagne right back into my glass, some of it

spraying onto my date's tuxedo coat. The mixture of him jumping and me trying to keep from choking earned the attention of some of the other nearby guests. I tried to give them all reassuring smiles, but my eyes were watering from holding back my coughs. I probably looked more insane than anything.

"We're in public, Lou," Alfie chided before he wrapped his arm around me, trying to assist.

"Yeah, yeah," his co-star said, brushing the comment aside with a few flicks of his wrist. "Speaking of good shags, have you met Sierra yet?"

I figured the blush wasn't from her make-up as Louie's date extended her hand to Alfie. She tried to offer it to me too, but I was still too busy trying to regain my composure. She pulled away slowly, offering me a smile similar to that which I'd originally given her. Sierra's might have been laced with a little more shame at her date's expense, though.

"Christ, you two know how to gather all the attention."

We all turned to see April Evans approaching, her strut akin to something that belonged on a catwalk. If she hadn't become an actress, I imagined that's where she would've ended up. She certainly looked the part in her designer dress, one that was more comparable to Nicole Fletcher's style than my own. The beads that adorned the red spaghetti-strapped, body-tight dress glistened in the ambient lighting of the museum. I imagined the only reason she could walk at all was due to the slit that ran up to her upper thigh.

"You jealous it's not on you for once, April?" Louie joked, nudging her playfully as she came to stand beside him.

"Ha," April replied, rolling her eyes. She took a sip of her champagne before her sight landed on me. "Oh, dear. Jordi, are you all right?"

I gave her a thumbs up. "Just choking," I managed to squeak out.

April pursed her lips. "Hm, well, when you're finished, I've got some touch-up in my bag if you need it." Her attention went back to the boys. "Are either of you donating this year?"

Alfie lifted his champagne. "I'm donating, but not my blood."

"I'm way too inebriated for that," Louie added.

"Figures." April nodded toward the nurse stations. "Gabrielle is donating now. And did you both hear that Elliott is no longer coming? Filming for that new project he's working on was delayed and now the little brat is stuck on the Amalfi Coast while we're here as spokespeople for blood."

"You play a vampire one time…" Alfie mused, shaking his head, and I smiled up at him.

"He's gotten to skip out on the last three conventions and now this," April continued, jealousy lacing her words. When she realized what she'd said, her eyes widened before they settled on me. "Not that those conventions are awful."

"I know what you mean," I assured her.

April rubbed her lips together before she pursed them again. "Jordi, why don't we go touch up your makeup? I believe it's smeared a tad around your eyes." When I reached up to try to wipe it away out of instinct, she continued by saying. "Oh, no. Don't worry. I'll get it fixed up for you. Alfie, don't mind me stealing your date for a moment."

One of my hands fisted the fabric of my skirt, lifting it so I didn't trip, the other trapped in April's sudden hold. When I glanced back at where we'd left Alfie, Louie, and Sierra, all of them looked equally confused. Alfie, at least, managed to give me the smallest shrug, letting me know he had no idea why I'd been whisked away so suddenly.

Then again, he wasn't doing much to stop it.

Maybe I actually did have makeup running down my face.

I was starting to believe it, wishing I could free up a hand to wipe it away, despite April's insistence that I not, when she looked back behind us, then dragged us to the nearest table.

She sighed as she took a seat.

I remained standing, my eyes scanning the area in search of a bathroom. I was sure there had to be one around here somewhere, but April had led us nowhere near it.

"Sit," she insisted, elegant as ever before. Not at all like a kidnapper, which was what this was beginning to feel like.

I slowly did as instructed, watching April as she took a casual sip of her drink, waiting for me to settle myself and the fabric of my dress.

"That's lovely, by the way," she said. "Suits you perfectly, and I'm sure Alfie loves the dark color."

"He does tend to favor black."

April offered me a soft smile before she took another sip, then set her drink down.

"I'm sorry to pull you away like that, but Louie is like a leech, and there was no way I was going to have this conversation in front of him."

My heart sank to my stomach. Considering how few times April Evans and I had actually interacted, I couldn't begin to guess where this was going. But if we'd been taken away from the boys…

Louie, I understood. For as little as I knew April, I knew him even less. Even so, it had been made very apparent that he had little to no filter.

But Alfie… I didn't know why we'd been dragged away from him.

Her posh composure broke, and April let out a small, nervous laugh.

"I'm sorry," she said. "I don't really know how to bring this up without being absolutely frank about it."

I knew she was trying to be polite, but her wording did nothing to help my own nerves. "It's okay. Say whatever you want to say."

She met my eyes then, and I immediately knew where this conversation was going. They were the same eyes she'd aimed at me when we'd first seen each other in the celebrity green room. The ones that told me she knew.

And, of course, Alfie had given me more details of how that happened, but I was suddenly very interested to hear her point of view.

"I wanted to let you know…" She sighed. "Alfie told me how upset you were after the last time we spoke. And please don't be mad at him for telling me," she added quickly when I opened my mouth to speak. "I kept bothering him because I could see it too. I truly commend you for keeping it together as long as you did. I'm not sure I would have been able to. Christ, I could barely keep any sort of composure most days."

My brows creased in confusion. "What do you mean?"

April sighed again. "I didn't know you were unaware I was the one who'd told Alfie to go find you. He only explained that a few weeks ago. I'd assumed you'd known, and that me asking you how you were…" She let out a huffed laugh. "Well, I suppose you did still figure out that I knew. I was always so jealous of how intelligent you were. *Are*, I suppose. But I promise you, Jordi, I didn't bring it up with the intention of upsetting you. I was only asking because I know what it's like to feel alone in these situations."

She'd just told me I was smart, but even I knew it didn't take a genius to figure out what April was insinuating.

"April…" I tried and reached out to her.

She pulled back instantly. "No, no, I don't want sympathy. I only wanted you to know that the same person who hurt you hurt me, so I understand. And I know we aren't particularly close, but if you do need someone to speak to about it, I'm here."

My eyes were watering again, and when April allowed me a good look at her face—she'd been keeping it down aside from a few quick glances, hiding her emotions—I could see hers glistening too.

This time, she didn't pull away when I reached out to place my hand over hers.

"Thank you," I whispered. "For being so vulnerable with me. I know it's not easy to talk about."

"It's so fucking stupid," April said suddenly, her voice cracking with her composure. "He's out there living his life, none the wiser that we're both here at a charity gala crying about something he did to us over a decade ago."

"It's unfair," I added. "I've been thinking about it a lot lately, for obvious reasons."

"Of course."

"And Alfie… he's been wonderful in trying to understand how I'm coping and how it's affected me." I rolled my eyes. "Sometimes he's a little *too* wonderful. He won't even kiss me in public without asking first."

April shook her head, a small smile curling up her lips. "He's one in a million, that one. As far as men go, that is. It's a wonder how he'd ever called that piece of shit his friend to begin with."

"You've got your one in a million too, don't you?" I asked, my eyes drifting to the giant engagement ring on her finger. "Your *Vogue* photographer. Gabriel, you said?"

April's forehead scrunched—well, it tried its best; she had wonderful Botox—before she smiled, her body shaking with silent laughter.

"You mean *Gabrielle*?" she asked. "The *female* photographer from the *Vogue* shoot?"

My eyes widened, more from embarrassment than anything else. I'd read the headlines about the engagement, and nothing more. And maybe I wasn't as smart as April had given me credit for because with all the talk about high-end fashion, my brain had immediately gone to *French man* when she'd said her fiancée's name earlier. The pronunciation would have been the same, after all.

"I'm so sorry," I said. "I didn't—wow, I feel like an idiot."

April smiled again. "You've been out of touch with our world for a little while now."

"I have."

She flipped her hand over and held onto mine, squeezing gently. "We're happy to have you back in it. Our cast is very close, if you haven't been able to tell. We're all enjoying seeing Alfie so happy again." Her eyes narrowed. "And we hope you're happy too?"

I squeezed back. "Yeah," I said. "I am."

AFTER AN ACTUAL trip to the restroom to hide the effects of our emotional conversation, April and I rejoined the others. Given that many of the guests were starting to take their seats, I assumed someone had come around—or was starting to come around—to request that we prepare for dinner. Apparently, they hadn't made it as far as the *Crimson Curse* crew yet.

I noticed the additional person in the group immediately. She was stunning, with pin-straight golden hair and eyes that would make the crystal-blue water of the Maldives jealous. Her natural-pink-tinted lips curled up in a smile at our approach, an inviting arm extended towards her fiancée.

April happily obliged, giving her date a kiss on the cheek, before pulling back one side of her open blazer—which left Gabrielle practically in her bra, seeing as that was the only thing she wore underneath the jacket—to examine where the blood had been drawn.

I watched them so intently, so obviously in love, that I hadn't noticed Alfie had found his way over to me.

He kissed the top of my head. "I told you you didn't need to worry about April and I," he whispered directly into my ear.

I watched for only a heartbeat more before I angled my head toward Alfie.

"I've never worried with you."

CHAPTER TWENTY-FIVE

THE REST OF the evening, post-dinner, was spent bouncing around, sipping on champagne, and meeting many people I probably could have gone my entire existence without meeting. Alfie appeared to feel the same way, given the way his smile faded as soon as we had our backs to whoever we'd been speaking to. He let out the deepest sigh I'd ever heard.

"Every single bloody year I come to this thing. It never gets better." He turned his head down to me, his hand squeezing mine. We'd remained in some form of subtle contact the whole night. "How are you holding up?"

"Good," I assured him, and it was mostly the truth. Aside from the blisters forming on the balls of my feet, I was enjoying myself. Alfie was the one doing the heavy lifting with the conversations.

Every so often, I glanced about the room, trying to spot Harry amongst the many people on security detail. The ones that had been assigned from the museum were more obvious, given their matching uniforms and CIA-level communication gear. Any private security brought by the guests blended in a little more.

Each time I did manage to catch him, though, he smiled and nodded at me, probably amused over my care for his whereabouts. It was his job to worry about Alfie and I, after all. Not the other way around.

But while I worried about Harry, Alfie worried about me. I knew that continual contact thing wasn't just a sign of affection. It was like he was making sure he constantly had his sights on me, as though I would drift into the sea of people and be lost forever.

What I loved most, though, was how happy Alfie sounded each time he introduced me to the people we spoke with. He knew most of them, and even when he didn't, Alfie painted me in a light that made me appear like the most important person in the room.

His favorite line?

"This is my girlfriend, Jordi. She's a soon-to-be bestselling author."

I'd gotten past blushing over the comment by the third time he said it. It was amazing that he'd brought it up at all, seeing as I hadn't even thought about anything publishing-related since I'd landed in London. I'd even deleted my email app so I didn't get caught up in work drama when I should have been cherishing my time here. For all I knew, Lynn had found me multiple offers for representation.

At worst, she'd found me none, and my life would go on as normal.

With all the champagne and socializing, it didn't take long before a yawn started to build. I tried to hide it, but of course Alfie noticed.

"Getting tired?" he asked me after we'd excused ourselves from a conversation with an actress from a popular British period drama. Mom was going to flip when I told her I'd met her.

I nodded. "But I can keep going," I assured him. "I knew it was going to be a long night."

"I'd say we've done enough damage," Alfie said. "I'm sure Harry wouldn't mind going home, either."

Given my attentiveness to his whereabouts, I hadn't even thought of that. He was due to head home after the gala's conclusion, and according to a quick peek at my phone, it was already nearing midnight.

I grabbed Alfie's hand. "Let's go home."

April's dress was like a beacon in all its glittering wonder, but it also made it much easier for us to find her and Gabrielle to say goodbye.

"I'll see you soon, I hope?" she said as we pulled back from our parting hug. "At one of those conventions at the very least." When I confirmed that I would, indeed, see her again one way or another, she smiled. "Brilliant. We can grab oat milk lattes."

Louie was a bit harder to track down. I probably could have gone without another comment about Alfie and I's very active sex life—not that he was *wrong*, but it didn't need to be aired at a charity gala. He was yet another part of this world that I would need to get used to.

A small price to pay if it meant being with Alfie.

Harry had managed to close the distance as we left the museum, trailing a few feet behind us. There were still some lingering cameras, though most seemed to have departed the premises. In fact, most signs of any formal event occurring inside the museum had disappeared. The faint hum of jazz music and polite chatter could be still be heard, but only until the door finished closing behind us. Some of the guests had stepped outside, the smoke of their cigarettes catching me as Alfie and I walked past and down the stairs onto the sidewalk.

"I'll go get the car, if you two don't mind waiting a moment," Harry said. "It's only about a block."

"We can come with you then," Alfie suggested.

"You sure?" But he wasn't actually asking so much as challenging. The nod at my aching feet set him up as the winner. "I'll be right back."

Cars drove past on a water-slick road. It must have rained

while we'd been inside for the event. Other Londoners were out enjoying their Friday night in South Kensington. I was sure many of them were headed home too, and if not, they were in it for the long run, hangovers be damned.

I'd acquired enough of a buzz where I knew I wouldn't suffer in the morning, but not enough to protect me from the autumn chill.

"Here you go," Alfie said as he removed his jacket and wrapped it around my shoulders. "We'll have Harry turn up the heat in the—"

"No fucking way."

I stilled, my whole body freezing in place—the third option after it decided it wanted no part of either flight or fight. I so desperately wished it wanted to partake in one of the alternatives, though. Particularly the former.

No. No, this couldn't be happening. I'd made it this whole trip without this happening.

Alfie's hands had tensed on my shoulders, his whole body trembling behind me. I knew it wasn't from the cold, either.

There were still cameras. Fewer, but they were still there. He needed to stay in check, and I was so worried he wouldn't be able to.

Alfie Fletcher wasn't a violent person. He was hardly ever an angry person. Yet, on the rare occasions I'd seen him get truly upset, it had been for one reason, and one reason only.

And that reason, dressed in worn out clothes and reeking of

beer and cigarette smoke, was stumbling toward us on the street.

"Alfie fucking Fletcher," Josh said. "Long time no see, mate."

"I'm sorry," Alfie said. His words sounded strained, like he was fighting against what really wanted to come out. "I'm afraid you have the wrong person."

"Oh, no, no, no." Josh came closer and I tucked my head into Alfie's shoulder. So far, it appeared he hadn't recognized me. "I know it's been some time, but I know one of my best mates when I see him."

"You're no friend of mine."

If words could kill, Josh would have been impaled five times over. Alfie's tone was made of pure ice.

As if he'd heard my thoughts, Josh clutched a fist over his heart, feigning pain. "Ouch. As if you hadn't treated me poorly enough already."

"Treated *you* poorly?"

Alfie was shaking, his hands in fists. I grabbed hold of his shirt, hoping that remembering I was there might ground him, just as his touches all night had grounded me.

It was the wrong decision. I shouldn't have moved. I should have stayed put and kept my head down.

"Oh, no way." Josh huffed a laugh. "*Jordi?* Jordi Wright?" He thrust his fists in the air. "The yank has returned!"

I felt sick hearing my name on his lips. Now, I was shaking

too, but my legs still refused to move. Given the pain in my feet and the fear that had taken over my body, I didn't believe I could unless Alfie helped me.

Harry, please hurry.

I tugged on Alfie's shirt, urging him to come with me. It was only a block, Harry said. I could make it one block if it meant getting away. I'd buy the whole bandage aisle in the morning if I needed to.

Thankfully, Alfie got my hint and wrapped one arm around my waist, his other hand on my hip closest to him so he could hold me upright while we walked.

"Whoa, whoa, whoa," Josh said. His hurried footfalls splashed on the wet sidewalk until he was in front of us once more. "Not even gonna catch up? It's been a while, Alf!"

"Leave us alone, Josh," Alfie seethed.

Josh's head tilted to the side, his lips pursed in a pout. Around us, the stragglers from the evening watched as they walked past. When I turned toward the museum, the smokers were surveying us, appearing half-torn between wanting to intervene and finishing their cigarette. Those of the photographers that remained were watching with greedy intensity, waiting for the money moment.

"Bit unfair, don't you think" Josh said. "You forgive Jordi, but you don't give me a chance?"

"Jordi did nothing wrong."

"It takes two to tango, mate."

I couldn't breathe. I clung to Alfie's arm, trying to drag him away from Josh, away from the whole mess unfolding in front of us, before it got to the point the cameras were waiting for.

"Jordi," Josh said when Alfie didn't answer. "How've you been, sweetheart?"

"Don't talk to her!"

Had I not been there, clinging to him, I imagined Alfie might have lunged. His shout rang through the night, earning the full attention of everyone within a reasonable distance. The smokers were finally stomping on the butts of their cigarettes, polished shoes clacking on the pavement as they made their way over.

Josh held up his hands in defense, taking a step back. "I'm not gonna do anything, bruv. But I do have to ask, Jordi. Who turns you on more? Me or Alf—"

I screamed as Alfie broke free of my hold on his arm and charged at Josh. The cameras flashed as fist connected with face and Josh stumbled back in pain. He grabbed at his nose, trying to stop the blood seeping past the gaps in his fingers.

My hand went up to my mouth as the scene unfolded in front of me. I wanted to help. I wanted to jump between them and pull Alfie away. But he wouldn't stop going after Josh, and I knew, realistically, I wouldn't have been strong enough, no matter how badly I wanted to make this end.

The smokers had finally reached us. One pulled me further away from the fight, while the other went to grab Alfie, defending one of their own. I curled into myself, still trembling, as the man who held my shoulders tried to calm me down. He had no idea—absolutely none—who I was and how I was involved. He was trying his best, but it was no use. Nothing he said would get me to relax.

I needed to get away.

"Hey! Hey—stop!"

The man shouted after me as I broke out of his hold, ignoring the fact that my feet felt like they might fall off, they were in so much pain. I lifted the skirt of my dress in both my fists, hoping I had enough balance to stay upright on the slick pavement.

"Jordi!"

Alfie called my name, but I didn't stop. Not as he or Josh or either of the men who'd intervened tried to come for me.

Get away. Get away. Get away.

I cut across the street, hoping the cars still driving this late would stop for me. The glow of the streetlights was just enough to reflect off the fabric of my dress, making it hopefully a bit easier to see the woman running away from her problems.

I kept going, ignoring the cars that honked as they passed by or the drunks who called out, "Clock strikes midnight soon, Cinderella!" I kept going and going and going, until I realized I'd gone so far that I couldn't even see the Natural History Museum when I turned back over my shoulder.

That's when I stared straight ahead, down the random street in London, and collapsed in a big black poof of polyester on the wet sidewalk.

And I cried.

I realized I had been for a while, the tears silently spilling from my make-up-covered eyes. I wanted to rip off the false lashes and run my hands across them, smearing whatever remained. But I let my tears ruin it all naturally, my hands going up to hold my head instead.

Less people passed by, the streets relatively empty in this part of town. It looked like I'd made it to a neighborhood. Those who did stroll past went in a rush, likely trying to get away from the crazy girl in the ballgown. I imagined I looked like an absolute mess.

I sure *felt* like an absolute mess.

All those years I'd spent trying to convince myself it hadn't been my fault had come flooding back—everything I knew I could have done to stop it from happening in the first place.

I threw my hands down, one of them landing on a rock. I clutched it in my fist, as I half-sobbed, half-shouted, "Josh, you fucking piece of shit!" and threw it down the street. Somewhere in the distance a dog barked. Someone else yelled for me to keep it down; people were sleeping.

I groaned up at the sky before I buried my face in my hands.

The memories of him haunting me would never leave me alone. Never. No matter how many years passed. No matter how many times Alfie assured me it wasn't my fault. He would always haunt me.

April was right. It wasn't fair. It wasn't fair that I was sitting alone and cold on a damp London street crying while Josh was going on living his life. Granted, I was pretty certain he was now doing it with a broken nose. That shouldn't have happened, though. None of this should have happened, because he shouldn't have touched me in the first place.

I lifted my head slowly.

Ten years. Ten years later, and I'd finally put the blame on him, not myself. And despite the fact that I was still crying and trembling, it felt like part of the weight had been lifted off my chest.

It hadn't mattered how many times Alfie had reassured me. I'd needed to realize what Josh had done for myself before I learned that I was the victim, not the accomplice. Me. And only me.

I heard the hiss of the tires on the wet pavement before the car came up beside me. It had hardly stopped before the rear door nearest me flew open and Alfie rushed out. Harry came around from the driver side shortly after.

Under normal circumstances, I was certain Alfie would have wrapped me in his arms as soon as he crouched down in front of me. Given what had just happened, though, he stopped himself and asked, "Can I?"

I curled my lips in, failing to fight off the fresh wave of tears as I nodded.

Alfie sacrificed his shirt, pulling me in as much as my dress would allow, so I could cry into his shoulder. I'd thought I'd run out of tears by now, but there was something about being held—more importantly, being held by someone who made me feel safe—that prompted a fresh stream.

We sat there on that sidewalk for what could have been hours before my tears finally subsided, and the rain decided it wasn't quite done yet.

Small droplets hit my head, slowly at first before the fall became steadier. I didn't know how much I cared. My dress, hair, and makeup were all already ruined. And my tears had indeed left a spot on Alfie's shirt. Had Harry not been there, I imagined we might have stayed out in the cold and rain even longer.

We were ushered into the back seat of the car, but our bodyguard didn't put the vehicle in drive once he hopped in the driver's seat. We stayed parked on the random street that I'd wandered onto, my head in Alfie's lap as he stroked my wet hair back from my face, my dress taking up more than its fair share of the back seat.

"Jordi, I'm leaving this one up to you," Harry finally said, his voice calm, soothing. "We can stay here as long as you'd like, or we can return home."

"Are you hungry?" Alfie asked. It was the first time he'd spoken directly to me since we'd run into Josh. "What do you need? We can find it."

I was numb, half from the cold, half from my emotions. But

when his hand stilled on my head, I reached up and grabbed it. Alfie winced, and it was just as I'd suspected. His knuckles were bruised and starting to swell from the punches. I had no idea how many subsequent punches he'd managed to get in, or if the bystanders had pulled him away. Maybe Harry had gotten there just after I'd left and put a quick end to the brawl.

Regardless, Alfie needed help. I was just tired and shaken. He was hurt.

"We need to get home," I managed, my voice raw from disuse. "You need ice."

"I'll be fine," Alfie assured me.

"No," I said. "That's what I want. I want to go home."

I didn't give a rat's ass about myself in that moment, my focus had shifted entirely to Alfie and getting him fixed up. The most I needed was a hot shower and some sleep. Given the rate at which his knuckles were purpling, Alfie might need an x-ray.

He started stroking my hair again. "You heard her," he said. "Let's go home, Harry."

CHAPTER TWENTY-SIX

I DIDN'T KNOW what time it was when I woke up the next morning, but it was bright outside, and Alfie wasn't beside me.

I was wearing one of his shirts, comforted by the sweet yet woodsy scent that clung to it, and the comfiest sweatpants I owned. When I sat up, my whole body ached as I stretched it, my eyes hurting from the light. When I touched them, they felt swollen, and I could only imagine the image I would see when I finally looked in a mirror.

I probably looked like roadkill.

I contemplated not getting up at all, but then I heard the hushed voices in the kitchen. None of them sounded happy, and among them, I caught Alfie. Was he yelling at someone? He was upset, that was for sure. And it sounded like Harry who was trying to keep him calm. I'd thought he'd have returned to the countryside by now.

Pushing the covers back, I crawled out of bed, my bare feet announcing my approach as they stuck to the hardwood floor.

There was, in fact, a crowd in Alfie's kitchen, and as I arrived all their heads turned to me. Aside from the tenant of the townhouse, I firmly recognized only three: Harry, Archie, and Nicole. One of the women had been at the event's red carpet the evening before, but I didn't know her name or who she was to Alfie. One of the people who'd been at the conventions was also there, meaning they were probably a member of Alfie's team. The third woman I didn't recognize.

Alfie's chair screeched on the floor as he pushed it back, standing up to greet me.

"Hi," he whispered. Like the night before, his hands—one of which was wrapped in white medical bandages—extended toward me, but stopped short. I took the initiative moving close enough to wrap my arms around him, my head resting on his chest. He kissed the top of my head as his strong, comforting embrace enveloped me.

"We didn't wake you, did we?" he continued. "We were trying to be quiet, but—"

"I woke up on my own," I interrupted, my voice just as soft but not on purpose. I imagined it was all I'd be capable of for a little while. "How are you?"

I pulled back and reached to take hold of Alfie's hands. I examined the bandaged one, noting how it covered most of the swelling that had developed the night before. One of his fingers had a small brace on it. He'd probably broken a knuckle, then. When I moved my eyes past Alfie, to the table where he'd just been sitting, I saw an ice pack.

"I haven't gotten it officially checked yet," he said. "But I can't move my middle finger."

"You shouldn't have punched him," I muttered, more because I felt bad that he'd been hurt than because I meant it.

"I'm glad I punched him," Alfie replied. "I should have punched him ten years ago too."

"No, you shouldn't have."

I looked past Alfie again to find the stern, brown-skinned woman I hadn't recognized watching him with a raised brow. Given the number of folders in front of her, I assumed she held a pretty high level of importance.

When her gaze drifted from him to me, it softened. "You must be Jordi. I'm Arushi, Alfie's lawyer." She stood up and walked over to me, extending a professional hand for me to shake.

If I hadn't already still been in a state of shock from the night before, I definitely was now.

"W-why are you here?" I asked.

Arushi smiled kindly at me. "If your boyfriend's hand is any indication, it seems like there was a spot of trouble last night."

I leaned on Alfie again. "A little."

"Don't be nervous. You're not in any sort of trouble."

"Alfie might be," Archie chided, his disappointed eyes set on his son.

"Yes, well, that's what we're all trying to prevent now, aren't we?" Arushi continued.

"What kind of trouble?" I asked.

Alfie rubbed my back as he said, "There might have been pictures that turned up online this morning."

"What?"

I knew it had been a possibility, but usually Alfie's team was able to pay off the photographers off so that they didn't post anything he didn't want out there. Before, that had been pictures of me. Now, I imagined he didn't want pictures of his fist connecting with another guy's face floating around.

"You said you didn't think the other man would press charges," Nicole chimed in, the worry over her son's well-being evident.

"No, I don't think he will," Arushi confirmed. "He would be doing himself more harm than good if he did."

"Why?" I asked.

Everyone in the room grew silent, all of them casting glances at one another. It was clear I'd missed a lengthy conversation while I'd been asleep.

"Jords…" Alfie started. "If he presses charges, there's enough evidence to prove that I did harm him." He lifted his hand to solidify his point. "But if we go to court, it wouldn't be in Josh's best interest."

I blinked, still somewhat confused.

"You're a key witness here, Jordi," Arushi added. "You were there for every moment that led up to Alfie harming Josh, and if you were called to testify, you would have to take an oath that requires total honesty. About everything."

Understanding dawned immediately.

"I would have to come forward," I said. "I'd have to talk about what Josh did to me."

"I told everyone it wasn't an option," Alfie added hastily. "If you don't want anyone to know then you don't need to—"

"I'll do it."

I don't know what Alfie had said before I'd woken up, but it must have been enough for my statement to shock everyone gathered.

"Jordi, *no one* is pressuring you," Arushi said. "This is your story to come forward with, and you're allowed to do it on your own terms."

"It *would* allow us to spin some of the stories in a more positive light, however," the woman from the night before said. Her caramel hair was in a tight bun atop her head, and she was wearing thick-frame glasses today. "Instead of Alfie being the assailant, he'd be the hero, defending his partner from an abuser."

"This isn't about me, Lucy," Alfie said. "I did what I did. And should I have perhaps thought about it more? Probably. But I'm willing to pay the consequences if Jordi isn't ready to come forward yet."

I swallowed the lump that was forming in my throat as I fought back tears. He hadn't spoken at all the first time. I'd left England and Alfie thinking the failure of our relationship had been my fault. But now, it seemed he'd learned from his mistakes. He was defending me, even if it meant legal action being taken against him in return.

Except Alfie wasn't the only one that had learned something this time around.

"I'm going to do it," I said, remembering the conversation I'd had with April, the brief moment when I'd put the blame where it rightfully belonged. "I'm going to come forward. He shouldn't be allowed to live his life while his victims spend their time having nightmares or afraid of even the simplest touch. From the people they love, nonetheless."

Alfie's arm wrapped further around me, and he pulled me into his side. I watched as everyone's faces shifted from one of concern to something akin to pride. I knew it probably wasn't that for everyone—most of the people in this room hadn't met me until this very moment—but at the very least, my willingness to speak had calmed some of their nerves.

It was when my eyes settled on Harry, his eyes glistening, that my tears finally spilled over.

"Look what you made me do," I said to him, finally managing a smile.

He returned it, along with a huffed laugh. "I'm so proud of

you, little lady," he said.

"No father wants to see any young woman he knows go through this," Archie added. "Don't think we're seeing this as anything less than it is."

"It's a massive decision," Nicole added, nodding along with what her husband had said.

"And don't think you're committed to it," Arushi said. "It *will* help, but if at any time you decide you want to back out, you can."

"I'm not going to back out," I assured them. I glanced up at Alfie before I returned my attention to the rest of the people gathered. "I've spent ten years hating myself when I should have been directing that hate elsewhere. Now, it's about time I did."

Arushi smiled at me, while Lucy got to work with the other members of Alfie's team sitting around her, all of them shuffling through their folders as they talked about how they would frame this story for the upcoming press release. Something needed to be done fast if they were going to beat Josh's potential lawsuit.

"Alfie told me you're due to return to the States in a few days," Arushi said.

"Tomorrow," I corrected. "I have to go back to work on Monday."

"Do you think you could possibly extend your trip?" she asked. "It might be helpful to have you around, and in the same time zone. I can contact your boss if you'd like me to make the request."

As terrifying a thought as it was to have a lawyer call Lynn and explain that I was now a key witness and potential solution for her client's assault case, I nodded. This release was going to hit the news the same way the pictures had: hard and fast. Lynn might not see them immediately, but given the interest surrounding Alfie from Starr employees and talent, something told me it would eventually happen.

After giving Lynn's contact information to Arushi, she rushed away to begin her work in conjunction with the PR team. Archie, Nicole, and Harry hovered around them, offering their two cents as it pertained to Alfie and I's well-being.

I leaned my head on Alfie's shoulder, somewhat overwhelmed by everything. His lips found the top of my head immediately.

"I'm so proud of you," he whispered into my hair. "My beautiful, brave girl." Alfie kissed me again. "Also, I can't say I'm thrilled about the circumstances, but I *am* excited to get a few extra days with you."

I tilted my chin up just enough to meet his eyes.

"Open and honest, remember?" I said. "Whatever it takes for us."

"When I said that, I meant it more as something between you and me, not you, me, and the entire world."

I chuckled. "I know. But this would've always been a burden

for us, Alfie. If it takes the whole world knowing what happened to make sure we can make it through this. I'm willing to let them know. Finally put this behind us and move forward. A fresh start."

Alfie nodded and wrapped me in his arms. "I like the sound of that."

CHAPTER
TWENTY-SEVEN

THE NEWS STORY hit with a vengeance just like I'd thought it would. Normally, Alfie wasn't front page material. Not since *Crimson Curse* had ended, at least. But in the age of modern feminism, celebrity news outlets were quick to pick up the statement his team and I had crafted.

"I'll throw an apology in there," he'd said as we sat around his kitchen table, all of us trying to find the absolute perfect wording, "but I'm a very minimal part of this all."

He didn't want to be painted as the hero, but this couldn't have happened without doing so at least in part. We created a statement about how we'd been antagonized, and only when verbal abuse started being aimed at me, did he step in. It was the truth, after all, and that's what we'd set out to tell.

I'd called everyone I could think of before Lucy sent it out: Mom and Dad, Liv, Grace, Tori. I didn't want them hearing about anything from anyone other than me. As far as phone calls went, I think the record for most crying done long-distance was broken. Even my normally steady dad's voice cracked on more than one occasion while we talked. But, unsurprisingly, it was Tori's call that delivered the most extreme reaction.

"Calm down, Your Highness," Alfie had said to her. I'd put her on speakerphone. "Jordi is in safe hands."

"She'd better be!" my colleague shouted from the other end. "If you lay one unwanted hand on her, Alfred, I swear I'll cut off your balls and feed them to the lions at the zoo."

My trip to London had been extended a week thanks to Arushi's help talking with Lynn and Starr's HR department. Despite the story breaking into the news cycle, we still needed to wait the legal duration of time for Josh to file any charges.

Seeing as April had also come forward with her story via social media as a stand in solidarity with mine, Josh wisely did nothing. His sentence for admitting he'd assaulted the both of us—and who knew how many other women he'd come in contact with over the years—would have been far worse than Alfie's.

By the time I was due to be dropped off at the airport, I was exhausted. I'd spent the better part of my second week in London on an emotional rollercoaster. And while having extra time with Alfie had been nice, we'd mostly stayed in and watched movies. Neither one of us wanted to brave the outside world. Even from inside, we could hear the occasional paparazzo shouting for us, seeing if we were home.

Needless to say, Harry had extended his stay in London too, claiming he wouldn't be able to sleep at night without knowing we were safe. He'd even claimed Alfie's second bedroom when he wasn't patrolling outside.

"Here we are," Harry announced as he pulled up to my terminal to drop me off.

He got out of the car to get my luggage out of the boot. Alfie and I remained in the back, neither one of us moving very fast.

"I'll try to come visit you as soon as I can," he said. He'd cancelled his last two upcoming convention appearances claiming a family emergency. I knew April had done the same, leaving Elliott and Louie to hold down the *Crimson Curse* fort. "I need to sort out a few more details with Arushi and Lucy, but I should be able to find a flight to Chicago soon."

I nodded. "Don't feel any pressure." We'd already talked about how we should take at least a week away from one another to allow me to adjust to my life and how it might have been affected by the news break.

I knew this was hard for Alfie. All week he'd hardly let me out of his sight. That was made easier given how we'd spent most of our time, but on the rare occasions we'd needed to step out, he'd become my shadow. I attributed it to him having the exact opposite reaction the last time I'd left London and wanting to make up for it. Show me that he cared.

The thing was, I'd never doubted that before. If he hadn't cared, he wouldn't have reacted the way he had. But unlike before, I needed to show him that I would be alright. That he didn't need to go around the world's comic conventions searching for a sign of life from me.

I slid across the back seat and onto his lap, wrapping my arms around his neck to keep myself steady. My lips met his for a tender kiss, another, before I pulled back and ran my fingers through his hair.

"We'll see each other when we can," I whispered. "I have no doubt about that."

"If you need anything for work when you get back, make sure you call Arushi. I've already warned her you might need paperwork."

"I will."

"And Lucy said she's willing to work with you for the time being if you find that you need any help on the PR side of things."

"Okay."

"And if you think anyone is following you, remember to—"

"Alfie," I said through a laugh. I leaned in to kiss him again. "I'll be fine. I promise. I'll text you right before I take off and as soon as I land, okay?"

He sighed before he rested his forehead against mine. "I love you."

"I love you too. More than you'll ever know."

And this time as I was leaving him, my confession didn't come with an apology.

WHEN I WALKED into the office on Monday, it was like I'd risen from the dead. It felt like it too, with my jet lag in play.

It appeared I'd been right. Everyone had seen the story.

I tried to keep my eyes ahead of me, even though I knew every single person I passed was doing little to hide the fact that they were watching me. Their eyes burned into my back like a brand, and I hated it.

I made my way quickly and quietly to my cubicle, eager to distract myself with work.

Wow, never thought I'd say that.

I hadn't checked my email at all in the time I'd been away, so I mentally prepared myself for what awaited me. It turned out to be over six hundred unread emails. Not impossible to get through, but I wouldn't be able to do anything but play catch up for a few days. Hopefully Tori could manage without me for a bit longer.

As I scrolled through, I saw most of the emails were from Lynn and HR, unsurprisingly. I filed those away, knowing I'd eventually have no choice but to deal with them. The ones that actually had action items I needed to accomplish were filed in a priority folder, then I started sorting through the rest.

My eyes widened in brief shock when I realized that many were from Lynn regarding the contacts she'd reached out to. I'd all but forgotten about that with everything else that had been going on. Some of them were her friends politely telling me they weren't looking for new clients at the moment or they didn't represent authors in my genre. Fair enough, and I appreciated Lynn keeping me in the loop, even with the bad news.

Some were more hopeful though—requests for partials and even a few agents asking to meet me over a video call.

I was in the middle of looking up some of the agents that had responded positively when my laptop pinged with a new email notification.

TO: Jordi Wright "jwright@starrpm.com"
FROM: Lynn Hauser "lhauser@starrpm.com"

Jordi,

Welcome back! How about you and I grab lunch today?
Lots to catch up on!

Lynn

Lots to catch up on, indeed.

A short, friendly message could mean a lot of things in the

corporate world, and of course my brain went straight for the worst-case-scenario meaning.

I was going to be fired. I'd caused too much trouble for Starr—even though no one knew where I worked; Lucy had made sure that remained a secret and they'd even removed me from the corporate site for the time being. Now I was paying the consequences. They couldn't possibly afford to keep me around, not with all the distractions I was causing and how much time I'd taken off.

Tori's visit to my desk didn't help.

"She's back."

Normally, I would have expected her to come with confetti and a shaken bottle of champagne for me to pop, but today, by Tori standards, the greeting was rather subdued.

Instead of jumping right into the gossip of the trip—not the gossip the whole office was talking about; the *actual* summary of the trip—she hugged me. I hadn't realized how much I'd needed a hug from a friend. Alfie had been great, of course, but there was something about the comfort of your girlfriends in this kind of situation that was just a little different.

"It hasn't been the same without you," she said. "And honestly without Alfie too. I've missed being called royalty at the last few cons."

I managed to chuckle. "Was Alexis from social media okay?"

"Eh." Tori shrugged. "She's fine. Won't have to be working with her much longer anyway, so I'm just sucking it up."

"I'll be back on the tour soon enough." If I remembered correctly, there were only a few stops left, anyway.

That's when Tori's forehead had scrunched up in confusion. "What?" I asked.

"Have you talked to Lynn yet?"

"I've been back in the country for less than twenty-four hours, and at this desk for maybe two so no. She asked me to get lunch with her today, though." I knew my worry was showing. "Is there something I should know about?"

Instead of delivering the office gossip, Tori tucked her lips in, ran her index finger and thumb across to metaphorically zip them, and scurried dutifully from my cubicle.

"Tori!" I whisper called. "Victoria Wilson!"

It was no use. I didn't see her again, and before I knew it, I was waiting in the lobby, trying to ignore the glances Sam gave me from behind the lobby reception desk. I gave her a soft smile, letting her know I wasn't stupid.

"It was really great what you did," she said. "Coming out with that story. And it's even better that you have a partner who supports it. My little sister..." Sam sighed. "I'm not gonna go into the details, but she wasn't so lucky. But she appreciated your bravery coming forward. She thought it was so cool that we work together."

Her admission stunned me into silence, and thankfully I didn't have to say anything because Lynn came through the glass doors to the lobby at that moment.

"Ready to go?" she asked, sounding lively as ever.

I nodded, and when I turned back to Sam, she said, "I'll see you later, Jordi. Have fun at lunch, ladies."

"Were you two talking?" Lynn asked when we were in the elevator. "You could have finished up. I wouldn't have minded waiting."

"No," I replied. "Where were you thinking of getting lunch?"

"There's that new taco place I've been hearing about. Want to check that out?" She smiled at me as she added, "And I wouldn't be opposed to mid-day margaritas while we talk all about your trip."

Margaritas to soften the blow. Nice.

I tried not to think too negatively as the server brought over the giant chalices filled with our drinks, attempting to be funny by saying something about day-drinking on a Monday. When she walked away again, Lynn took a sip and made a face.

"Now I get what she meant. This is strong."

I stared at my own drink before I pushed it away with a sigh. "Lynn, I'm sorry."

I figured I might as well cut to the chase. If I was about to be scolded for any number of reasons, I might as well try to get my side in before Lynn had a chance to say anything.

Her brows came together. "For what?"

"For scheduling that tour." I might as well start at the beginning, if I was getting my chance to talk. "And for taking so much time off and causing all this office drama."

"Office drama?"

"Yeah, with Alfie visiting, and I feel like I put a rift between you and Mr. Singh, and now this." I flicked my wrist gesturing to the space around us, which I then realized didn't clarify anything. "All the new information about me."

Lynn's face softened. "Jordi," she started. "Why do you think I asked you to lunch today?"

I mentally hit pause on the speech I'd prepared about how, while irresponsible, I'd brought Starr more business with this tour than we'd seen in years for Jackson's books. I'd given up most of my weekends to make sure our events were a success. How I loved having her as a manager, and would never, *ever* find a job that came even remotely close to this one.

"To... fire me?"

I hadn't thought it was funny, but Lynn threw her head back and laughed. I only stared, probably making the tables nearby wonder what in the hell was going on.

When she came down, Lynn said, "I can tell you right now, Jordi, that when someone's getting fired, they don't get gourmet tacos and jumbo margaritas during work hours. Didn't you read my email?"

All fifteen words of it. "You said there was a lot to catch up on."

"And there is. For some of the reasons you mentioned and others."

I hated the suspenseful pause as she took another sip of her drink.

Lynn sighed contentedly when she finished, then folded her arms on the table, all business.

"You're right that there's a lot going on right now, and you're at the center of most of it. I've had more discussions with HR in the last two weeks that involve your name than I have in all your years of employment with Starr."

I hung my head. I knew she was just being honest, but it didn't make me any less embarrassed.

"We're not talking about you because you're troublesome, Jordi. While, yes, some members of the executive team are conflicted about how to handle your employment at the moment, I've made sure no decision is made without my express approval. And that's approval I'll never give. I know how much this job means to you, and I know you would never prioritize your new boyfriend over your duties." She rolled her eyes. "Men just don't understand sometimes."

She hit the nail on the head with that one. "I'll go to whatever meetings I need to in order to sort this out," I volunteered. "You're right—I love working for Starr. It's been a dream of mine since I was a little girl. I couldn't imagine working anywhere else."

Lynn sat back in her chair, wearing a smile. "I was afraid you'd say that."

Now it was my turn to be confused. "What do you mean?"

"I told you there was a lot to catch up on, right?" She reached for a chip and started breaking it apart on her plate. Was Lynn nervous about something?

"While you were gone, my husband let me know he got a promotion. It's going to come with a large enough raise that will allow me to quit working."

Wow. That came out of left field.

"That's amazing. Congrats," I said. "But I have to say I'll miss you at the office."

"That's very sweet of you, but I'm not going to stop working."

My eyes widened. "Oh really?"

Lynn shook her head. "I got into this side of the publishing business because I thought marketing would be where I'd make a difference for our authors. I wanted to see them succeed. In reality, I have very little direct interaction with them, and half the ideas I propose don't get the budget needed to fulfill them. Then you came along and gave me your wonderful manuscript." She huffed a laugh. "Jordi, I *still* want that sequel. I haven't stopped thinking about that cliffhanger for months."

I chuckled. "I've been a *little* busy, but I promise it's in the works."

"I know. You're doing a lot right now. All that to say, I realized I'm in the wrong part of the industry. So while I was reaching out to my connections about your manuscript, I started having conversations with some of my friends who are agents. Mostly the ones who said they couldn't offer you representation at this time because I wanted to let them know they'd helped me decide what I want to do."

"I don't understand."

"I'm leaving my position at Starr to work at a literary agency," Lynn announced. "And *I'd* like to offer you representation, Jordi."

My hand went up to my mouth to cover it while I stared, awestruck, at my boss. Well, I guess she wouldn't be my boss much longer if this was her plan.

"Wait," I finally managed. "Lynn, this is massive! Are you serious?"

"Very," she replied, nodding. "I've already secured a position at an agency. Everything will be commission-based, so with Robert's new role, I don't need to worry about having a salary. I signed the paperwork late last week and will be handing in my two-week notice with Starr this Friday.

"As for where you come in, I was open in my interview about having a project I wanted to represent right away. It was a young author who wrote an inspiring story and has an even more inspiring background. That was my one stipulation I gave during the whole process."

Lynn reached across the table to place her hand on my forearm. I couldn't think of anything to say, the tightening of my throat making that much more difficult.

"I know you want to earn this deal on your own, and, in my eyes, you have. I fell in love with your story before I knew anything else about your boyfriend or"—she rolled her eyes again—"*celebrity endorsement opportunities*. This story was pure and magical, and I know readers will enjoy it just as much as I did. So, it's your choice, of course, but that's my official bid to be your agent."

I hadn't even had the slightest chance to look at the other offers Lynn had passed my way. But given our previous conversations about my story, I knew she was speaking from her heart, not from a business standpoint. Even as her employee at Starr, she'd been in my corner from day one, coaching me and supporting me. Probably because I was trying to do the same exact thing she'd tried to do with her career.

I *knew* I'd earned this offer on my own, and just like Lynn had faith in me, I had even more faith in her to help make my dream a reality.

"Is it a conflict of interest if I say yes?" I asked, my voice breaking as I fought against my emotions.

Lynn chuckled. "I'm sure we can work something out. Or at the very least keep things under wraps until the manuscript officially sells," she added with a wink. "I'm not even considering Starr as an option, so there should be no trouble there."

"And my job here?"

"Again, you're welcome to keep it, and I actually suggest you do. When I leave, Tori will be taking my position. I've already discussed everything with her and HR."

Now it made more sense. No wonder Tori had been so

secretive earlier—and had made a comment about not working with Alexis. She wouldn't be working on events anymore at all. She'd be the head honcho.

A bubble of excitement for my friend blossomed in me, but it was nothing compared to the volcanic eruption that was building as a result of the news I'd received.

I nodded, slowly at first before it became more excited as I truly realized what was happening.

"Then yes," I said. "I'd love for you to represent me."

Lynn lifted her glass to me then. "To new beginnings," she said.

I clinked my margarita against hers. Oh, Lynn, you had no idea.

FIVE YEARS LATER

"THERE YOU GO," I said as I finished scrawling my signature on the title page of my latest book. "I hope you enjoy it, and thanks for coming out."

The excited reader smiled as she thanked me and walked away, clutching the third book in my series to her chest. My smile remained even as I moved onto the next person in line, all anxiously waiting to see me at my comic-con booth. Not my publisher's. *Mine.*

I didn't think I'd ever get over the fact that I'd earned enough success to have an entire booth dedicated to only my books.

Pop-up banners and promotional materials surrounded me. Readers had been coming up almost non-stop, which was both flattering and exhausting. I'd never considered myself *main attraction* material, yet here I was, feeling like a celebrity guest. And while I considered authors celebrities in their own right, I'd never expected the attention I was receiving.

Maybe it had something to do with the guy somewhere else on the con floor, up to his old tricks as he signed copies of his headshot and various stills from the recently trending *Crimson Curse*. Except now Alfie Fletcher wasn't there to promote a show only available on streaming services. No—he was there to promote a new project. One based on the debut novel by J.M. Wright.

With Lynn's help, I was able to move through the publishing process much faster than most people would. We'd gone through a few rounds of edits, changing the story just enough to market it as a story of growth and overcoming trauma. Fitting, given my personal story. She only pitched the book to female editors, too, hoping they would see me as more than the celebrity partner I was frequently photographed with during our back-and-forth visits across the pond.

Those had stopped since my manuscript had been picked up. Alfie chose the night of our celebration to also tell me he officially wanted to move to Chicago.

Despite the relocation, however, it wasn't long after my first book's release that a copy conveniently fell into the hands of a screenwriter at a production studio in London. The same one responsible for *Crimson Curse*. Even more ironically, it was the same screenwriter that randomly showed up to the same restaurant Alfie and I were getting drinks at one evening.

She'd told me her people would get in touch with my people who were actually Alfie's people—and Lynn.

And so the story of Alfie finally getting to star in an adaptation of one of my books came to be.

I greeted the next person in line with a big smile. One glance at her con-gifted bag told me she'd already gotten her photo-op with Alfie.

"Your ring is so pretty," the girl complimented.

"Thank you," I said before stealing a glance at the giant diamond on my left hand. It nearly put April's to shame. And it didn't matter that Alfie had proposed months ago; I never got tired of looking at it. "Happy reading," I added as I passed the freshly signed book back to her.

"Last few, Jordi," Amanda, the event manager from my publisher, told me. "Then you get a break."

I nodded, knowing I couldn't say how relieved I was. I loved what I did, but my wrist grew tired after a while. And I sometimes forgot my signature after doing it so many times.

I couldn't believe how much I sounded like Jackson.

The rest of the signing line went quickly—some more teenage girls, a couple who read my books together, a mom and daughter duo—until the last person finally came up to the table.

"Can I have this one personalized?" Alfie asked. "To J.M. Wright's biggest fan."

I chuckled as I took the copy of my book from his hands. I did as he'd requested on the same page I signed everyone else's, then turned to the second title page where I had a bit more room to write.

"Alfred William Fletcher," I recited as I wrote. Alfie laughed at the use of his full name. "The search is over. You finally found my book, open parentheses, and my heart, close parentheses. Love Jords."

I always signed his books the same way. He kept them all on his nightstand in our bedroom, and I caught the way he'd smile at them from time to time when he thought I wasn't looking.

I slapped the book cover shut and handed it back to him with the same, "Happy reading," I gave to everyone else.

"I'll cherish it always," Alfie said, hugging the book to his chest like a starstruck fanboy. Oh, how the tables had turned. "And now that there's three, I'll actually start reading them."

"That's what you said when the second one came out."

"Well, I have to read the first one, don't I? I'd be a pretty shit star of a TV show if I didn't."

"Crazy how once you aren't the only one who gets to read my books anymore, you aren't interested."

"That's not true," Alfie defended. I raised a challenging brow, and he amended, "Okay, it might be a little true."

I laughed and shook my head at him. Around us, con-goers watched, realizing exactly who we were. One excited attendee called out to Alfie, waving frantically before running over to ask for a selfie. His bodyguard stepped in, but being the kind human he was, Alfie obliged the request.

We didn't waste much more time after, though, not wanting to cut into our lunch break.

"It's okay that I'm not the only one who reads your books anymore," Alfie picked up where we'd left off, his hand finding mine as we laced our fingers together. "Just as long as you promise me something else."

"What's that?"

"I'm the only one who gets your heart."

Now that was one promise I knew I would always keep.

ACKNOWLEDGEMENTS

Considering my favorite part of any story I've written is the romance, it was only a matter of time before I wrote one that was entirely focused on it. But my decision to start publishing in this genre didn't come without the help and general support of so many amazing people.

Thank you to my parents and little brother who continue to be so supportive of this journey. I love you guys so much, and couldn't do this without you!

Thank you to my beta reader, Meghan. You continue to not only be one of my best friends and cheerleaders, but someone who gives some of the best early feedback on my books. I'm so thankful for you taking the time to help me (and fangirl with me over my characters). Love you!

Thank you to my editor, Emily, for taking this project on and offering your insights and the finishing grammatical touches. Thank you, also, for formatting the ebook!

Thank you, Nicole, for stepping in and creating the cover illustrations of Jordi and Alfie. You helped me bring my vision to life in a way that exceeded anything I could have imagined!

Thank you to my friends and family who continue to show

support for all my projects.

Thank you to my colleagues at my full-time job for cheering me on while I work this "part-time job" of mine.

Thank you to the online writing and bookish communities for your endless support. You all continue to give me the courage I need to put my stories out in the world, and I cannot thank you enough for that!

Thank you, Elena, for creating such lovely character art of Jordi and Alfie.

And thank you, dearest reader, for picking up this novel and giving it a chance. I appreciate you endlessly for helping me achieve my dream!

ABOUT THE AUTHOR

MCKENZIE BURNS is a multi-genre author from Chicago with a passion for writing stories that involve different cultures, witty banter, and women who don't take 'no' for an answer. Her spare time is spent drinking copious amounts of coffee and searching for obscure music.